CW00589543

AU PAIR

EXTRAORDINAIRE

ABOUT THE AUTHOR

Mariki Kriel is the pen name for the author who was born in South Africa. She emigrated to the United Kingdom in 2012 and still moves around often. She writes in English and Afrikaans. A selection of her poetry has been published.

First Published in Great Britain in 2021.

A CIP catalogue record for this book is available from the British Library.

For my family;

my children and grandchildren

and all my supporters on this journey.

The light at the end of the tunnel

is not an illusion.

The tunnel is.

Unknown.

AU PAIR

EXTRAORDINAIRE

The bizarre tale of an extraordinary au pair looking for light on the other side.

Mariki Kriel

CONTENTS

Page

1. A Hole in the Wall   1
2. Keith Leaves   14
3. In Limbo   25
4. The Letter   34
5. Flying at Last   39
6. A new home   54
7. Wales   62
8. Goodbye Wales   76
9. The House of Curry   89
10. Going Home   116
11. The Tunnel   141
12. A Cell for a Room   164
13. The Attic   187
14. Escape from the Attic   213

15. A River in Front of Her   222

16. A Safety Net   245

17.   Closer to Home   266

18. Feast or Famine   280

19. Up in the Air   297

20. Leave to Remain   306

21. Magic and Magicians   321

22. The Lie of Hope   340

23. Disillusion   355

Heading South   371

ACKNOWLEDGEMENTS

MARIKI KRIEL

Chapter 1

A HOLE IN THE WALL

Most people write down their New Year's goals. This year, 2012, is a newborn baby, with thick eyelids and swollen cheeks. It resembles someone in the family. There are reminders of previous years: the same January heat, the same hope. You notice a familiar nose, a look in the mother's or father's face, but you know this one is going to be different. It has a personality entirely of its own. Somehow, she knows this year is going to change their lives forever.

'There is of course a third option...' Keith's voice is strong in the beginning of the sentence, then dwindles, and towards the end, it becomes hesitant.

'I do not know if I should share this with you, but I see it as an option.'

She stands in front of the sink, washing the dishes. Her back faces him. And she has just been wondering if it would be easier to take sleeping tablets before one last walk into the ocean. Perhaps the drowning part will be easier if she's slightly drowsy. She hates cold water and usually takes her time to get immersed.

'What is the third option?' She wants to get straight to the point. It is not going to help if they cannot be open and honest with each other. No secrets, no half-truths. She stops scrubbing the pan in which he fried their supper an hour ago and turns to face him. They ate steak and chips. Rump, bought at Woolworths; lightly fried with the pink inside, almost red. The Woolworths shopping card still has a long way to go. It was their last opportunity to buy on credit, so they treat it with great respect. The smell of fried oil hangs darkly in the tiny kitchen.

They might have had something to celebrate tonight, and normally they celebrate with excellent food. Since they do not drink alcohol, they make a point of eating well. Only once, since they moved into this house, have they had a disastrous meal. That was frozen tuna that turned out to be tasteless and dry. Every morning, they plan the evening's menu together. Keith shops for the ingredients and cooks their tasty meals. She eats, washes the dishes, and tidies the kitchen. Who is she to complain?

She realizes they must take things slowly. It is only two days since the reality of the brick wall struck and nearly buried her. How can she expect to have direction and clarity so soon after their life- changing decision? She wants to believe she is a positive woman and finds it hard to accept failure. She does not know whether this is good or bad. When is something a failure? So often one reads about people who gave up just before they could have been rescued. She and Keith have held out and hung on; perhaps too long. How will they ever know if help was just around the corner?

'In a way, we should take our hats off to ourselves,' says Keith. He joins her in the kitchen and pours another cup of coffee from the filter machine. 'It has been two or more years now that we juggled accounts and money. Somehow that, and our hope that things would change for us, kept us going. The three sales we made during 2011 were way too few to cover our daily expenses and mounting debt. If we want to be fair with ourselves, we must admit the writing has been on the wall for a while.'

She knows exactly what he is talking about. She is the one who clicks the computer's keys to move money around so that the credit cards get 'serviced.' Not to mention the fact that in 2009 they dealt with a breakup in their relationship, and for him, two stints of rehab, and a three- week stay in a clinic.

'Yes, it has been a long and hard battle. You know, right up to this week I felt if we could just keep the ball rolling, this will eventually gain momentum, and gradually we would get out of this deep hole. But, when that idiot ducked out of his wonderful 'offer', it finally snapped my hope, like a twig pruned off a tree. Shucks man, there I was: dressed up, and waiting for three o'clock for him to arrive to sign the documents. Once again, our hopes were dashed.'

'Also, Conrad doesn't want to pay us an advance on our commission. Just think about it, it's not even a loan. It's our own money, due any day now. What makes me angry is he does not say 'yes' or 'no'. We ask, and he ignores us.'

Different things push different people to the brink. For Keith, it was this last issue that turned his rosy hued future into a grim and dark palette. For her, it was the dashed hope of a certain, sure sale that would have 'bought' them more time. One can stretch one's hope only so far, and no further. Eventually the elastic must snap. But it is incredibly significant that they came to the same conclusion on the same day.

'This is it! We cannot stay here any longer under these circumstances. By ignoring the facts, we are going nowhere fast. The fiscal dragging on our finances is killing us. The gate is barred, and the moat is filled with crocodiles!'

The next morning, when she steps into the office, she sees Keith is upset.

'I received the first text from the bank to remind me I exceeded my overdraft limit. They will soon revoke the car payment.'

She knows him well enough to tell he feels defeated. She says nothing. What can she say? They have not paid their rent for January, and it is already the eighth day of the month. She feels ashamed about that, because they sold their house to a young British couple in February last year, and now they rent it. The rent is very reasonable, but even so, they could not pay the couple yet. The thought that they let them down concerns her.

She swivels her chair around to face Keith where he sits behind his laptop. 'Do you know what I think?'

'No, what do you think?' They look into each other's eyes, and she knows this is a defining moment which they might remember one day as 'the day they decided.'

'I think we will be better off to take leave, rather than being here at the office every day.' She is shocked to hear these words come out of her mouth. She, the hardworking, dedicated, loyal Kiki, has just voiced defeat.

Countless people walk past their enticing office each day. Returning to their cars, their childrens' faces are painted, and they carry balloons from Spur, right next to the agency office. They fill their trolleys with Woolworths' shopping bags.

Those who occasionally step into their office are often not buyers, but prospective tenants, looking for an apartment or a house, to rent. They invariably have pets, and pets are not welcome in apartments. Then they want it furnished, when it is unfurnished, or vice versa. To complicate things further, they want to move in while the property is still occupied.

'Our industry is probably hit hardest by this economic crisis. It is sad when you think how experienced and qualified, we both are. We each have NQF5 certificates in Property, and just the other day we received our PDE (Professional Designation Examination) exemption for estate agents. There are few couples in this country who can offer what we have, even so, we struggle to survive. I feel we should leave everything and run away. Why don't we go to the Transkei? Yes, let us go to live in the Transkei! We are finally at the end of our road. We are facing a wall.'

It's as if Keith gains energy. As he speaks, he waves his arms above his head. He has a vision now. He stumbled upon Plan One.

'Nobody wants to buy a house now. Would you want to? Well, you know how we burnt our fingers! Humph, so much for experienced estate agents, buying at the peak of the bubble just waiting to burst.' He was referring to the beautiful apartment they bought on the Garden Route a while ago. It forced them to sell their home for less than their outstanding mortgage. There was no point enjoying endless sea views from the deck when they could not even afford the mortgage.

About seven years ago, they spent ten days at a quaint hotel on the Transkei coast. It was a laid back, peaceful experience. They spent their time reading by the pool, sitting in the pub, fishing, and enjoying a great time. To get there, one drives past mud huts, roaming horses, goats, and cows. Unattended herds cross the road and wander off to the other side of the gravel road to graze on unfenced land. It is rural, a basic existence, and an incredibly beautiful part of South Africa. They rested and ate plenty of freshly caught fish and oysters.

Should she switch off her phone, nobody will be able to get hold of her. But is that where they want to spend the rest of their lives?

She tries to picture them: they manage a small, run-down hotel, next to the ocean. She will be working in the kitchen as the housekeeper, receptionist and cook. Keith will oversee the kitchen and staff, do the shopping and draw up the menus. Her recovering alcoholic husband will also run the pub.

Hm, she isn't sure how that would work. The only positive thing she can see in this scenario is that there might be an equally run-down truck provided with the position, which they might use to get to the nearest village or town. But the fact of the matter is, the banks will soon close their accounts, and their car will certainly be repossessed. Soon they will not be insured, and they will have to cancel their medical policy. That is not a pleasant prospect for an estate agent couple!

They are busy digging a hole in the wall. It goes much faster than she expected. Her children and all their family are shocked beyond belief when they tell them of their plans. Although they had been aware of their plight and their battles to survive the economic crises, there was not much they could do to help them. They hold a family gathering to discuss their plans, and finally the children reluctantly give them their blessing.

'We are going to sell all our possessions. And then, we are going to live in England.' There, the words slipped out of their mouths. Keith's British Citizenship will be the tool, the key, to get through the wall.

The following day they resign their positions, and Keith phones the Home Office to find out what procedures to follow to get his wife a spousal visa. They estimate that it will take roughly three months to get their act together.

When sleep eludes her at night, she pictures them, sleeping on a beach, clinging to their rucksacks, filled with their earthly possessions.

Oh God, I do not want to give up this life. I do not want to let go of my home, my clothes, and my beautiful things. What about my mother and my family? If there is any other way, please show us.

'Everything in this house is for sale! Just show me what interests you. Everything, yes everything must go!'

She pretends to read the newspaper at the kitchen counter. Though her back faces them, she can feel the woman's knowing eyes dart over their possessions like laser beams detecting a target. She has a quick eye. She already spotted the paintings she bought in Israel in 1982. Since then, they have hung on a wall wherever she lived.

'How much are these two paintings?'

'Fifty Rand for both', says her husband, who she knows is quickly calculating how many meals it will pay for in Europe. They need every cent they can put together for their plane tickets, her visa, and for reserves until they find work in the UK.

She winces but does not react. She reads about the Voortrekkers in their local newspaper, Die Burger. Apparently, these brave people who trekked across the Drakensberg Mountains to avoid conflict with the British in the Cape in the 1800s were dope smokers. There was also a lot of sex involved, says the writer of the article. *And I always thought they were such God-fearing people,* she muses.

'I'll take the two blue couches. I also want this boudoir stool. How much is this plate?'

She does not hear what her husband says. She wants to shout 'That plate was a wedding gift to my parents in 1939! It is not for sale. I promised Cathy she has the first option on the blue couches. I bought the boudoir stool at an antique shop in Knysna. I love it! How can anybody else sit on it? It belongs under my dressing table. I love the cast iron legs, the seat with the tassels, swinging elegantly when one pushes it underneath the table.'

The prospective buyer left her open handbag on their dining room table. The promise of money is there: their passport to breaking through the wall. She walks from room to room, her eagle eyes sweeping over everything they possess.

'This blue rug will go well with the blue couches. How much do you want for it?'

'Fifty Rand' replies her husband, the salesperson.

'No, no, no!' she cries inwardly. Finally, she opens her mouth: 'That is a Persian carpet!' Her voice sounds weak and rough.

'This is not a Persian. I don't recognize the weaving pattern.' She already looked at the back of the blue and white rug that used to lie for many years in her mother's home. Somewhere in the study, she has certificates to prove her claim, but the room is in a mess. This morning, she threw everything she kept inside the Jonkman's cupboard onto the floor. Hercules, the antiques dealer from Bredasdorp, will come tomorrow to collect the Bentwood chairs. He indicated he might want to buy the cupboard, too.

She rummages through the papers lying on her desk.

Keith shouts: 'Kiki, how much is the red rug?'

'Oh, please Lord, not that one, too,' she mutters. She finds the certificates and a measuring tape. To prove her point, she must measure the rugs to ascertain which one, is which.

'What do you have in your kitchen? Do you own an electric beater? And what about your linen and your towels? What are you going to do with that?'

They stand in the kitchen, and Kiki smells the woman's perfume. The husband is bored, and pages through a glossy magazine their high-end Property company publishes each quarter.

Kiki frowns, but says nothing. Her husband deals with this much better than she anticipated. It shocks her to watch him open the cupboards and reveal his Holy of Holies. One thing she knows for certain: nobody will get his knife. The knife is the one he ordered from the Kitchen Chef over the internet. They fought about the knife for many days. To her, a knife is a knife, and she could not understand why he wanted to spend so much money on a stupid knife. In the end, he won the argument, and will surely pack it into his suitcase to take with him when they leave.

'Here Kiki. Wrap this and write which items Christa wants to buy.'

He puts his favorite salad bowl on the table, and for the second time that day, their eyes meet. They are really doing this thing. They are selling their possessions. Not only are they soon going to be homeless, but they will possess hardly any worldly goods.

Her phone rings. 'Hi, this is Brendon speaking. I saw your advertisement on Gumtree. Is your double bed still for sale?'

'Sorry, no, we have sold both our double beds and a single bed.' Once again, she thanks Michael for the deposit he put down for their queen- size bed. He will fetch it when they leave the house. He understood they need their bed until a day or two before they leave. He is from Ghana, he told her. He, his wife and their two young children live with his wife's parents in Cape Town. He buys furniture and stores it in a garage, until they one day have their own home.

She immediately felt empathy for him. She imagined him arriving in South Africa with a suitcase, and a rolled-up blanket. *He is probably a professor in literature or someone of importance, struggling to find a good job,* she thought.

When he arrives with his truck, she helps him to move the fridge from the garage to his truck. She holds on to the one end, while he climbs on the truck from where he pulls it up. She feels a bond develop between them, an understanding, a knowingness. Soon Keith and she will be the ones to arrive in a strange country with their rucksacks and sleeping bags.

Her bare feet burn on the hot tar. 'You should give me a tip for helping you!' They laugh, and he waves at her as he drives through the gate of the security complex.

She returns to the garage to collect the frozen food, now lying on the floor. She carries it to the kitchen to put in the 'new' fridge.

She walks towards the patio doors and faces the swimming pool. It surprises her to see Keith lying on the lounger, ready for a tanning session under the warm South African sun.

'Better make the most of this opportunity,' he says, as he turns onto his stomach.

She sighs, shakes her head, and goes inside. After she puts the frozen food into the freezing compartment of the fridge, she goes to her study to sort out her CD's.

Chapter 2

KEITH LEAVES

'Should I have my case wrapped?' asks Keith as they walk past the wrapping facility at Departures. They have not been to the Cape Town International Airport since it has been revamped, and everything looks and feels different.

'When you wrap your case, it looks as if you have something special inside. Recently I heard of someone who found the wrapping inside his empty suitcase.'

Kiki feels anxious and does not want him to waste time wrapping his case. She wishes he were already on the plane. If only the 'goodbyes' could be done with. As far as she is aware, there is nothing in his suitcase valuable enough for anybody to steal. But, then again, she is not a smoker, and the four cartons of Kent Special Mild might entice someone.

'I should be able to fit two more cartons of cigarettes into my cabin bag. Cigarettes are much cheaper at the duty-free shops. You do not know how much they cost in the UK.' She thinks she does but would rather not comment on this contentious topic.

He looks relieved when his polka dot suitcase disappears on the luggage line. He puts his boarding ticket inside the pocket of his new denim jacket. Once he decided to leave for the United Kingdom, things got hectic. There was no time for a haircut, and his dark brown hair looked somewhat unruly.

'Let's have a coffee and a final chat before I go to the departure hall. But first, I need the bathroom,' he says.

She realizes she also needs the bathroom before she drives home. Her legs feel weak, and her hands shake. It dawns on her that the time has come for him to leave her behind. So much must happen before she can also board a plane to London. *Oh, to sit next to her husband and eat a meal served on a plastic tray!* She wants to experience the enormity, the extent of their decision to leave South Africa: a conspiracy concluded between two desperate people. She wants to fly over her beloved country and say "cheers" with a glass in her hand. However, her companion is leaving her behind to manage life on her own, and who knows when she, too, will be able to escape.

A few days ago, they received the news they have not approved her Settlement Visa. Not only did they lose a few thousand Rand for the declined visa, but she now must reapply. This time she must write and pass an English

Language test, which consists of a written and oral examination.

After the news, it was as if nothing could hold Keith in South Africa. He had made up his mind. He had to be in the UK as soon as possible. Previously, when they went their separate ways, it was supposed to be for just three weeks. Yet things went horribly wrong, and they didn't get together again for nearly eight months. After that, she was convinced they would never be apart again for so long a period. She has a bad feeling about this separation though, and is reminded of Hilda, his mother, who said: 'Do not let him go on his own Kiki.'

Her husband looks dapper in his new jeans, smart boots, and Kilimanjaro jacket draped over his arm. This is not the way she pictured their departure. They had planned everything to be completed by the end of the month. But everything - the banks, the car, the phones - everything is going to come tumbling down soon, and she is not quite ready to deal with it on her own.

'Do you know what? I think I'd rather leave now than later. The sun is setting, and I feel a bit nervous driving from the airport. Somehow, I always end up in the Cape Flats,' she says with a wry smile. He agrees it is best that she leaves now.

When they part, they say all the usual things: 'Have a pleasant trip.'

'I'll phone you when I arrive at Heathrow.'

'Hopefully, you'll sit next to a wealthy lady who will ask us to take care of her mansion in the country. Tell her we'll accompany her on her holidays to France too.'

'Make sure you phone Conrad and ask him to pay our outstanding commission into our new bank account.'

He holds her tightly against his chest, and she smells his cigarette breath. The reality of being left by herself on this side of the wall hits her in her stomach. He is going to crawl through, and she might not be able to find him again on the other side. Her composure crumbles, and unexpected floods of sobs, tears and sadness, overcome her. She knows it for a fact now: he is leaving her, not only for a few weeks, but possibly for a few months.

Dusk falls fast, and she worries about the exit roads leading from the airport. Luckily, she makes it to the car where it is parked on deck C.

Reaching home, her two polka dot cases mock her as she walks into their bedroom. Whatever fits into those cases is all that she will possess in her new life. At this moment, another polka dot case is being loaded into a Boeing heading for Heathrow Airport. It belongs to her husband who holds both a British and a South African passport.

Apart from her luggage, only their queen-sized bed is still in the bedroom. It has not been sold, and she wonders what to do about it. Who would want to buy their bed? The one where they made love, where they breathed onto each other's skin, nestling closely? Who would understand that the salty taste was from her tears, and the stain was from a glass of white wine filled to the brim?

She goes to the half empty lounge and stretches out on the yellow couch. This will be the last time she will watch Grey's Anatomy on their own TV.

Pat will arrive shortly to fetch the driftwood, the water feature and the succulents that used to decorate their patio. Getting rid of their belongings has become a challenge. What was dear to her does not mean much to someone else. She gave and gave, and it will not go away.

Does it hurt to not have possessions anymore? When they made the initial decision to leave, the thought terrified her. She felt like a tortoise without its shell. She had never previously considered life without material possessions, and now it was becoming a shocking reality.

It's so easy to embrace the idea that they judge you on what you own, the car you drive, how you dress, and what your home looks like. But reality was offering different thoughts.

The one thing that keeps her from self-pity is the prospect of a new life in the unknown. She thrives on change and adventure, but right now she must admit it feels scary not knowing where they will live in the future. They just must get through the hole. She is filled with false bravado. If they can do it, anyone can. It's fine. Go ahead. Sell your possessions, give up your home, resign from your job, and put in another application for a settlement visa. There you go, open the can of worms.

On her last day at Morning Place, she wakes up early. Nobody is lying beside her. Her 'somebody' is now close to Heathrow Airport. Soon he will rent a car, put his cases in the trunk and take off. Where to, she has no idea.

She turns onto one elbow and takes stock of what they left in the house. There is still plenty of stuff to get rid of: their bed, an eight-seater table with chairs, and the yellow couch. Before she can hand over the keys to the new tenants at two o'clock, she will have to make at least two trips with the last bits and pieces to Bellville, where she will stay with her daughter and family until she, too, can leave.

When she finally deposits her cases in the bedroom of her daughter's house, she is exhausted but feels relieved. The house is strangely quiet; no dogs in sight; they're boarding at the kennels. The family will not be back from their holiday in Knysna until Sunday afternoon, which gives her time to rest, and to prepare for her English Language Test on Saturday.

She does a 'Google Maps' search to study the route from the house to the examination hall on the campus of Cape Town University, a route with which she is not at all familiar.

Her future life in England and being able to live with her husband depends on this exam. She still finds it difficult to grasp the fact that they do not regard South Africa as an English-speaking country. There are eleven

official languages in her home country, but the one that
opens doors all over the world, the one that she
instinctively understood from a young age, the one that is
more acceptable than her mother tongue- that one- is now
holding her back. How ridiculous! She had to pay two
thousand rand to prove that she comprehends and can
speak English. The fact that she holds a degree in which
one of her subjects was English means nothing, because it
was taught at an Afrikaans-language university.

'Am I allowed to park my car here?' she asks a man
who looks at ease with his surroundings.

'I always park here, and then I walk up those stairs to
the exam hall.' He points in the direction of the famous
statue of Cecil John Rhodes, who sits on his horse, peering
in a northerly direction.

It relieved her to know she arrived at the right place
and parks the car behind his.

'Sorry sir', she asks. 'Why do you say you *always* park
your car here?'

'I want to emigrate to Australia, and all that stands in
my way is this darn English Language test. Today will be
my fourth attempt.'

Can it be so difficult? She wonders.

She meets other Afrikaans-speaking people who plan to
emigrate to Australia. *Why are you going to England? The
weather there is appalling!*

'That's true, but my husband is a British citizen. Also, Australia sounds like a boring country to me,' she says, feeling slightly irritated.

Question 5A: Give your opinion about the extravagant parties held for baptisms, weddings, and other major occasions. Do you think it is worth it, or should it be scaled down? Write three paragraphs. That is a simple question. She has strong opinions on this topic. She thinks this is a ridiculous expenditure, and she will give them a piece of her mind.

She sets out full of energy and ideas. However, soon her confidence takes a blow. She finds her sentences become long-winded and clumsy. How can she correct them? On her laptop at home, she can just delete the mistakes, but her paper has become a war zone - deletions and crammed handwriting with changes. She is shocked and feels ashamed. If she were the examiner, she would not even want to read the mess.

After the examination, she drives to the Victoria and Alfred Waterfront. She wants to exchange clothes they bought there before Keith left.

It feels unnatural to walk around on her own at this beautiful place. Though the sea is calm, the boats sway gently while tourists board them. She nearly bumps into a mime artist while staring at tourists. For a moment she wishes she could sit down at a table and sip a glass of cold Sauvignon Blanc.

Feeling relieved, she ticks off another task on her list. When she arrives home, she consults Google Maps again. Tomorrow at noon, she must be at the Downs College in Observatory to do the oral examination. There is not a lot she can do to prepare, considering that she has spent her whole life trying to master the English language. If she cannot speak English by now, she never will.

'I'm in Cornwall,' says her husband later that evening on the phone. He sounds happy and excited. 'I drove all day, and I'm going to sleep in a Bed and Breakfast tonight. This is a beautiful town with a Roman bridge, a pier, and sailing boats in the harbour.'

Somehow, he manages to make her feel sorry for him. He has rented a car for a month and will drive around until he finds a place where he thinks they would be happy. She looks at Google to find the place where he is. Looe is a tiny seaside village.

'Too small for us,' he says. 'Good luck for tomorrow's oral. Believe me, you speak better English than some of the Brits here in Cornwall.'

She reaches the exam location almost one and a half hours too early. She steps inside the building to make sure she is in the right place and meets the assistant. He says she can come immediately, as there is an opening.

The examiner fiddles with her tape recorder.

Oh, dear Lord! What if my speech is not recorded and I must redo it in a few weeks' time!

She peers at Kiki over her glasses. *What on earth makes a woman come here on a Sunday, to listen to candidates who display their lack of English or, hopefully, their proficiency?* Kiki wonders.

'Tell me about one of the most difficult decisions you had to make, and how it affected your life.' The woman is business-like, and she settles deeply into her chair.

Kiki is forced to think fast. *What comes to mind, what can I tell this woman?* A waft of her perfume tickles Kiki's nose, and she sneezes. She needs time to think. She must have enough to talk about; no point in running out of steam after a few minutes.

Shall I talk about the decision to leave South Africa? The problem is, beside the fact she must wait for a Settlement Visa while her husband travels in Cornwall, she does not have enough evidence yet of what the impact on her life will be. Should she tell her about her decision to leave Keith, while he was still drinking, how she had to leave him to start a new life, knowing it was going to break her heart? No, the impact of that decision, too, is not yet sufficiently clear.

At last, she decides. She will tell her how she concluded that she had to leave her first husband and give up her marriage of twenty -eight years. *Oh Lord, what a messy life: drama after drama.* She squirms. Time is running out. At least she knows the outcome, and what the effect was on her life. She takes a deep breath, connects her eyes with the examiners', and starts talking.

'So, even though it was a tough decision, I know it was the right thing to do. I know now that life is not always straight and predictable, and sometimes one must take life into one's own hands,' she closes lamely.

She smiles, nods her head, and sits back on the hard chair. Hopefully, she has displayed her skills in her vocal use of tenses, grammar, and vocabulary. Whether her take on life has shocked the examiner does not concern her. At least Kiki noticed she had been extremely interested in her juicy story, and hopefully she would give her a good grade.

Not long after she arrives home, she hears the engine of a car drive onto the property. Car doors are flung open, followed by a volcano of voices. She rushes to a window from where she can see her daughter, her son-in-law, her four grandchildren, sweet wrappers, empty cool drink bottles, books, and toys tumble out of their minibus. They are home from their holiday.

The next phase of her departure arrived. There is no way to tell how long this could last.

Chapter 3

IN LIMBO

A mixture of emotions haunts her: fear, boredom and loneliness. She misses someone, something. She misses belonging to a place or to a person. Where she is now, despite all intentions, has become her temporary home.

She *owns* three dogs who adore her. A white Labrador, a black Labrador, and a little bed warmer who has become her best mate. They have a great understanding. Each of them instinctively knows what the other is planning to do. Last night, as she repacked her belongings into the red suitcase - Emirates' thirty kilograms limit - he acted like a lover who knew he was soon to be scorned. As she prepared for bed, he nudged the lid of the suitcase, showing that he wanted it to be opened. She knew he wanted to sleep on top of her clothes. Should she leave during the night, he would be inside, and she would take him with her.

Don't worry Little One, I am not going anywhere. Yet! She feels guilty. Kiki knows the day will come when she leaves. When that will be, she just does not know yet. She turns a blind eye to Tommy, the Labrador, who sleeps curled up like a kitten on the couch. Bonny lies by her feet and wherever she goes in the house, two shadows follow her. It annoys her when she bends to pick up something and finds a dog in her space. She does not have the heart to put them outside in the cold and the rain. She now understands why they sleep on the veranda floor. The first night after her family left for Europe, she gave the dogs blankets to sleep on, and the next morning, opening the curtains, she was treated to a show of white fluff and pieces of fabric strewn all over. She supposes they do not really feel the cold through their thick skins. With the dogs by her side, she is not afraid, bored, or lonely. They wait outside while she goes shopping, and in the morning, after she deactivates the burglar alarm, they hug her when she opens the doors. Tommy plays games with her and gives her warmth. If only he could whisper in her ear that he loved her, he would be her perfect companion.

Keith phones her almost every day. He talks, and she listens. When she manages to get a word in, it sounds insignificant and empty to her. Who would be interested in her life as it is now?

I made vegetable soup, I worked in the garden, I cleaned and polished the coffee table, I played computer games, and I went to the shop to buy electricity and dog food.'

He tells her about the apartment he rents in Norwich and his new job with all the challenging administrative work.

'Tomorrow I should have my first sale,' he tells her.

She is glad for him. But how can it be that he doesn't need her help? There's no mention that he misses her as his work partner. That is just the way it is. He is ready to excel on his own. Their Skype conversation lasts an hour, and not once does he enquire about her feelings or wellbeing. She has no idea whether he still loves her. Tonight, when he speaks to her from his apartment in Norwich, he is bare chested. She sees his torso and she longs to give him a hug. She does not mention this. First, there's no opportunity, and second, he would not encourage her.

A door has closed between them. There is a sliver of light shining under the door, but it comes from a dark moon on the opposite side of the universe. He tells her about Sirius, the bright star in the Northern hemisphere that he conversed with. That star does not appear in her part of the world. She does not feel any benevolent rays lighting up her way. Where she lives, in Limbo, God, as a star, does not exist.

Kiki thanks Eckhart Tolle for his book *'Living in the NOW.'* She savours her moments. Today she laps up the minutes and drinks in the day. She has light only for today, but the past has uncanny ways of invading her empty thoughts. When she worked as an estate agent, her mind was filled with clients, apartments, contracts, and phone calls. Now, the mischievous past steals her and takes her to places and situations irrelevant to her current life in Limbo. What does she care about the day when they moved from Durbanville to Cape Town? Does she really need a reminder of the boyfriend she jilted when she was seventeen years old? What is happening to her mind?

Here she is. It is only her, without Keith, enjoying peace and quiet. She recently started to wear glasses and had her hair cut in a style she does not think suits her. She has few needs and drives a car (albeit the bank's) to take her to the shops. If she wants to, she can visit her mother who lives in Stellenbosch in a retirement home. Kiki sleeps in her granddaughter's bedroom, where every few nights, a poster of either Justin Bieber or Selena Gomez slips off the wall, misses her head, and flops onto the bed.

At least twice a day, she visits the British Embassy's website to follow the progress of her visa application. It stays stuck on the original message left on the fifth of May 2012: *'Visa application received and under process by British Embassy in Pretoria.'*

She writes down and numbers each day until the beginning of August. This way she can draw lines through three months' worth of days.

She does not need to visit old friends. Ideally, she should contact people she has not seen for a long time. What is really the point of speaking to old friends? The chance of seeing them in the future is minimal. What will she tell them about herself? She feels like a failure. She and Keith abused their credibility in this country. After so many years of valiantly battling, trying to keep her head above water, she has capitulated.

'Aha, but surely your children will not allow bad things to happen to you!' friends exclaim.

That is just the point! I do not want to look into their eyes for support. It is their turn to support their children and not have to worry about their mother.

Would anyone enjoy a conversation like that? No, it's boring and leads nowhere.

Oh, this country is really going downhill. Did you read in today's newspaper, about the nineteen people who were killed when two Putco buses had a race? One bus crashed into a bridge. What a joke! They are destroying tons of schoolbooks, while a huge percentage of schools are still waiting for new books for this school year. One of the tender corruptions again….

No, it's bad manners to talk like this to people who have to stay here with nowhere else to go. This wasn't the reason for Keith and her to leave. But since they decided, there is so much negative press in the newspapers and on TV confirming the declining situation in South Africa.

Yesterday she noticed a parked car with an open boot on a street corner in the suburb where her family lives. A handsome man crossed the road carrying an 'On Show' sign. *Oh,'* she thought: An *estate agent preparing for lots of visitors on this rainy, freezing Sunday. Well, good luck to him. May I never have to do that again.*

She wonders what work she will do when she has settled in her new country. Keith had made it clear he was happy in Norwich; she would have to find her own thing to do.

She is in a reflective mood when she sets the timer of the walker in the gym downstairs. She can walk two- and-a- half miles comfortably in thirty minutes.

After about three minutes' walk, she tightly grips the handles of the machine. She closes her eyes and takes a few deep breaths. Repetitive thoughts jump into her head. *I cannot be sure that my new life will be perfect.* Then, the question: *Will I be able to live this kind of life of being separate, rather than in a union, where nothing is allowed in between?* She is reminded of the letter Keith sent her yesterday by email. Oh, he wanted to get back at her! A hurtful letter, sticking a knife where she had put hers. What sweet revenge!

The further her legs take her on the machine, the tighter she grips the handles, and then something urges her to release her thoughts. It becomes a clear light in her head and the Ring-a-Rosie circle of negativity makes way for a specific thought, a message.

'There is a task for you. It is something you yearn for. It is something you have been prepared for by going through difficult circumstances. Your life has been a preparation for this. Always, you want to give and share your experiences. Showing the way and helping others without feeling used, is what you yearn for.

There is a place waiting for you. It is being prepared. You will not have to look for it, it is already secure, and it will come looking for you. Here, you have been living a life of searching for opportunities to share, but circumstances have been hard and unforgiving. In the soft soil of a moist country, there are open hearts, longing for the comfort you can give. In your hands, sitting like a dove, is a special gift for you, waiting to be released and fly home. Young child, you are healed. It is not your task to fix broken things. You are free to go, and you are ready to release him, so that each of you can excel; individually and separately.'

The tears she cries are a release, not of sadness or anger. It is a relief to know the tears streaming down her cheeks, wetting her new spectacles, can flow freely. The dogs run to her side, concerned about the noises coming from her mouth.

She peeks at the meters on the bike and sees she walked for twenty-five minutes, burnt sixty-five units of fat and one hundred and fifty-five calories. Her blood pressure is one hundred and ninety-three. She took ten and a half strides in a minute, and she climbed a hill, measured at a figure of eight.

There is no gauge to measure her mental state after this epiphany. She completes her set time of two point seven miles in thirty minutes and stops the machine. She wipes her eyes with toilet paper she finds in the adjacent bathroom and walks upstairs in a daze. Has this happened so that she can act as if she did not care? *Can you see, I found my own job? Don't you worry about me, I'll find something to do.* Is that what she ultimately wants to show the world?

One part of her must admit it would be nice to be wanted. They have been so good together. Even working in harmony as a couple for so long is a monumental achievement. Few marriages could sustain that.

She needs to get to the UK and live her new life. Kiki knows it will be quite different, but she thinks she is ready now. No doubt it is going to take another miracle to rebuild their relationship. He told her in no uncertain terms that once she is there, she would have to change. He has changed, and he cannot live with her if she stays the way she is.

This morning, as she prunes the shrubs and trees in her daughter's garden, she cries. Growth; stems growing skew, greenery sprawling on the lawn way out of line; it must be cut back and tamed. Her heart aches. She is sad because her best friend is not hers anymore, and he might never be that again. She realizes she cannot tell him how she feels. She may never speak out again. If that is what she would like to do, she is barking up the wrong tree. Either she must become totally free from her needs, or she must learn how to be happy as an individual in their relationship. When the Dutch built dikes to keep the ocean at bay in the Netherlands, they tried to fix much more than a hole in a wall. They had to claim and reclaim land from the ocean. With her and Keith it is different – they needed a hole in the wall to close in on them. First, they had to make a hole, and then they had to climb through it, without knowing what was on the other side. But only he got through in time. He has left her behind, worrying that the hole is closing fast again, leaving her in doubt that she'll get through.

Chapter 4

THE LETTER

The letter. The letter that had burst into her email messages. An arrow fired from afar.

The hole is so big now; she is afraid that she might fall through it and end up on an unknown planet or in a dark hole. Kiki is tumbling fast, right through her head; she's filled with pins and needles, she goes right through her stomach. Down her jelly- like spine she glides, and finally splatters like rain on a windowpane, onto the floor. Maybe her head will explode, and the thoughts tumbling through her brain might get caught up in the tangled mess her hair has become.

If only she could find answers or a glimpse into the future on the Internet. *Dear Internet God, does he still love me? What has changed between the last time I saw him and now? What kind of love is this I have for a man who committed himself to accompanying me through the wall, but now needs space?*

The Internet has always supplied her with answers to everything. Think of a topic, then Google it. Whatever information you need, you'll find the answer there. How long will it take to fly to the moon, or to dig a hole in their wall? She demands an answer and knows she will find it.

But this time there are no answers. What is the future of a woman who loves a man who has deserted her? There is no information about her tomorrow, where she will live or work, whether she will be happy or sad. She suffers from a modern disease, but unfortunately there is no remedy for Internet withdrawal. Typical symptoms are shaking hands, sweaty palms, racing heart, pins and needles pricking your face. She displays them all.

She was spoilt before the construction of The Wall. Always she had contracts for two mobile phones and enough time and data to enquire about anything she wanted. Now she must buy airtime. This business of buying time is a totally different story. Once she paid for two gigabytes, not knowing how big or small a gig or a byte was. She must type a trillion figures into her PC. Or no, maybe on her mobile phone? With shaking hands and impatience brimming over, she gives up. She gets into her car and races to the shopping mall to ask for the shop assistant's help. She urgently needs a fix.

The car that she drives belongs to the bank. They do not know it yet, but soon she will leave the car and the keys in an envelope at the bank. The person in whose name the car is registered does not care what happens to it. But the car knows it has been deserted; it plays tricks with her. It does not want to release the key when she wants to lock it. She has become good at leaving it, nonchalantly, with the keys still in the ignition. Who is she to force the car to release a stupid key? She just gets out and walks to the shop without looking back.

What does she have to lose? She has sold everything she owned. Treasures and trinkets, which travelled with her over years of joy and sorrow: now all gone. She can pack her life into two suitcases. They, she and her husband (who now needs space), have so much debt, they cannot repay it without a miracle. If he ever wanted to wave goodbye to her at an airport and never see her again, he could not have chosen a better time.

Once there was a Wall and they did not know how to get to the other side. They were supposed to dig at it together, and follow plan one, plan two or maybe three. Somehow, her husband dug alone, while she was busy applying for her visa, organizing an English language test, and recovering from a cataract operation. He dug a hole, just big enough for himself, so that only he could slip through. While she was sorting and selling their belongings, saying her goodbyes, he dug into their bank accounts, squirreled away their winter stock, bought a one -way plane ticket, and slipped through the hole.

She hadn't realized that there was a plan four. She had never expected the letter. The letter with the ultimatum: she had to change or stay behind in South Africa. How could she possibly stay behind? Without him here with her, her life would be a misery. No, no! The whole idea is preposterous. He also does not realise it, but without her by his side, he would struggle to live a fulfilled life. It is clear to Kiki that Keith would never return to South Africa, so there is only one thing for her to do and that is to go to him. She? She had to change. How? She has no idea how to change. All she knows is that she has given up her life here, that she no longer has a job or a home. She is on her way to the UK. And now, he tells her to change or stay here in South Africa!

All that is left of her old life is a gaping wound. She is slipping down its bleeding sides. Her fingers are oozing, her nails look strange without their protective shield. But she hangs on because she believes the wall can be rebuilt.

She fears, though, that there might be a hidden secret door somewhere, and even if she could hide behind the wall's protection, he might slip away again. Each brick in the wall has a story to tell. This one, the cornerstone to the left, is their love for each other. Then she spots a crack that she had previously never seen. How did it get there without her noticing it? She must consider that she might never be able to see what is on the other side of the wall.

And yet she can hear the droning of a barge in the distance. Chug, chug! And is that the call of a swan, searching for his mate? She hears the footsteps of a lonely man walking to his new apartment. In this home, there is nothing to remind him of his life on the other side. She notices a green carpet on the floor with matching curtains. There is a down duvet with a nautical cover on the double bed in the main bedroom. She wants to believe that he chose it with her in mind. There are new plates in the cupboard in the kitchen, and a special coffee machine stands in the kitchen. In her packed suitcase, there is the knife sharpener for Keith's chef's knife. He has the knife; she will bring him the sharpener.

Chapter 5

FLYING AT LAST

After months of thinking herself onto this plane, Flight TK 638 from Cape Town International Airport to Istanbul, it prepared her well for the flight. Everything she needs for her travels is in the bag lying on the floor at her feet. Her South African passport, stamped with her precious Settlement visa, she keeps in the small bag against her body. After all she went through to get permission to stay in the United Kingdom, nobody must be able to take it from her while she sleeps.

She goes to the tiny bathroom to brush her teeth. The droning noise of the plane as it flies across Africa makes the gulping sound of the flushing toilet less threatening. She swallows the sleeping tablet she put into her purse weeks ago, and sighs. Is this true? After tonight, the next time she falls asleep will be in their apartment in Norwich in her husband's arms.

She hopes she wakes up in time to prepare for their landing at Ataturk Airport in Turkey. There is not much time to find the departure lounge for her flight to Heathrow Airport.

Do not think about leaving South Africa tonight, she tells herself. It's a big thing for her - leaving her family and her life behind – and it's almost too much to bear.

Maybe she should rather think of her husband. How will it be to experience the pleasure of their closeness? She wonders if he would like to hold her the minute they walk into the apartment. No, probably not. Knowing him, he would first want to show her the ins and outs of the new coffee machine.

Her mind struggles to come to rest. Until now, she had purposefully denied the memories of the weeks leading up to this flight. What happened between them during their four months of inevitable separation was so unpalatable that the only way to deal with it was total denial.

She realizes she is taking a chance going to the United Kingdom. But she is confident they will work things out between them. She will deal with the hurt and disappointment once they are together again. They have been through so much during the ten years they have already been together that they will deal with this too. Their love is sound enough. She is convinced that within a few weeks at most, everything will be back to the way it had been before Keith left.

The flight attendant bumps against her feet. She pulls her legs closer to her body and takes a couple of deep breaths. In a few hours, Keith will get up to drive to the airport to fetch her. The trip will take about three hours. She knows he will not be late.

The Lord alone knows how hard it was to whittle down her belongings to a laptop, carrier bag, and one medium- sized suitcase. Thirty kilograms, no more! Her granddaughter accompanied her to the check-in counter. She wanted to make sure there would be no problems with her luggage. She was the last family member Kiki saw in South Africa. One last hug, and the girl headed towards the exit where her father and youngest sister waited for her in the car. Her straight, long, blond hair fell down her back and bounced in the sunshine as she disappeared through the door. When Kiki sees her again, she will probably be a young woman. Who knows when that will be?

In a retirement home in Stellenbosch, her mother would be fast asleep. She did not tell her she was leaving the country. It made no sense to upset her. While she waited for her visa to arrive, Kiki had visited her occasionally over a few weeks. Each time she thought it would be the last time she might see her. Now, half lying, half sitting on the empty seat next to hers, she visualizes the 92-year-old senile woman. She had lost everything except her sense of humour. There she was sitting on her red rocking chair. The gentle frown on her face matched the distress she experienced each time her daughter said goodbye.

'Please take me with you. It is so boring to sit here day in and day out.'

'I love you, Mom. Sorry, but I must go now. See you soon.' Until a few months ago, her mother would have accompanied her to the front door of the home, pushing the walking frame, her movements uncharacteristically slow. She would then stand there by the door, waving at Kiki as she drove away in her car. A while ago, the nursing home staff had warned her that her mother had an acute case of pneumonia. She had been coughing for weeks on end. When Kiki hurried there, her mother denied being sick.

'Sick? Me? I am not sick. I am just sick of sitting around in this room. Nurse, do you know my daughter? Look, she came to visit me.'

When she wakes up the next morning, the plane has been flying over Turkey for a couple of hours. She goes to the bathroom to freshen up. *What will go through Keith's mind when he sees me again,* she wonders?

In Cape Town, her grandson will wake up now. He will want to come to her bed to lie with her, the way he did the past few months. What a splendid little sleeper he is! No kicking, no moving around, just nestling in her arms, emanating warmth and personality.

She watches the screen in front of her to see how the plane is drawing a line. It is edging closer to Ataturk

Airport. She is not a seasoned traveller, and her heart pounds in her chest. Soon she will be on foreign soil, albeit just for a few hours.

Keith flew straight to London on a more expensive flight. None of this 'stopping over in other foreign countries' for him! 'It makes the flight too long,' he said.

Well, at least I am saving a few thousand Rand this way. That will make up for the coat and shoes I had to leave behind, she thinks. Also, don't forget, she is the bringer of goods. Cigarettes, much cheaper in South Africa, take up a sizeable chunk of space in her suitcase.

She wonders for how long her energy, her 'space' will be remembered in South Africa. Who was she to those she left behind? A daughter, a mother, a grandmother, an employee, a friend, a daughter-in- law, a sister- in- law, a Facebook contributor, a quitter, an example, a co-dependent? Life goes on and the void she leaves will be filled quickly. Will she be able to build new relationships, will she mean something to new people in her life again? Her husband made it clear in *that letter* that she was to live her own life. He had changed, and he wanted to move on. From now on, *fit in or leave, do your own thing*. That was his attitude towards her.

She had booked a window seat for this leg of the flight from Istanbul to Heathrow. She wants to observe the rivers and farms spread like veins across Europe. Clouds obscure the small towns and villages, but somewhere across Bulgaria, she detects a river that seems to direct the plane towards England. For a long time, the plane follows this river.

She wishes that the plane would cross the channel from Europe to England at Dover. It would be wonderful to see the White Cliffs of Dover from the sky. But the plane seems to make a loop, then it enters England from a northerly direction. Villages and green, then green and greener, then roads. And finally; tarmac! The plane touches down. Here she is on English soil at Heathrow Airport.

He will be there, waiting for her. All the anger and stiffness will be gone once their warmth rubs off onto each other. She comforts herself and makes sure she has all her belongings with her. She brings her African heart, her wisdom, and a bag filled with cigarettes. He brings with him his stubborn loneliness, his fear, and the keys to their new lives.

The 2012 Olympics begin in two weeks in London, and Customs is slow and thorough. She is entitled to live and work in the UK for two years until she can apply for Indefinite Leave to Remain. She will have to pass a test called 'Life in the UK'. Her husband is her sponsor. She will not be entitled to Government Support until she has Permanent Residency. Because she will travel on a South African passport, she will have to apply for a Schengen Visa, should she want to visit another country in the European Union.

While she waits in the long, winding queue at Immigration Control, she looks forward to getting through the hole, but somehow, she dreads the finality of the moment. She remains apprehensive without reason. Will she be allowed to go through?

There is a commotion at the Customs counter. They ushered a Turkish family who does not have details of their intended address into a cordoned area. Kiki watches them in shock. Her heart pounds in her chest. They make phone calls on their mobiles.

'What is your physical address?' The official sounds tired. She hears the panic in the man's voice. A young girl, sitting by herself, wipes the tears off her face with the back of her hand. She has nobody to phone in the UK.

Kiki feels very vulnerable. If she were sent back to South Africa now, where would she even begin? Her life there is over; there is no turning back now. When she finally receives a stamp on her passport, she goes to find her suitcase at the carousel. Her legs feel like jelly.

'Please sir, have you seen a suitcase with polka dots?'

It feels as if she stood in the Immigration queue for hours, while in fact it was only ninety minutes. Her handbag tugs at her shoulder and her new shoes pinch her swollen toes.

'Yes Love, I have been watching that dotted case circling round for a while.'

His friendliness is a welcome contrast to the sullen official she saw on her departure from South Africa. She needs his friendliness as much as she needs to be optimistic about the future in her new country of residence. She is on high alert, picking up signals and signs, fully aware that her future survival is based on taking cognisance of her new surroundings. Although she is in no imminent danger, she feels uncomfortable when she is in a strange place. Keith will be impatient by now. She should not keep him waiting any longer.

She walks towards the rows of trolleys waiting to be used. The hall is eerily quiet. Most of the passengers from the Istanbul flight left a while ago. She extends her hand to free a trolley from the line. It moves slightly but stays stuck. The trolley will only be unchained once she pushes a pound through the slot. A pound! She does not own a pound. Yet. Without a pound, she is stuck. How on earth can she carry her suitcase, bag, laptop, and handbag? She must hurry, though. Keith is waiting for her. She finally puts her laptop and bag on top of the case and pulls it on its wheels towards Arrivals.

She notices him immediately; he looks like a stick man. They embrace briefly. She is shocked to see how thin he is now. The angry words spoken on the phone and the harsh letters exchanged on the internet left sharp edges, and it is hard to make contact across these landmines.

The distance he created between them in his new life makes her departure from her loved ones seem insignificant. He has already lost interest in the past. He has sacrificed his free day to drive all the way from Norwich to the airport to fetch her.

He puts her belongings into the boot of the red car he bought a few weeks ago without asking for her opinion or blessing. To her, it is just a red car, but she is also incredibly grateful that they did not have to board a bus or a train to get to her new home.

The landscape is flat and as they drive into Norwich; she has no vantage point from which to make a judgment or form an impression of the town. She viewed it on Google maps many times and knows the Wensum River runs like a snake around the city. One can see a castle on a hill from the patio doors of the apartment's lounge, but when she sees the first boat going past their apartment, she is unprepared for the sight. The semi-deserted factory buildings squatting on the riverbanks create a picturesque backdrop, while houseboats rock gently on the waves. A pair of swans and their three cygnets glide past as if on cue. How beautiful! She slips her arm around Keith's waist, and she hugs him. He stands next to her, waiting for her reactions and approval.

'I told you that you would like it.' He seems pleased with himself. 'So, what do you think about the place?'

'I love it. You did well to find this home for us. It is not exceptionally modern but seems comfortable. With a few of my feminine touches, we will make it more homely. Wow, this bedroom is large! Oh, yes, your choice of duvet is brilliant. And this floor lamp, did you buy this too?' She is keen to see how he managed on his own.

'Yes, but then I broke it and had to buy a replacement. It cost only ten pounds. And here! Ta-da! The coffee machine! I'll show you a bit later how it operates.'

The kitchen is compact and small but seems well equipped. But it seems that his cooking comprises of pre-cooked meals bought at Marks and Spencer. To her, the shop sounds like a typical Woolworths in South Africa, and she wonders about the price of these easy meals. Wisely, she does not comment, but makes a mental list of things to buy that will enhance the appearance of the apartment.

She takes another look at the second bedroom. There is a double bed without a duvet but covered with documents and clean washing. A new printer stands on a nest table. It must have been a struggle for him to keep a hold of everything. Setting up home and finding a job.... It could not have been easy. But she is here now, and they will soon get back to normal.

'So! Are you ready? Let me show you your new town.' He is in a hurry to leave the apartment.

He first shows her the shops closest to their apartment.

'Here is Matalan, Curry's, Boots, Poundland and here - oh you'll love this one - is Hobbycraft.' They go inside a two storied building filled with painting materials, scrapbooking tools, knitting wool and needles, (do people still knit?) embroidery materials, whatever one would need to make a doll's house, puzzles and much more.

'Wait,' she says, as he tries to steer her out of the shop. 'I want to look at the mosaics.' She is alarmed. 'This shop sells rubbish mosaics. Look, these tiles are plastic.'

'Never mind, you can order proper tiles through the internet.' He grabs her arm and pulls her towards the exit. She thinks of her cutters, tiles, pieces of broken mirror, and the patterns she packed into a box, and left at her youngest daughter's home. Keith is on a mission, and she must walk extremely fast to keep up with him.

They walk over a footbridge crossing the river which flows past their apartment. Then, they turn right into a street lined with typical town houses. A group of young people passes them. Though she catches an English phrase here and there, their conversation sounds unrecognisable to her.

'This is typical Norfolk dialect,' Keith says. 'This is the way they speak here.'

'But will they understand my English pronunciation?' she asks, feeling puzzled.

'Of course! Just speak clearly and slowly. Come this way, follow me.'

They cross a road and pass an old church before they arrive at the entrance of a castle. Keith is a man on a mission; like a marathon athlete looking out for the next refreshment table en route. He seems oblivious to the effect the old church building has on her. A poster advertises weekly Karate classes. She decides to visit the building again on her own. The beautiful doors and gates deserve to be appreciated and photographed.

After another short walk, they get to a shopping mall. 'Here is another Boots, and this is where I bought the lamp. The NHS doctors are on the upper level. You come here to register as a patient.'

'Me? May I? But they say on my Visa that I am not entitled to public funds?'

'Yes, you cannot get aid, but you may see a doctor and get free medication.'

'Wow, you mean to say I can get my medication for free?' she repeats sheepishly; but surprised about the positive information.

Next, he shows her the centuries old outdoor market where they buy two pork rolls dripping with applesauce. 'There is the Forum, a modern building housing the public library, and this is Debenhams. Jamie Oliver is opening a new restaurant here. This is Next, here are Wilkinson's and Matalan. Let me give you some advice, buy nothing from this shop. It is a bit like Pep Stores in South Africa.'

She tries to take in all the unfamiliar names of shops and instructions. As they march through the shop, she smells the cheapness of the wares, not realizing that soon it will be one of the few shops she would visit frequently.

'You will soon find out where to shop for the best prices. Don't buy anything without comparing prices. First, look around, compare and only then you should buy something.'

She is relieved when they arrive at the apartment again. It feels strange to be educated and informed like this. He is miles ahead of her. Her head spins like the beans crushed in the new coffee machine in the tiny kitchen. This might be harder to adjust to than she anticipated. She struggles to get in tune with him. Although she thanks him repeatedly for setting up a home for them, it is as if her words don't reach his heart.

After a brief rest, she unpacks her bags. The mosaic mirror with its stand is unharmed, and the wire cross only needs a firm pat to straighten it again. She will have to put her clothes in the other room. The wardrobe in the main bedroom is almost fully packed with Keith's clothes. He bought three new suits and now owns thirty long sleeve shirts. She has never seen him wear pointy shoes like the ones he wears now.

'I received a letter from the school informing me they appointed someone else for the position as assistant librarian,' Kiki tells Keith. Though she is disappointed that they did not consider her for the position, she is not too concerned.

He takes her bank card to put into his wallet, and she realizes that he now has complete control of their finances. It also does not look as if he plans to relinquish any of that control to her soon. It worries her that she does not know what their current financial situation is.

The next day he does not have to go to work, and they take on another excursion. He shows her the remains of the wall around the city, erected in the fourteenth century by a nobleman to protect it from invading enemies. They walk alongside the river until they reach a tower, and from there they walk past the beautiful old cathedral.

'And here is the South African shop where one can buy Provita, Mrs. Balls Chutney and other South African products.' He knows the shop owner and introduces Kiki to him. The shop is small and crammed with produce. The two men talk about the South African Society, a group of patriots who meet once a month in a restaurant in the city.

The next morning, she wakes up to the sound of the ironing board being opened. Keith should be back from work at seven o'clock tonight. She is tired, and her Achilles tendons ache.

As he leaves the apartment, he hands her a twenty-pound note. She takes it, albeit reluctantly. It does not feel right. She is used to handling her own finances.

'What is this for?' she asks with a frown on her pre-makeup face.

'When you are in town, you might want to buy lunch.' Dressed smartly in his dark suit, he looks different from the person she has known for nearly ten years. She feels puzzled and confused.

Isn't it strange how things have changed?

Chapter 6

A NEW HOME

She wants to buy a throw. She saw one that she liked a lot in the shop, but she will have to ask the 'purser' for pounds to pay for it. Until now it has not been an urgent addition to their meagre possessions, but she thinks it is about time that she broaches the subject and makes her need for a warm covering known.

Last night was the second time that she put on her flimsy dressing gown and lay down on the fawn green leather couch in the lounge. A fluffy throw would have kept her warm and helped her to fall asleep. Soon it will be winter, and even though the central heating is turned on, she would enjoy the soft embrace of fabric on her skin.

After she took a sleeping tablet, time passed quickly. Kiki thinks she hasn't moved a muscle since she had lain down. She jumps when she hears Keith's voice. She is now fully awake and opens her eyes to see him standing above her.

'Why are you lying here? Don't you want to get up and go to the room to sleep in our bed?'

She feels sheepish and walks to the bedroom with half-closed eyes. As she snuggles in underneath the duvet, she decides. Before she works again, she will write a book. Maybe she will view writing as a job and prove to herself that she is worthy and disciplined. Kiki realizes nobody will encourage her, rub her back, or praise her for her diligence. She wants to write for over three hours each day. Yes, less than three hours is not negotiable. There needs to be a balance between work and play. The beautiful historic city waits to be explored and all the wonderful shops need her admiration. She is unstoppable. Finally, she has a goal, something to motivate her.

After fluffing up the pillows, she lays her still sleepy head in the new hollow. She makes another decision. While she writes, she will listen to music. She knows what Keith will say. 'But you don't have any CD's. You left them all in South Africa.'

'I have unlimited access to thousands of CDs in the library,' will be her reply.

She is getting good at preparing her short conversations. It's easy. Just listen and then agree. Do not argue, do not voice an opinion.

Look at you! When in your life have you been able to sit by a river, and draw pictures of houses and boats floating on a river? What did you do to deserve the luxury of sitting in the sultry sun for hours in a magical old world?' The English voice inside her head has become her only companion.

Yes, yes, I know! I wish I had learnt to paint years ago but be reasonable. I am a novice who needs plenty of time to practice. These thoughts and emotions, rummaging around inside my head like second-hand clothes at a jumble sale, must be folded into neat piles – each item needs a price tag. Only once that has been sorted, can I consider other entertainment.

She remembers with satisfaction the painting of the woman with the pink hat that she completed yesterday. It is only half a face. And should she make copies of the picture? She could place four or five of them next to each other in a frame. Yes, that is what she will do. That will be unique and look awesome.

But only **her** opinion of the results will count because nobody else will notice her efforts. Or, if he does, Keith will not show any appreciation. She found a 'paint by numbers' set at Wilkinson's sale and that inspired her to paint. After she bought the cheap set and followed the instructions, nothing could stop her. Her new hobby is as creative as mosaic making, but less messy and much more convenient.

Kiki hopes she will pass the ironing test this morning. Without realising, she drifts off into a confusing world where she is half South African, and half English. She can hear the water running in the shower. It seems as if she finally succeeded in eliminating each tiny crease on Keith's shirts. Many mornings, the sound of the ironing board is like the crack of a whip to her fragile ego.

'Look here. I did it perfectly? Why can't you?'

She has run out of excuses: 'It is the iron's fault. These cotton shirts are difficult to iron. It must be the washing machine. It causes permanent creases.'

She also knows (since she has been told) that she never listens, is paranoid and buys the wrong biscuits, coffee, cheese, and bread. She 'broke' the expensive coffee pot, and she does not use the washing machine according to the directions in the booklet. *Oops, ouch.*

With her new resolve firmly cemented in her mind, she finally slips into an early morning sleep. She abandons all negativities. The prospect of a new day makes her feel relaxed and calmer.

Last night though, lying next to her husband's motionless body, the frustration and anger grew like over-inflated balloons and overwhelmed her. She fled to the couch in the lounge. This thing, which she may not tackle with her bare hands, throttles her. It overpowers her, and because she does not have any weapons available, she finds it easier to flee like a coward with no action plan than to stay put.

If she could find a soap box to put out on the town square, she would not even put out a cap or a hat to collect measly copper coins. No, she will deliver a speech for free. Oh, to get this obstruction off her mouth! Speak no evil. Hear no evil. See no evil.

Nowadays, when her phone rings, she jumps in surprise. Will she be able to understand the caller's accent? She never knew that the English language has so many pronunciations. Some people speak fast, and then they suspect that she is hard of hearing.

'Sorry, can you repeat what you just said?''

'Is that Mrs. Kiki Brown?'

'Speaking.'

'I am phoning from Bright Care for the Elderly. We received your application for a job as a live-in carer. Before we can process your application, we need more information. You didn't specify what type of job you are applying for. Our carers work two week shifts and then have a break for one week. Will that suit you?'

*No, it will not suit me. Then I will not have a place that I can call my own. What will that week be like? The week at home, I mean. How far removed from each other will we be then? I'll leave on a train after taking care of some old sick person and arrive at a place where I will do the washing and the ironing and be free to do "my own thing." All the time, I will be wondering, what this **thing**, of becoming separate entities, is about? Where will my home be?*

She cannot tell the Bright lady what she is thinking.

'Yes, I will be available to work two weeks and then take one week off.'

'We need your National Insurance Number to complete the forms for tax and banking purposes.'

Oh dear, more formalities and obstacles. Kiki has never heard of a National Insurance Number as a requirement for work, though she knows Keith keeps his NI card in his wallet.

'I hold a Settlement Visa and a South African passport. I do not have a National Insurance number yet. But I have a bank account.' She is proud of her account and is grateful for Keith's assistance in registering it. 'I'll apply for my National Insurance Number as soon as possible.'

'It might take a bit longer to process your application now, but I'll work with the information you have given me. Thank you very much. Goodbye.'

It disappoints her that the conversation is over so soon. These words could be the only ones she would utter today. Kiki puts the phone down on the bookcase. She sent her resume and application forms to many job advertisers. Once she even had a telephonic interview with a representative of Summer Holiday. It did not go well. The Estate Agencies advertising for positions, all bar one, ignored her excellent experience and references. The Israeli jewellers in the mall might call her if their staffing does not work out. She does not hold out too much hope that they will accept her as a carer. All she can do is to wait and see, just as she'll have to wait and see what the future of their marriage is.

Their marriage has the potential of a popular novel displayed in a bookshop. In the beginning it waded happily through rivers of white and red wine. Eventually it got soaked like a wet blanket. Then it was strung up in the sun for all the world to observe. It dried out and lost weight, shrivelled up like biltong and then, miraculously, it breathed again. It was more supple and brought hope to two people who were close to giving up on themselves. But the novel can't be written until the last chapter has been lived, and only then it is time to decide – should it have a hard or soft cover?

'I think it's time that you give the anti- depressants a break.'

'Doctor, I don't think that's possible. Do you realize I have been taking these tablets for nearly twelve years? I tried at least three times to wean myself off them but found it too difficult. It's such a pity they don't sell the brand I used to take in South Africa here in the UK. Maybe I should ask the doctor to post them.'

'Let me help you wean yourself off. See how it goes. I know you have a lot on your plate right now, immigrating, and by the sound of it, your husband is unsupportive.'

Somehow, against her better judgment, Kiki is persuaded to stop taking her medication. In her heart of hearts, she would love to be free of the chemicals that kept her going through troublesome times. Now, she must live her new life in the UK, and she is told to give up her trusted crutch, albeit one that took as much as it gave. Could she cope without it?

She does not have too many options. Since the brand she uses is not available in the UK, she would have to switch to something new with different side-effects. At this stage of her life, it seems silly to experiment with medication and she also doesn't want to depend on other people to send her tablets from South Africa.

Keith is not happy with his job selling static homes in Norfolk. He has resigned without securing another position. Luckily, he is invited to an interview in North Wales. It all seems exciting, but Kiki feels sad and is reluctant to leave Norwich so soon. Sure, they must move from their apartment once their lease has expired. And it's not good for their wellbeing to take sleeping tablets to drown out the noise from the nightclub across the river. But Wales? What will she do there? It is just as well that she has not yet found a job in Norwich.

Will she be able to find the hole again in the green hills where the ancient Druids lived?

Chapter 7

WALES

It's a short walk from their home to the Post Office in town. But after a few hundred yards, her toes freeze. She has noticed lately that when she goes outside into the cold, her feet become white, like blocks of ice. To protect her face from the cold, she covers her mouth with the thick woollen scarf she knitted during their travels between Norfolk and Wales prior to their move to Abersoch. This cold though, goes deeper than her physical body; its long, thin fingers grope at her heart and probe her brain.

She hopes the Post Office does not close for lunch like most shops in this tiny village. The clothing shops, boutiques catering for the wealthy and famous summer holiday visitors close their shop doors for the whole winter. Some of them open at weekends for a couple of hours, but that is it. She has been into a few of these shops, but the brand names are so expensive that, disheartened, she stopped going inside. Even items sold on the winter sale are unaffordable.

'This time of the year, we usually have extra post days, but because of the increased price of stamps, people don't send as many Christmas packages.' The lady behind the counter weighs Kiki's large brown envelope and puts stamps and a sticker on the front.

'That will be six pounds. Are you satisfied with that?'

'Yes, that's fine. How long will it take to deliver it to South Africa? This is all I can send to my family this year,' she adds lamely, feeling slightly embarrassed.

'Oh, it should be there in five days. What is the value of the contents of the envelope?

'I don't know – nothing, I suppose......'

'Right. Then I will write here: nil pounds.'

'No, no! It is not worth nothing. Say... mmm.... Say, five pounds.'

She spent many hours trying to paint something unique for each of her grandchildren. Sure, she is not really a painter, and the canvas and the paint weren't for free, so she thinks the value she put on the contents is justifiable.

No, one could say the value of my envelope is at least five pounds. In a strange way she feels relieved when she arrives at their warm home. She enjoyed making those gifts and felt sorry having to send it away, but it is one thing less on her imaginary list of things to do.

She scanned and sent the rental agreement of the flat they vacated in Norfolk to the Dispute Committee. Now it is for them to decide if their deposit should be returned to them. So that was another task she could tick off her list.

It went relatively well, though it was hard to resist the impulse to bang the slow computer with her fists.

Tomorrow is Keith's day off, and they plan to go to the neighbouring town to do their weekly shopping. He will select and put the purchases into the shopping trolley. Kiki will trail behind and study the other shoppers. Whatever she buys will be the wrong brand or too expensive, so she follows Keith as he moves from shelf to shelf, comparing prices and items.

On his next day off from work, they do more sightseeing in the region. She marvels at the stunning beauty of Wales and cannot stop tears welling up in her eyes. But then, slightly annoyed, she asks herself: *Why, Wales, why are you such a lovely place but so cruel to me?*

Staring at the grey, nondescript day through the window, she remembers it was about this time last year that they realized the full extent of their troubles. Their future at that time looked as bleak as this Welsh road outside their rented house. It did not matter that then she could admire one of the most famous views in the world. Table Mountain, covered with a white cloak, looked foreboding and angry. Cargo boats, sailing past on the crest of foamy waves, their goods destined for a distant and foreign country, seemed safe. At least, they had somewhere to go. They had a purpose!

Summer started late in 2011 and Spring winds blew sand from the beach across the parked cars in front of their office building. The end of the month was relentlessly marching towards their bank accounts. Each month, matters became worse. Her faith in their ability to make a living out of sales shrunk, just like the diminishing size of the boats as they became smaller and sailed away to far-off countries. She and Keith were both getting weary of their mantra: 'Maybe tomorrow something will happen to make things better.'

Their second car was sold a few months ago, and the cash injection has long since been depleted. The thought of lapsing their medical insurance was unthinkable but becoming inevitable. Life in South Africa without medical aid was not really an option. It would also be a pity to cancel her life insurance policy after diligently maintaining it for so many years.

With little else to do in the neat home, she has time to daydream until Keith comes home from work. It is easy to remember what brought her here, but it is her future that confuses her. She tries to make sense of it all. She must find the reason she feels so stuck and without hope for her future in Wales. When fingers of desperation choke around her throat, they force her to consider its effect and the source: *Is it because of withdrawal from the anti-depressants? Is it a fresh attack of depression? Is life worth living when I feel like this?*

Thoughts of the past become compulsive to her. The nice car they drove - should they have traded it in for a cheaper one? Would they then have ever been able to get finance for another car? Perhaps they should have cancelled their rental home and looked for a smaller and cheaper one.

The extent of the type of 'down-scaling' they required for survival would have depleted her faith completely. She passionately believed in and advocated Suze Orman's 'make space' principle. Today, after posting the brown envelope to South Africa, she wonders if they had looked at things through the right lenses. If she had known then what she knows now, she might still have been able to dress nicely, and leave their home each day to be part of 'something', albeit in the struggling property industry. By now, a year later, they would have been better known in the area, and their growing rental portfolio would have provided a reasonable income. With the odd sale, they might have been able to sustain themselves. But could they really?

She must be realistic and tries to imagine the type of life they would have led, dodging phone calls from the bank, worrying about food money; this is why she is here in Wales today. Her mind feels cloudy from going through the endless list of debt they left behind on the other side of the wall, and she goes to the kitchen to make a cup of red bush tea.

But today her mind will not let go and it forces her back to the time before they moved to Cape Town from the Garden Route. If only it was not for alcoholism! They had done so well in the Garden Route, where they regularly won prizes for the couple with the most sales in the region. But things could not continue the way they had, and though it was heart-breaking and a shocking thing to do, she left him there in the apartment, handing over to him her home, her career, and their future.

Encouraged by her new belief in 'self', instilled by antidepressants and psychologists she had met at her three-week stay in a clinic, she fled to her mother's cottage. A move that was bad, unbelievably bad, for their finances.

Something soon whittled away her optimism in creating a life on her own in the village of her forefathers, the French Huguenots. A dead property market and the lack of support from friends, proved to be her undoing. Also, the knowledge that Keith's mask of bravado was slowly slipping away, became more pressing. Like a cockerel announcing the birth of a new day, it was as if he was crying out for help. They argued and cried on the phone, with only one result: an ever-increasing phone bill. Oh, how they fought! Only the Lord kept count of the late-night calls after many glasses of white wine!

Kiki learnt to switch off her phone after ten in the evening, and most mornings there would be a message from the previous night. No wonder their 'divorce' attempts got no further than Keith's disdain for her 'pathetic' lawyer.

She befriended the gardener and his helpers. Before they started work on a Saturday morning to fix the broken paving, she gave them tea and toast. When they painted her bedroom a metallic grey, they showed interest in the mosaic mirror she was making, and soon she taught them how to 'paint' with pieces of tiles. She cooked lunch for them all, and they built a wood fire in the lounge. Then it was time for them to go home to their shacks in the township on the outskirts of the village, and she spent the evening crouched on the carpet in front of the fire.

On Sunday mornings, she went for walks in the main street of the historical village. She pretended to be a tourist. She sat in the sun, sipping wine at a pavement table of one of the many restaurants. The usual cars were parked at the Dutch Reformed Church. She was reminded of the days when her first husband and their young family parked their car under the huge plane trees every Sunday. They would file into the historic building where she had got married and where her four children had been christened. She visited her mother in the retirement home and spent happy hours chatting with her.

But this interlude did not last long. It caught her completely off guard when she received a call marking the end of her short-lived single life. The possibility that it could happen was always there, but the blow of the inevitable shame surprised her. It could have been a car crash, or Keith might have fallen off the balcony and died. But no, it happened as he bought cigarettes at the petrol station after spending the afternoon at a village pub. He was apprehended and put into the back of the police van.

'You will not believe what a terrible night I had! It was definitely the worst night of my life,' he exclaimed on the phone.

'What happened?' she asked nonchalantly. Kiki did not know what could have happened to him.

'I slept in prison on Saturday night, and I was released only a few hours ago. I had to hitchhike home.'

This was exactly what she had tried to prevent for such a long time. This was the reason why she hung into their existence for so much longer than she should have. She feared it would only be a matter of time before the wheels of pretence fell off. And my oh my, how the mighty have fallen! He did not take it well that he had to sleep with his head centimetres away from an intoxicated cellmate. Keith explained he was leaving the shop when a female officer put her icy hand on his unsuspecting shoulder. Though blood tests taken at the hospital registered a horrendous figure in excess of the legal consumption limit, it was certainly a mistake. He had drunk a little.

Not knowing how to deal with this shocking turn of events, she hung onto her daily existence. She pushed herself harder at work and decorated the cottage as if it were the last place where she would ever live.

She did her sums, and her faith was still intact. Things would work out, she told herself. After a further three months of freezing her butt off in a dead office during the day and stoking the cottage's fireplace with wet logs in the evening, she took a position in the suburbs near Cape

Town. At least she would live closer to her supportive daughter, who had carried her over more than one 'life is not worth it' occasion. She could still visit her mother in the retirement home in Stellenbosch every other weekend.

To her surprise, they offered her two positions, and she chose the one that offered a small basic salary. She was brave and drove into unfamiliar neighbourhoods and areas. She had to walk into strange homes and often sat in empty show houses where not a soul came to visit.

In the evenings she drove home to another rented cottage where she poured herself a glass of wine. She wandered down the aisles of a strange shop as if she were exploring a forest, searching for an undiscovered plant species. Gradually she could feel the fear of food shopping dwindle and her purchases became more specific and purposeful.

Like a shawl, it draped the sadness of her loss over her shoulders. But she had to prove to the world and herself that she was more than a partner in a dysfunctional marriage, a marriage that refused to go away. There was no rush to get divorced, but they were no closer to a solution to their dilemma.

She had to come to terms with the fact that he loved white wine more than her. She did not hold her breath at the possibility that the recent public humiliation was enough to make him change his ways. She had to move on and position herself to become a separate person.

Before she left the office one morning to list a house, she finally listened to his voice mail from the previous night. He was very drunk, but his words sent a chill down her spine.

'I don't want to wake up again. I took sleeping tablets to help me go away.'

Was it serious? Was it a way to get her attention? With trembling hands, she phoned his office, only to hear that he had not come to work that morning. After her third unanswered call to his mobile, she called their neighbour and asked her to investigate. Kiki then phoned their medical aid and explained the situation to them. They would send an ambulance to take him to hospital.

When he finally answered his mobile phone, it relieved Kiki. He could not remember much but asked her to leave him so that he could sleep. Shortly after this call, the medical aid called back and told her he refused to leave the house.

She alerted his family, and then there was not much else she could do, apart from getting into her car and driving four hours to go to him. She did not think it was a good idea though and decided against it.

The following day, he called her. 'My sister insists I come to Cape Town this weekend to see them. I still feel groggy, but by tomorrow morning when I leave, I should be all right. Can I see you, please? I mean, when I'm there, can I please visit you?'

She did not want him to see where she lived. He was not supposed to be in her life in any personal way. But, how childish would it be to say 'no.' And if she had to be perfectly honest, she missed him and wanted to see him. How many times in the last few months had she not wanted to get into her car and drive to him? Eventually she decided to meet him on neutral ground. Then, if she wanted to, she could leave and go home.

'Fine. Let me know when you're here, and we can decide where to meet.' Maybe she imagined it, but he seemed relieved to hear her decision.

They met at his mother's home. As he reached out to embrace her, she glimpsed his gaunt face. There were circles under his eyes, and his smile was slow and stifled.

I shall probably never know what he went through. But also, he will never know what I had to go through. I shall keep my heart intact. I've worked so hard to become free, and there's no reason to get caught up again, thought Kiki as she felt his familiar body press against hers.

She stiffened her back and withdrew from his tight embrace. She knew she looked good. Her hair had grown and was slightly longer than when he last saw her, and her skin was tanned a dark brown. After drinking tea with his mother, he suggested they should go to Prince's Pub, where they often used to drink a beer shortly after their original meeting. He ordered white wine for them both.

'You will never know how horrible that night in prison was.'

She allowed him to talk. He needed to get his story out of his system.

It is a good thing that it happened. This had to change the course of events. This was the intervention she had been waiting for. But did she still desire it? It might be too late for them.

'I want to give rehab another chance, but I realize the medical aid might not pay again. What do you think I should do?'

She was taken aback at how easily he rolled over - like a cat begging its owner to scratch its back. This was not what she expected. She made a quick decision. She would support him, but not get invested.

'Perhaps someone at the clinic where I was treated will guide us. I don't think you should return to the same rehab where you last went. I'll phone Danie on Monday and ask for his advice.'

She wondered what Danie's reaction would be when she told him she had seen Keith again. He had worked so hard to set her free, and just being together today, drinking wine, showing him understanding and sympathy, might put her own recovery in jeopardy. But she decided that since he was still her husband, the least she could do was to help him with his recovery.

They both felt lighter once they decided. They discussed the events that had occurred while he was staying alone and dissected the shocking event again and again. But strangely, in her heart she still felt extraordinarily little sympathy.

'Will you please take me to your home? I want to see where you live.' How could she decline? Six weeks later, her home became his home as well.

Kiki goes for a walk to see if Keith is free to accompany her to buy a cup of coffee at the little shop close to his work. She needs to get out of the house, which they rent from the South African couple who emigrated to Wales years ago. Perhaps a walk in the cold will rid her of the awful memories that are terrorising her so relentlessly.

She walks past pastures awash with grazing sheep. She notices one black lamb amongst flocks of white sheep. A gorgeous owl peers down at her from the branch of a tall, lonely tree.

Standing at the gate of the lodge where Keith works, she phones him. She can see him where he stands, smoking. He waves at her when he notices her. But he informs her on the phone that it is impossible to join her for coffee.

'Things here aren't like in South Africa. I can't let you come here, or just leave for coffee with you.'

'Oh, that's a pity. I'll just go on my own then.' She tries to sound positive and happy. Last week too, he could not meet her at the shop on the beachfront. He said he was busy with clients. She would love to see this woman at his work, the one he talks about every night. It would have been good if she could meet Kiki. Maybe if she could see who his wife was…….

'Why don't we have a little party at our home? If you invite the people from the office, we could have a barbecue and show them the typical South African way of entertaining our guests. We might even invite our landlord and his wife to join us.'

She can see that Keith is not interested in her suggestion of inviting guests and listening to her small talk. Doesn't he notice how desperate she is for conversation? Although she keeps as busy as possible with painting, watching TV, doing the ironing, and cleaning the house, the days become tediously long and lonely. She experiences many moments of desperation. She worries she might slip away and never return to this life.

Chapter 8

GOODBYE WALES

She does not keep track of the overcast and rainy days.
Now and then thin rays of sun peek through the clouds like
slivers of broken glass, but they cannot change her
mood. The day lasts for just an hour or two and then it is
dark again. In this small town, shops are still closed for the
winter; the job applications she sent on email will remain
unanswered. Each day will still comprise of ten lonely
hours until Keith returns home from work. Her paintings
are still unnoticed, unappreciated, by the one other
person who can see them.

Last night, like an unattended moat, she was caught
off guard. Something in the movie they were watching
triggered her emotions. With her back turned towards
Keith, she allowed tears to run down her cheeks. He did
not have to know how sad she was. And then, suddenly
she was brave and uttered the words that matched her
beating heart: 'This movie made me incredibly sad. I feel
like that girl, you know. Lately I have been wondering:
what is the purpose of my life? I mean, what exactly do I
mean to anyone?'

She turned around to face him. He stared at her with his piercing blue eyes and unsmiling, uncomprehending face.

'What do you mean?' he asked warily. 'As related to when, what?' He frowned and seemed totally confused.

'No, not related to anything else. Just as it stands today. What is my purpose in life? I must ask myself: What do I mean to anyone? Why am I here, sitting in this bleak house every day without hope or a future?' She did not wipe the tears streaming down her face, but realized she had to check the hysteria building up inside her. *Control, control yourself. Don't let go,* she admonished herself.

That was the moment that he should have said something like: 'But you mean something to me. You are important to me. Without you, my life would be lonely and meaningless....'

But she waited in vain. He just looked at her, got up from the couch, and left the room to smoke a cigarette outside. She stayed there, lying on the couch, perplexed that even now, tears streaming down her face, she could not get the reaction she desired from him.

When he returned to the lounge, she said: 'My, look what time it is! We should have been in bed already.' She folded the throw and draped it over the armrest of the couch. She picked up the used cups, took them to the kitchen, and prepared the coffee machine for the next morning.

Later, when she woke up in the middle of the night, damp with perspiration, her heart racing, and her dry tongue chewable like a piece of toast, she tried to remember his exact words. Nothing! The fact was that he had nothing to say or did not wish to convey his nothingness. His emptiness, his lack of feeling; that was what choked her up. She must accept the truth: he has nothing to say. A person needs feelings to be able to create words. As usual, the room was overheated, and that didn't help her hormonal imbalance. She turned towards his prostrate body and put her hand in his. She felt relief when he pulled her close to him.

The following evening, when he returns home from work, he tells her how his colleagues did some research on the internet to find information about the cluster headaches he suffers from periodically.

'They rate the pain worse than childbirth or a fractured bone,' he informs her. As if she didn't know that. Was it not she who had stood by his side through all those terrible episodes, those cruel attacks? Was it not she who had rushed to the pharmacy to buy the injections, who had taken him to the hospital to be given intravenous drips? She bites her lip and says nothing.

His colleagues also understand now why he hadn't taken home the bottle of red wine that was gifted to him today. When a person is susceptible to cluster headaches, he or she should not drink alcohol, it says in the article on the internet.

Good. Let them think that. It's important to him to have an acceptable excuse for not drinking.

He was so busy today, explaining the cruelty of cluster headaches that, he did not have time to think about his wife's little emotional outburst of last night, she thinks, while she listens to his version of his day. Never did it occur to him that she had had to stretch her endurance, like a piece of bubble gum, from five o'clock to seven o' clock that evening, because he had been to the pub with his colleague after work. She can't blame him for her bleak outlook on the world, or that words congeal in her mouth because he won't hear her. Why does it never occur to him to invite her to join him at the pub, just a few minutes' walk from their home? That she spent a few hours longer on her own, waiting for him, made no difference to him.

He must also never know that she put on her thick coat and walked to the pub where he and his colleague sat drinking. She stood outside like a beggar wishing for alms, watching them through the window as they sat by a table, facing each other, talking amicably. It was only because she feared his wrath that she did not go inside and order a drink at the bar. Her fingers, frozen like twigs on a tree, fingered her wallet nestling inside her coat pocket. Eventually she decided against it and ran home to the security of the only place she had to go to.

This morning she stands in the sitting room, staring through the window at the emptiness outside. In a few days, the Mayan calendar will end. The ad on the television urges her to send money to help keep the snow leopard alive.

At first, she thinks she imagines it. In South Africa, the earliest anyone will see a spring blossom is at the end of July. So then, this is right. The end of December in Wales marks the same season as the end of July in the Southern Hemisphere. This is as it should be. The flower of the Prunus Persica in their neighbour's garden, sheltered by a white plastered wall, is an indicator of the beginning of change. The pink blossom sits proudly on the naked branch, boasting like a young ballerina in her new tutu.

She decides to buy a fluffy pink jersey when they go to the shop again. She wants to show an allegiance with the brave tree, pushing forth buds despite the cold, bitter winter. If the bud can do it, so can she.

Later that afternoon, she lies on their bed and listens to a recording of the sound of ocean waves on her slow laptop. Somehow, she transports herself to another world where there is hope. For half an hour, she slips through an open door and returns refreshed and energised.

Keith will soon be home from work. She puts on the television and watches a Sky Arts program. She paints a picture that she started with the previous day. *What a pity he can't be asked to comment,* she thinks, while she scrutinizes the developing scene.

'I'll be late tonight. There's a function after work.'

She tries hard not to let him hear her disappointment, but she knows he can sense that she feels let down. He does not tell her where the function will be held or who else will be there.

After supper, she takes a sleeping tablet and climbs into bed. She realizes she will be unable to put on a cheerful face when he eventually arrives home. It will be better for them both if she leaves; exits the day and escapes to a dark place of nothingness, where there will be no clock watching, no wondering where he was, or what he was doing.

She feels like a rag doll, being pulled this way and that. Her sleepy head protests from the aggression. She opens her eyes with extreme difficulty.

'What are you doing? Why is the light on?

'Move up! You are lying on my side of the bed!'

To ensure that she does not accidentally touch Keith in her sleep, she moves to the furthest side of the bed and then turns onto her tummy. In the morning when she wakes up, she wonders if what she experienced last night was a dream. But the deep ache in her being told her it really happened.

'So, what have you done recently about finding a job?' he asks her the following evening from the kitchen where he is preparing dinner.

'I sent at least thirty of my resumes to apply for estate agent positions and countless more for carer jobs, but nothing has come of it yet. If only I could find something to do here in this town.' She sighs and turns around to face the television.

Just recently, he had tried to involve her in his quest to shop for decorations on the internet. She had to research prices of ornaments, throws, kitchen utensils and decorations to be used in the static homes he marketed. It soon became clear to her that, with the limited allowance the company put toward it, there was barely any margin for profit and that it was not worth all the effort she'd put in. The internet in this part of the world is ridiculously slow, and it had frustrated her going through endless lists of products.

'Why don't you try to find a position as an au pair?'

'I have thought about that, but you realize I am way too old for that. It seems the average age for an au pair is about eighteen years. Who would want to employ a woman of sixty-two to take care of their child? I notice on the websites that they are mostly European, and their chief aim is to improve their English. Also, it's not financially rewarding – au pairs are mostly paid pocket money, plus food and lodging for their services.'

'Sure, but at least you will have a roof over your head, and food on your plate. Who knows, there might be a family who would like to employ an older woman to look after their children; a type of grandmother....'

'But that will mean I'll have to leave you here in Wales. Have you given any thought to the consequences of such a move on our lives? Do you think it will really be worth the price to pay?'

'At the moment you are a fiscal drag, and we simply cannot afford for you not to work.'

She says nothing but can't help to think about the annuity money she receives every month and puts into his account. It doesn't seem to count, even though she has no access to it.

The website for au pairs that she discovered recently requires a fee to enrol. Out of concern that it might be a scam, she has not put her name on the list as a prospective employee. But tonight, everything is different, and with new resolve and a coldness around her heart, she fetches her bank card, pays the required fee and completes her profile. Within half an hour, she is a prospective employee, looking for a position as an au pair; her experience is that of a mother of four children and a grandmother of seven. Who cares about her extensive resume as an estate agent with twenty-five years of experience?

She doesn't tell Keith what she has just done, so when the house phone rings half an hour later, she still doesn't explain to him why someone was looking for her regarding a position as an au pair in Gillingham, Kent.

You don't have to do this,' she tells herself. Don't let him push you out of your home. It is as much yours as his. Don't leave unless you are completely ready.

The following day, she receives a call on her mobile phone. She struggles to follow the Indian man's accent. They noticed her profile on the au pair website; he tells her. They think she would be the ideal person to look after their three-year-old little boy. He speaks only their dialect of origin, but if Kiki could teach him to speak English, that would be wonderful. Could she please work for them early in the New Year when their current nanny must leave to have an operation? They will pay her one hundred and twenty pounds per week and yes, they will buy a double bed for when her husband wants to visit her. They banter and laugh, and it is hard to resist the open and pleasant man's request. Just the simple fact that someone needs and wants her, persuades her to accept the position.

'And, oh yes, I notice on your profile that you drive a car. Would you assist my wife with driving lessons? We plan to buy a car soon.'

'Yes of course I will help her. I got my driving licence forty years ago and I taught each one of my four children how to drive.'

Later in the day when she speaks to his wife, Shona, she confirms her husband's request. 'I want to buy a car, and I'll be pleased if you could help me get my driver's licence. We'll be able to visit places then, and even drive to Wales to visit your husband. We have never been there, and apparently it's a beautiful place.'

A car! That sounds so cool. Kiki will also be able to use their car for personal outings. Keith will not let her drive their red car. He says it is too expensive to insure her as a driver. The implication of a learner driver as her responsibility does not register yet. She would have agreed to anything - if someone asked her to lead an elephant through a jungle, she would have complied!

She needs to escape from Wales in a hurry, and if this family wants to employ her, she is ready to leave. She was going to look after a little boy not even three years old full time **and** be a driving instructor. Maybe it wasn't such a good proposition, but despite her misgivings, this was the door that had opened and presented itself to her. Who knows what the consequences would be if she **did** not walk bravely through it?

Keith seems slightly taken aback when he hears her news. She has less than a week to pack her clothes, sort out the house, iron his shirts and get her head around the fact that she is on her way, heading off into the unknown to experience an alternative way of life.

Unperturbed, Keith spends the evening on the internet to buy a train ticket for her journey from Bangor to St. Pancras International. From there she will have to take two tubes and then she'll take another train to Gillingham. It's all very easy to manage, says her husband who had lived in the UK for three years before she met him in South Africa.

She will pack her painting materials and some bits and pieces into a box and post it to her new address, as she won't be able to handle too much luggage on the train. And she will leave behind a vast gap, filled already. Keith tells Kiki that night that he will look for a smaller house once she has left.

The following day she carries a box filled to the brim to the Post Office. On her way there, she finds Keith, who stands looking at the local estate agent's window displays. He seems embarrassed when he sees her. When she returns home, she must bite back the tears threatening to break a dam wall in her eyes. Wow! It did not take long for him to move on! But whether he stays in this house or moves to another one, it won't affect her.

She irons his shirts, cleans the house, and packs things in an orderly way so that it will be easy for him to move. They have been together for twelve years and he had never had to pack one single box whenever they moved to a new house. Maybe he will ask someone to help him.

It reminded her of a book she read once: it is about a woman who prepared to leave her lover. 'What do you do; how much do you do once you decide to leave for good?' the woman wondered. Kiki wasn't yet sure if she was leaving for good; only time will tell. One thing is for sure; she will never return to this house. It is impossible to take all her belongings with her and she leaves paintings and drawings, books, summer clothes and shoes in a drawer. She wonders how long he will leave the small mirror on the cast iron frame displayed on the wardrobe. He, the minimalist, will probably deem it superfluous and a reminder of her.

On their way to the station in Bangor, Keith startles her: 'Well, at least now you will have something to do every day.'

'Yes,' is all she dares say. Kiki bites on her lip. The temptation is enormous to tell him she had no lack of inspiration about what to do each day in the white house. She stares at the green pastures littered with white sheep as the red car drives past them. What is the point of telling him it was their barren relationship, the hollowness of lying next to each other at night that had made her run to the car earlier? She felt glad and relieved that she could still walk on her own legs and not carried out on a stretcher, her face covered with a blanket....

At Bangor station she is determined not to cry one tear. She will not allow him to see that her heart is broken because he opened his hand so easily to let her slip through to the unknown. While they wait for the train to arrive, he hands her twenty pounds. She puts it into her wallet. At the end of the month, she will have earned her own money which she will put into her own bank account. She does not know, though, how long she could make the twenty pounds last.

'We are in a position of fiscal drag,' he had repeated last night. He fried onions for spaghetti bolognaise, their last meal shared in the white house. In the background she heard the familiar tune of Idols. She wondered if there would be a television where she was going. Maybe they would watch only Bollywood programmes?

They have been through the same argument many times, but once again she tried to reason with him: 'Are you sure this is worth it? Have you considered what this "fiscal drag equation" is going to do to our relationship?' But Kiki realises Keith has decided.

In her imagination, she pictures herself: lost and destitute, she drags her polka dot suitcase from station to station. She holds a printout of her train schedule in her one hand. The fast Virgin train to Euston Station will take her to St. Pancras Station where she will take a tube. Finally, she must find the South-eastern line that will take her to Gillingham. She must be on time for her employer, who will wait for her at the station.

She does not know what the outcome will be, but she realises she must now close her eyes and dive into the hole. She is determined to enjoy the exit ride through the beautiful Welsh countryside. Her experience as a single woman living and working in England has just begun.

Chapter 9

THE HOUSE OF CURRY

It is time to take a realistic look at herself. She is sixty-three years old. Her hair is reddish brown and cut into a sleek bob. Her eyes are dark blue. She is slim, tallish, and has an infectious smile (so she is told). Her husband recently dumped her. Since her mother tongue is Afrikaans, and she learnt to speak English in South Africa, she has a strange accent. Apparently though, most people find it interesting and attractive.

She currently works as an au pair for an Indian family. The family comprise of a tall, attractive father, a petite, beautiful mother, and a sweet little boy. Kiki does not always understand how to blend in with their lives and plans. For instance, when she mentioned on Saturday that she intended to go to the shopping mall during her free time, they suggested she went the following weekend. They did not give a reason, but she had no choice and must wait until next Saturday, when hopefully she will be free.

But the following Saturday morning they tell her to drive them to the mall to do their weekly shopping. Their shopping usually comprises of buying fresh herbs and spices, rice, and a variety of leaves that Kiki does not recognize and has never used before. They start at Tesco and finish hours later at the Indian shop in Gillingham.

After living with them for a few weeks, she feels desperately lonely. She wonders how to make new friends. Living by herself in a strange country, with people from a different culture, makes this task really challenging. Her husband, who lives his ordained life in Wales, is adamant that they live separate lives and suggested that she should make her own friends in the Southeast of England. But how? If she does makes new friends here, all she hopes is that they will provide some affirmation that she differs from the person who her husband thinks she is.

Her original wish of embracing a different culture and learning about it has been realised but has boomeranged spectacularly. Within weeks she realised that however interesting the venture is, it's extremely hard to adjust — their dialect, their food, their customs — they are all so different from her background.

She meets Shanti, their neighbour, a Pakistani single mother, on the day she arrives in Gillingham. Kiki had never known an escapee from an arranged marriage previously. She listens in awe as Shanti tells her about her life experiences. She is fearful that her son's father's family might abduct him. The UK Government subsidises them and it is amazing to see how she survives and make ends meet; she is an example to Kiki who admires her for her strength, kindness, intelligence, and tenacity.

It does not take long before Kiki finds herself in a predicament typical of many au pairs. As part of the family, she receives certain privileges. If she joins them in the evening in their bedroom to listen to music or read or talk, she is one of them. She is just an employee who insists on reasonable working hours and on privacy once the night creeps in through the windows. But she endures their disapproval when she retires to her bedroom. She realises that she has much healing to do and needs time to be on her own.

When finally, after a long and tiring day, she relaxes on her bed, she compulsively thinks about her life, and of all that happened, leading up to her arrival in this position.

Recently, she opened a locked door and fell hard. She fell and fell till she could feel solid ground beneath her limp body. Strangers, giving and caring, but just as lonely as her, picked her up. She met people as hungry for life as herself, prepared to share their love, their stories, and their pain. How strange that strangers touch, caress, and feed her, while the one person who should protect and savour her, kicks and punches her. She reaches out to old friends at home, who show forgiveness for her neglect and pull her close to them again.

Her first fall happens as she is on her way to Gillingham. She trips on the stairs at Euston Station and twists her right leg. She tumbles ungracefully down the stairs. Her polka dot case is left stuck three steps below her. A Polish speaking angel helps her to get up, and a stranger carries her suitcase to the top of the stairs. Her knee aches and she is convinced that she has damaged it permanently. Because of her anxiety and the shock of the fall, she misses her next train. She panics. But a kind official tells her not to stress, the next train will arrive within ten minutes. The last leg of her journey begins.

Should I not have been brought here in our car? Why do I have to go through this today? she thinks angrily. Soon, the train rushes around a bend, and a river appears. The water is dark and dirty; she notices a few small boats, and then briefly, a beautiful castle is exposed. The train is nearing her new hometown.

She expects an Indian welcoming committee to wait for her, but the station is eerily empty. Feeling nervous and anxious, she carries her luggage from the platform, down the stairs and outside to the street. Still, she can't see anyone waiting for her. She phones her new employer, and minutes later, Shona arrives. She is much prettier and more petite than Kiki imagined her to be.

They debate briefly whether they should walk home or take a taxi. To Kiki's relief, Shona hires a taxi, and she puts her luggage into the car's boot. After a brief ride, the car stops in front of a house in a street dotted with similar looking houses. As she steps out of the taxi, she notices the neighbourhood's neglect. Like small mole hills, dog faeces lie spread on the pavement. Overflowing dustbins decorate the entrances to the houses.

As she walks into the dimly lit lounge, the smell of spices and curry overwhelms her. Although she had prepared herself for something similar, it is more intense than she imagined. She hardly notices the small boy with the black curly hair and huge brown eyes who sits quietly halfway up the stairs. At the bottom of the stairs, the boxes she sent from Wales stare at her like stuffed coffins ready for their graves.

The stairs are too steep for her to carry her case unassisted to her room. She empties the contents onto the lounge floor before she gathers a load of clothes into her arms. She carries it to her bedroom, sidestepping the little boy who watches her keenly. The shelves in the mirrored wardrobe are full of someone else's possessions. Shona says it will be removed in a week. Shona makes her bed, and Kiki notices that instead of a sheet, she covers the mattress with a thick cloth. Kiki is concerned that it might be too hard against her soft skin, but she is so tired that she can't be bothered by it.

To befriend the boy who followed her to her bedroom, she allows him to play with her jewellery. He calls her necklaces 'mala' and she takes a picture of him with her 'mala' hanging around his neck like harmless baby snakes.

For supper they eat biryani on their laps in the lounge. Lika takes turns to eat from his parent's plates; he opens his mouth like a tiny bird to be fed. Shortly after the meal, Kiki goes to her room to unpack her case and boxes.

Keith phones to make sure she arrived safely. While speaking to him, she tries to be brave, though her stomach feels hollow, like a dead tree trunk. She is aware of her heart beating way too fast.

'What did it feel like to arrive home to an empty house tonight? Did you miss me?' She knows she should not ask him this, but she hopes he will tell her to come home tomorrow.

'Oh, it wasn't a big deal. I cooked some curry and watched television.'

In the shared family bathroom, she notices a plastic bucket placed in the bath. The shower does not work properly and there isn't a bath plug. *Maybe she should use the bucket to rinse herself?* she wonders.

Somehow, perhaps because she is so exhausted, she falls asleep after initially tossing and turning. She wakes in the morning to the sound of a vacuum cleaner. It dawns on her that she isn't waking up next to Keith in Wales. It feels as if someone punched her in her stomach.

After breakfast of dhal and rice they walk to the town. Lika oversees his parents. As they walk from shop to shop, they indulge him. When he sees something he desires - a puzzle, a book, or a toy that he wants - they buy it for him.

There is a quaintness about the town. They eat lunch in an Indonesian restaurant, and she tries to observe the parents' interaction with their son and each other. She is overcome by their generosity and kindness and feels optimistic about her future with the family.

Then, on the second night in her new home, she has another spectacular fall. When it finally is her turn in the bathroom, she feels desperately tired. As she returns from the bathroom and walks to her bedroom, she forgets about the irregular step, and falls face down into the floor. As she regains consciousness, she can hear herself curse in Afrikaans. There is a red puddle on the floor, and blood streaks her clothes. It takes a while to ascertain the amount of damage to her face and body. Her bottom teeth cut through her lip. Shona presses a towel against the open wound to stem the blood flow. For the first time in her life, that night, they transported her to the hospital in the back of an ambulance.

On her second night away from Keith, she sits in the emergency room of a strange hospital, unable to express her disdain and horror. She knows for certain that these falls signify her entry into her new life. She holds her husband responsible for this. How could he allow this to happen to her? Has he no pride? She should lie on the couch in her home in Wales, feeling safe, happy, and protected. And here she was - sitting in a hospital amongst drunks with knife wounds on a Saturday night.

Soon they become the outward signals of her emotional famine: the bruises on her cheeks and chin, her inability to eat because of her swollen lip, the face decorated with a black eye. All evidence of her fall from grace from her marriage, and her sacred and precious home life is in tatters.

Here she is, a stranger in a home where she doesn't belong, caught up in a culture she doesn't understand. The couple's superstition, that two falls in three days is an omen, a sign of bad luck, hangs eerily in the house like a charm on a chain.

The following day, after her second fall, she rests in bed nursing her broken face and ego. Rashid presents her with a pomelo for breakfast, which she accepts warily.

On Monday, to help her settle in, and to ensure she and Lika get acquainted, Rashid stays at home. They sit in the lounge all day and talk and talk. He shares many things about India and their new lives here in the United Kingdom. Like Kiki, he loves classical music, and she nurses a fragile hope that they might get on well. To her surprise, probably because she can talk freely for the first time in a while, she shares things with him that she previously had been too shy to discuss with anyone.

Shona's mother is a natural healer, and her daughter follows her principles. Later, when Lika has a severe cold, she concocts a potion comprising of leaves and herbs, and hangs it in a pouch around his neck. When his condition improves, Kiki can't help to wonder if it happened because of the potion, or because it was just time to heal.

Kiki compiles a list of Indian words that she might need when left on her own with Lika. She pastes the list against the fridge door. 'Mummy' is 'Ameni', and 'Daddy' is 'Oepa.' Currently he is lost to her and to the rest of the world that does not speak their dialect. She feels protective towards him, but he has a strong, almost defiant character. Somehow, over those first days when they're left on their own, she manages to feed him and learns the words for 'rice' and 'hungry'- words that she would hear repeatedly.

When his mother bathes him in the evening, Kiki takes a seat on the floor and watches them. Shona takes the brown plastic bucket filled with lukewarm water and rinses him. Kiki makes a mental list of the things she would like to change in the household.

On their first outing in the buggy, Kiki searches for a shop where she can buy a bath plug. She wants to introduce him to the luxury of a warm, deep bath. Because his skin is extremely dry, he needs to be covered with a special ointment prior to the bath. Once he is dry, a different prescribed ointment is used. Kiki chooses his clothes from a cupboard in his parents' room but loses her fashion and colour sense when she sees the disarray of trousers, shirts, and coats.

'Where do you keep his pants?' she asks Shona when she must dress him for the first time. He is partially potty trained, but Kiki soon realizes that his parents have little faith in his bladder control. He does not own pants and only wears nappies. It is up to Kiki to see how soon she can get rid of them. He wakes up minutes after his mother leaves the house in the morning and then stays awake till ten in the evening when his parents go to sleep. He sleeps with them in their bed and splits the couple apart, where he lies between them like a little prince.

When she opens a drawer in the kitchen in search of a dishcloth, she is confronted with various objects - a plastic lid, spices, Sellotape, user manuals, and quail eggs nestling in a box. In dismay, she opens the other cupboards. Chaos! No order at all. It blew her desire to learn the art of Indian cooking to pieces.

The little boy is hungry whenever he gets emotionally distressed. She feeds him rice with yogurt and fried plantain, which she mistook for bananas that were past their prime. She nearly threw them into the rubbish bin, but wisely decided against it.

'Because of his skin allergy, he can only drink boiled goats' milk. He is also allergic to chicken eggs. He only eats quail or duck eggs. I am on a gluten- free diet and eat nothing prepared with flour,' his mother explains. Shona is also a firm believer in eating mostly organic produce and will search far and wide to buy what she requires.

Often, Kiki's work hours stretch till eight in the evening. As soon as Rashid comes home on the train from London, she is supposed to be 'free'. She longs for when she can close the door to her bedroom and escape to her private domain. But there is no lock on the door, and Lika may come and go as he pleases. He jumps on her bed, opens her wardrobe doors, and takes whatever he fancies to play with or destroy. Often, on her days off, Shona makes herself comfortable in Kiki's bedroom where she then sits and reads while Lika plays with Kiki's jewellery or paint brushes.

She finds the days become long and tiring and she yearns for company; anybody who knows her, or will understand where she comes from, or remember who she was in her previous life, would do.

Teaching the boy how to communicate with her becomes draining and tiring. Although he is intelligent, he repeats questions, and she must tell him things over and over.

The first snowfall of winter does not deter them, and they go for daily walks. They brave the slippery and icy sidewalks. Kiki is amused by the sound of the crunchy snow beneath the soles of the new, sturdy winter boots she bought in South Africa. She needs all her strength to push the buggy. She takes the boy to the local library where the weekly toddlers' group attracts mothers and children from all walks of life. Initially Lika is shy, and he sits on Kiki's lap, clinging to her for support. After their third visit, he gains confidence and takes an interest in the books. She enrols him as a member, and they can take home five books at a time.

The monotonous diet of rice and spiced food soon becomes a battle for her. Within the first week of life in the House of Curry, she loses weight. She gets thinner and thinner, till she packs away her size twelve trousers. It is a good excuse to buy size ten clothes at the local shops. Her heartbeat is fast and irregular, and Shona insists she pay the doctor a visit. To keep the peace, she eventually goes to the practice near to their house. The doctor suggests that she wears a heart monitor for five consecutive days and nights. She must press the green button as soon as she feels a fluttering of her heart, which descends like a swarm of bees on her unsuspecting body.

'Rashid and I want you to know that should you ever be sick; we'll look after you. You can take care of Lika, and we'll get someone else to clean the house and do the cooking.'

Taken aback, Kiki says: 'But I am not sick. I know what the matter with me is. I have had tests done before. This is just the release of too much adrenaline into my bloodstream. I promise you; I am fine. The doctor prescribed tablets for me to stabilize my heartbeat.'

They are concerned for her which makes her feel wanted. Keith phones her religiously every night at exactly nine o'clock. It feels to her though, as if he has no interest in her schedule, nor cares about what she does. He must soon go to Devon for a work conference, and since it coincides with her birthday, he promises to visit her in February.

She is not sure who is more excited about Keith's impending visit – her new family or her! Shona buys a table and matching chairs from the charity shop in town.

The Biryani has been cooked on his request and they lay the table with delicious Indian treats. They spend a lovely evening with their generous hosts, and that night they sleep in her au pair bed, stiff and unrelenting like strangers who are afraid of becoming too familiar with each other.

Saturday and Sunday, she and Keith take the train to go to London. It is as cold as February can get, but they are dressed warmly and have an enjoyable weekend. Sometime, during their time spent together, it feels like the old days again; their camaraderie and intimate relationship becomes more of a reality and less of a faint memory. Keith knows London well and takes her to many places of interest, including the Chinese neighbourhood where Chinese New Year is being celebrated.

On the last evening of his visit, they watch a movie in the lounge. She has a sense of approaching doom. They had a good time together, but surely, they should discuss their future before he leaves again tomorrow. Has he thought about their future? Does he want their marriage to continue? She must discuss these issues with him.

'What if I find a job closer to you? Say, if I move to Manchester for instance. At least then we can see each other more often. It is much closer to North Wales than Kent is.'

She looks pleadingly, hopefully, into his blue eyes. She moves her legs from the couch and places her feet on the carpet. Her body is tense; it has quickly shifted into flight or fight mode. Surely, he must see how desperate she is to

get out of the House of Curry? After spending two nights
here, he must have experienced her sense of doom, seen
how much she misses her own space and noticed her
desperation?

'No, stay here in this region. It is important that you find
your feet, so that you can live your own life and be happy
on your own.' He stays remarkably calm and looks into her
eyes. It is as if he had rehearsed this speech and she had
tried her best the entire weekend not to raise this – her -
important life issue. The dreaded words finally
tumbled unaided from her gaping, broken mouth: 'But I
want to live with you. I am here in the UK because of you. I
need my own home and space. Please, I cannot continue
living here. Can't you see what it's doing to me?'

He stares at her but does not give his thoughts away
for one moment. She can't believe how hard he is. In
despair she grasps for another weapon trying to break
down the wall between them. Sadly, there is none left in
her arsenal. They stare at each other.

Finally, he speaks: 'Have you ever considered that the
reason you are here in this position is to learn lessons
about humility?'

Once again, she is shocked beyond belief. 'Please, tell
me now, before we go to bed, and you leave again
tomorrow-how do you see us living our lives apart like
this?'

With this question she has arrived at a sickening
realization: her husband who lives on his own in a two-

bedroom house, drives his own car, sleeps under the best quality duvet, watches DSTV every night, and eats whatever he desires, thinks that she, Kiki, should learn lessons in humility! She, who is the mother of four grown-up children and eight grandchildren, who has given up all but her life, must learn lessons in humility? Please! She must rest her case.

The reason then he is content that she works here and looks after a young child, is clear now. So, therefore she must clean the family's home, eat rice each day, and get confused by their contradictory orders. She must learn lessons in humility!

Had she not left her beloved country because-together-they lost the battle against the banks? Had she not given away or sold all things dear to her, so that they could have enough money to settle in the UK? But no, she must learn lessons about humility....

'I understand now. You don't need me anymore. Why don't you just admit it? You get the emotional support you need at work. You make people laugh and you love it when they find you amusing. They stroke your back and fulfill your needs. I know how it works. Remember, I worked for twelve years with you in the same office? When you look at me, I remind you of your past. Each time you look at me, you see yourself and the appalling way you have treated me. '

The sound of her voice has risen, and she remembers that the family is sleeping upstairs. *Oh, what the heck! They never consider me when they argue in the middle of the night. This now, here, in the lounge, is the rest of my life. I must know where I stand, and I need to know tonight.*

Unflinchingly and uncharacteristically, he looks straight at her. 'You are probably right. But, if that is all you have to say, please excuse me. I'm going to sleep now. You have become nasty, and I don't want to discuss this anymore.'

He gets up from the couch and leaves her, crumpled and defeated in a heap of misery. While he smokes his last cigarette of the day outside in the bitter cold February night, she gets up, goes to the bathroom, and cleans her teeth. She gets into the double bed that over the last few weeks has become her private frontier. Tonight, maybe for the last time ever, she must share it with her husband, whom she realizes now she might never see again in her life.

Her grief is so overwhelming; she flattens her body against the mattress. Keith comes to the bedroom and undresses quickly before he climbs into the bed to lie down beside her. Then, for the first time that evening, he shows emotion. He holds her head tightly in his chilly hands. They lie like this for a long time until she eventually turns to switch off the light standing on the bedside table next to the bed.

She whispers in the dark: 'How does one go about getting divorced in this country?' She is not satisfied yet. She needs to know how serious he is. Does he really understand what he is doing? He has said before that she was 'an all- or- nothing person.' He should realize now that he is pushing her off a cliff. Her cliff is the UK, and she will have to return to South Africa as soon as possible. The mere idea of her 'making the most of life here in the south of England,' as he suggests, is preposterous. It does not surprise her when he replies in a whisper: 'I don't want to think about it now.'

But then she thinks: *What if I want to become a British citizen? Then we should not divorce. That will mean we will have to maintain our farcical lifestyle for a further eighteen months.*

This thought fills her with even more despair, and she weeps uncontrollably. He holds her tighter, but during the night, she hears his breathing deepening, and she realizes he has fallen asleep. She lies on her back, staring into the dark for hours. Eventually, she notices daylight peeking through the curtains.

'Take care of yourself.' Those are the last, unoriginal words she directs at her husband as he walks down the slippery, icy pavement. He drags his wheeled polka dot suitcase behind him as he walks towards the station.

The first day after he left, she is still brave. She pulls herself together and somehow does the chores for which she gets paid each month.

Of course, they will fix this terrible misunderstanding. He will repent, and eventually they will live together again in the comfort of their home. He will think it over and realize that he is too hard on her. Now that he has seen the circumstances under which she lives, he will soon ask her to come home. Then she will proudly display her things; put her brush and mirror, her makeup and trinkets on the dressing table. She will go home to him and eat food that will put some fat back on her increasingly thinning body. She will paint and read and watch proper television.

Let him go to this training course in Devon, and by the time he returns to Wales, they will talk about all of this. Soon they will be back to their usual relationship - possibly dysfunctional and awkward-which is better than anything else in her life right now.

But when she phones him later-not once, but twice, he puts the phone down when she speaks. It gradually dawns on her that he really does not want to hear her voice. The house is unhappily quiet at nine o'clock each night, the time that he habitually phoned her.

She develops an allergic reaction and directs her frustration and hurt towards her employers whose house she believes is infested with some mysterious insect that has taken a liking to her flesh. Through a swollen eyelid, she glares at them coldly; her humiliation in knowing that her life and her looks have slipped away is now obvious for everyone to see. She has no leg to stand on; nowhere to escape to. Her third fall is final and completed.

Keith sends her an e-mail which is direct and to the point: 'From now on we can communicate via e-mail.'

No more phone calls then. He does not want to hear her voice. The truth, too hurtful, is too much for him to bear. She submits to her enforced silence; her tongue is plucked from her mouth. She tries her best to close the door to her memory storeroom whence thoughts regularly burst out to tease her mercilessly. Like little gingerbread men they run around wildly, and the farmer's wife tries hard to put them back into the oven.

The heading of her e-mail to her children in South Africa reads: 'Bed bugs.' Kiki tells them about Keith's visit and their separation and about the allergic reaction she struggles with which she suspects is caused by bed bugs. She laments at her despair of living under the circumstances she is in. Their replies vary: one answers immediately, one takes a day or two before encouraging her and one does not reply. The advice from her youngest daughter sounds the best. She lived in the UK for two years after school. 'Mom, it will only get better. You'll see, the second year is awesome!'

Good then, she decides. She will stick to her original plan. That means that she needs to accumulate enough money to apply for her Indefinite Leave to Remain application.

And then, dear Husband of Mine, I'll make the best of my stay...... and be happy.

Before she will consider throwing the towel in, she will give it a bash, stiff upper lip or no lip at all. The fact that her daughter lived in a house with a group of fellow South Africans and that they frequented pubs and music festivals, does not dawn on her till much later when she realizes she has set herself an almost impossible goal

She will stay in the UK until she gets her British passport. Kiki does not discuss this decision with anybody. Only she knows about her plans. She believes that the kindly Indian family imagines her lying on an operating table and since they know her husband does not want to live with her anymore, she will become a permanent member of their family. She also realizes that Shona believes firmly that she is the key to her future driving license!

Kiki tries hard to dissuade them from buying a car. She warns them about the cost of double insurance and the responsibility of car owners whose vehicles stand outside in the street. She warns them about accidents and what could happen to a driver out on the busy road. But Shona is not to be deterred and Kiki now worries even more about her future in this home.

Soon the search for an appropriate car intensifies. A friend of a friend knows someone who is selling a car and on her afternoon off they must go to look at this car.

'Why can't the man bring the car to us to inspect?'

'No, it is raining today, and he said he can't come here when it rains.' Kiki looks outside and notices clouds but it does not look as if it is going to rain soon.

'Where is the place where we must meet him?' She wants to know where they are going to walk to-not because she does not like walking in the freezing cold with a child in a buggy - but she has learnt that there is a probability they might play guessing games if they do not do proper research prior to their walk about.

Shona clearly does not know where they must go. 'I will ask Shanti. She will know where Agapanthus Road is.'

Shanti, their living, walking encyclopaedia and Google maps, joins them with a reluctant Sian in tow. Shona and Kiki take turns to push Lika in the buggy. Shanti directs them in the opposite direction from where they originally planned to go.

They walk past a school, various pubs, shops, houses, and more houses. Sian complains he is tired and lags. They walk further and Kiki asks Shona to take the buggy from her. They walk for what feels like hours and finally Shanti finds the right street. There, in the driveway of a house, they notice a man standing beside a blue Mazda. This car is going to be her Nemesis. Kiki's spirit cringes.

Of the three of them she is the only one with car experience and today she will have to do the typical wheel kicking of a prospective buyer.

'Can I see the engine, please?' Freddy opens the bonnet of the Mazda, and she notices the engine is rusty and dirty. She gets into the car and sits behind the steering wheel. She asks the seller of the car about the mileage. Her heart beats irregularly, but she chooses to ignore the signs of stress. She has not driven a car in the UK yet, and now she, an uninsured driver, plans to test drive a car on behalf of a prospective buyer.

She surprises herself at the ease with which she handles the car and navigates the unfamiliar roads. *Wow, it feels good! Remember me? I am the one who has held a licence since the day I was eighteen. I am the one who has owned and driven more than a few cars in my lifetime.*

When they park the car in front of the house again, she opens the driver's door and smiles inwardly when she notices Shona's and Shanti's admiring faces. Finally, she has done something that gained their respect. She will have to tell Shona about the things in the Mazda which concern her.

'It seems to lack power when you go uphill. But then, one just has to work the gears. I noticed a scratching noise, and I am concerned that there might be something wrong with the clutch.'

Shona is not interested in any of her warnings. She wants to buy a car, and this is going to be the car. Kiki supposes it is her decision and if she is prepared to pay nine hundred and fifty pounds for this old car, who is she to be negative?

The following day, research for car insurance quotes begins. Kiki does her own research but soon backs off. Shona's friends at work advised her to look at a certain website that compares prices. It seems wise to let them do their own thing. The amount to insure her as a second driver plus Shona as an owner driver with a provisional license, is huge. It does not however deter the excited new car owner.

Shortly after the insurance is sorted out, the seller brings the car to their home. That night Kiki hardly sleeps at all; she is nervous about what is going to be expected of her.

The next day Kiki sits behind the steering wheel, trying to stay calm. Shona attempts to secure the baby seat with the crying child who is already sitting in the seat. It is designed for infants and faces towards the back of the car, but Kiki does not comment. She is the designated driver, and they are on their way to buy leaves and rice at the Indian shop.

Soon, she lives in fear. Kiki does not get much time to prepare herself for the next outing on unfamiliar roads. Every night she must fetch Shona from work after a late shift. Often, she must drop her off in Maidstone for a training course. Weekends she must take her and Shanti to the shops to buy groceries. Her life has become a misery, regulated by a demand to go to the shops.

'But I am off tomorrow,' she says wearily. 'I have an appointment to meet someone.'

'What time is your appointment?'

'At one o 'clock,' she replies, knowing they don't believe her.

'Fine, then we shall leave at nine o'clock. That should give us enough time to finish our shopping. You can wait for us in the car. I know you hate food shopping.'

Kiki has not told her she arranged an interview for a position as an estate agent. Eventually she must cancel her appointment; it is too stressful. They drive to the shopping centre, where she drops them close to the shop's entrance. She then drives further until she finds a parking space. There she waits in the parked car until they return with trolleys filled with shopping.

'Kiki, now you can drive to the Indian shop in Chatham. 'Turn right here,' she instructs, pointing towards an exit road to their right. Kiki must make a quick decision. She notices a sign prohibiting cars from turning right. Behind them, a car hoot. She needs to be on the other side of the road, but she may not turn right there.

'Turn Kiki! Go up that road. We'll find parking there.'

'No, I can't! It is against the traffic rules!' she says, irritated at Shona's attitude, and continues on the road.

'Why don't you listen to me, Kiki?' Shona asks angrily. 'You never listen to me!'

'One day, Shona, when you have your own license, you can drive as and where you wish. But, while I sit behind the steering wheel, I decide.'

112

The day, the weekend, her stay there is spoilt. They have many fights about driving and the car. Their relationship sours and becomes thick, like curdled cream.

'Everything has changed since Keith's visit in February. You used to chat with Rashid, but lately you hardly talk to him. Now, you are unhappy and quiet. You say nothing, and we do not know what you think. If only you would talk Kiki, but you pull faces and sulk. We have had to take a lot from you. You have been sick, and we had to handle your personal problems as well.'

Shona sits on the chair in Kiki's room. She faces Kiki, who uses her laptop as a protection shield. She knew she was going to be given a thrashing tonight. Though she does not understand their language, she knew what Shona was saying to Rashid: 'This woman is going to get a piece of my mind! I am going to tell her off! Who does she think she is, telling me she will not let me drive my car! Yes, the police pulled me off the road, and they gave me a warning. What is the big deal that they asked to see her South African licence? Really!' she said as she barged into Kiki's room.

'It is fine if you refuse to drive with me. I still have enough money to pay for driving lessons and eventually I will get my licence. From now on you will only drive me to the shops and to work. You do not have to take me for driving lessons. But we are disappointed in you because when we appointed you it was because you said you taught your children to drive. Rashid is planning to take his provisional licence exam shortly, and we thought you would teach him as well. You were rude to me today. I know you were uncomfortable with my driving but that does not give you the right to be rude to me.'

Kiki decides to speak her mind: 'No, Shona, you are wrong. Everything changed when you bought the car. My personal problems have nothing to do with the change in our relationship. The car has changed everything. And if you think today was all right for me, you make a great mistake. You did not know where you were driving to. And yes, it did upset me to be pulled off the road by the police. Anybody else would have called it a day and gone home to think about the incident, but no, you continued driving around, looking for a health shop and you had no idea where it was! You are a dangerous driver, and I am not prepared to risk my life. When I taught my children, I had the right to instruct them, but you are my unteachable employer!'

It is difficult to resolve a conflict with Shona because she does not stop to listen. If the driving lessons and the car are going to cost her a bed, food and a hundred and twenty pounds paid into her bank account each week, then, what must be, must be. She will say no more but look into Shona's eyes and carry on as if their conversation did not concern or distress her. Before she acts, she needs time to decide what her next step should be.

The following day she hits the button of every advertisement on the Web for vacancies as an estate agent. If she could secure a job with a proper basic salary plus commission, she should be able to afford the rental of a place of her own. An advertisement for a position as a Senior Property consultant in Aberdeen, attracts her and she applies.

Would that be Aberdeen in Scotland? she wonders, as she closes her laptop.

Chapter 10

GOING HOME

A few days after Keith leaves for Dover and she had sent him off with the parting words 'take care,' it dawns on her she must do something drastic about her mood and her views on her current situation in the UK. Things don't look good for her and Keith and it is clear that she must take her wellbeing into her own hands. Since he ignores her phone calls and shows that he doesn't want anything to do with her, she'll have to be tougher on herself.

She forces herself to wipe away her tears, literally and figuratively. However, this is easier said than done! On Sundays, Rashid plays their favourite CD. The haunting melodies carry tears and despair up the stairs towards her bedroom, like a floating cloud of cheap perfume. Despite her resistance to indulging in melancholy, the music causes tears to stream down her face.

She understands her limitations in the House of Curry and feels increasingly vulnerable. Rashid decides that Kiki should help more with the cooking. Their request for her to prepare and cook dhal for dinner leaves her panicking.

She consults the Google God and finds a recipe with instructions on the internet. But the process remains foreign to her. Shanti immediately comes to her assistance when she calls her. Gradually, she gains confidence and soon speaks with authority about dahl cooking methods. Rashid enjoys the meals she prepares. 'You are artistic, and it will inspire you to be an innovative cook.'

The weekdays are long and tedious. Lika requires constant attention, and she must feed him frequently. She never knows when Shona will arrive home from work. When she fetches her in the evening, Kiki must wait for hours in the dark, sitting in the car till she eventually appears from the recesses of the building and appears at the car door.

Kiki is exhausted after the long day. It is hard to keep her composure when Lika follows her to her bedroom without a lock. If only they would realize that she needs time out, some privacy. Most nights she finds it hard to sleep, knowing that the family lies on their bed on the other side of the thin wall, right next to her head. The couple often talk to each other late into the night and Kiki wakes up with her heart racing, unsure where she is.

When the couple announces that their friends from Margate are coming to visit this weekend, it is clear she will have to sacrifice her bedroom.

'I don't mind sleeping on the couch in the lounge,' she says.

'No, you can sleep with me and Lika in our bed. Rashid will sleep on a mattress on the floor. He prefers to sleep there. It was his custom, growing up as a young boy in India.'

She tries tactfully to dissuade Shona, but nothing convinces her. Kiki's wish to sleep on the couch in the lounge does not carry any weight. This must be a cultural thing. She knows she should feel honoured to be invited into the family's bed: she is part of the family.

Kiki likes the visiting couple immediately and enjoys their company. She takes clothes from her room and changes in the bathroom. She sleeps in the family bed for two nights. When she must go to the bathroom in the middle of the night, she carefully sidesteps Rashid where he lies on the floor, his head covered with a sheet. He is oblivious of Kiki who tries to avoid falling over his long legs and spreading arms. The little boy, used to sleeping between his parents, is surprised on waking up in the morning to find Kiki lying next to him. It relieved her when she can move into her bedroom again on Sunday afternoon.

One Sunday afternoon she walks to town and after visiting a few shops, she bravely enters a pub. She orders a cup of coffee and after a while she buys a glass of wine. She savours the white liquid and sips it as slowly as possible. She must make it last so that she does not have to go outside in the bitter cold too soon. She observes groups of people sitting at tables and standing at the bar. *Why do they look so happy? How is it possible that she sits here alone, feeling like a beggar, hoping, praying for a coin?* she wonders.

When she leaves the pub to walk back, she does not yet feel ready to go home. Kiki knocks on Shanti's door and receives a warm welcome. She embraces Kiki and invites her into their small room. Kiki sits on the bed while she listens to Shanti's woes of arranging a visit for her mother from Pakistan to the UK. Kiki enjoys the freshly baked chapati that Shanti offers her.

'I dare not go home to Pakistan to visit my mother. I miss her so much and the only way I can see her, is if she comes here. She sold her gold jewellery to raise funds, but it is still not enough to support her while she is here. The Border Control requirements are high.'

Kiki learns more about her plight and her quest to be freed from her unhappy, arranged marriage; how she escaped under police escort and eventually gained British Citizenship.

When she leaves Shanti's room at eight, the lights in the lounge and kitchen of their home are turned off. She holds on to the wall, stumbling along in the dark to get to her bedroom. They made it clear that she stayed out too late and broke unspoken rules.

After three weeks, Shona and Kiki must take the 'Life in the UK' test. It is one requirement to qualify for 'Leave to Remain.' They study whenever they have time. Shona enjoys reading the subject material out loud, while Kiki needs quiet to focus.

Finally, the dreaded day arrives. They travel by train to Stratford where they must take the test. Rashid says he knows where the building is and he and Lika accompany them. They are well prepared, and the test seems ridiculously easy. It relieved Kiki when it is over, and they can return home. She and Shona smile broadly when the official tells them they passed.

Soon it is Rashid's turn to study for his exam. Shona and Kiki feel superior and have doubts about his chances of passing on the first attempt. He surprises them by not only passing but says that he also found the test easy. The family is now ready to apply for Indefinite Leave to Remain. Kiki believes she will have to wait until she has lived in the UK for two years before she may apply for this. It is an enormous relief though to have overcome this hurdle.

One evening she opens her laptop to find a few 'hits' on her recently joined dating website profile. At first, she was too shy to put a profile picture on the site. Soon though, she feels brave and daring and she decides to either do it properly, or not at all. Within days, she makes four new friends – John is from Folkstone, Kit is from Southend-on-Sea, David lives in London, and Kurt is from Brighton. It amuses her that people are interested in her. She explains she is South African and why she now lives in the UK. She enjoys chatting to them and through the banter she learns lessons in communication, albeit via the safety of online messages.

David is the first potential 'date' who phones her. He invites her to meet him in London. She takes the call in the bathroom; her heart beats fast like a drum and she hopes no one hears their conversation. She feels embarrassed; though she realizes her marriage is over and dead, it still feels disloyal to speak to another man. David loves theatre and drama and has an expert knowledge on music. They finalize her trip to London to meet him.

She tells Shona of her plans, and she and Shanti decide Kiki needs a new coat. On Saturday, Shona buys her a red coat with a hood and duffel buttons at a charity shop in Chatham. While traveling to London, Kiki notices dog hairs sticking to the coat like thorns. She nervously picks them off, one by one.

Kiki did not know that the underground tubes could be so unpredictable on a Sunday. The one to her destination does not run today. When she finally arrives at their meeting place, she feels anxious and relieved simultaneously.

He is a keen talker, and soon she listens, while he talks. David asks her why she is single and to her horror tears well up behind her lashes and soon stream down her face.

They drink coffee and talk more over lunch. But on her way home she tells herself that they are not suited.

John becomes her virtual friend. He seems genuinely nice, but she is hesitant to meet him. She finds Kit a real challenge. He is a widower and a practicing accountant. They joke and banter on the phone and she enjoys his company, though there is no indication that they will ever meet. Southend-on-Sea is too far away.

Kurt is the one person who manages to make her heart beat faster. At first, she thinks he might be dyslexic because his spelling is atrocious. When she finds out that he is originally from Iceland, she understands. He tells her that though he is still married; he is not happy. Though Kiki had vowed never to get involved with a married man, he bowls her over with his direct approach: 'I like you'.

Initially, their conversation is limited but when he phones her to tell her he wants to meet her, she realizes that his spoken English is much better than she had imagined. They arrange to meet on her next free morning. She does not tell anyone about this rendezvous. When she sees him for the first time as he walks into 'her' pub, she has a good feeling about their future as friends. Like a thirsty, lost soul in the desert, she laps up every warm gesture, every smile and kind word coming from his lips.

'My darling,' he says, 'be careful of the steps.'

'My darling!' She has not been called that for a long time! It does not take long for her to fall for him hook, line, and sinker and soon her other friends on the dating site become less significant. She does not have to wait or beg for Kurt's attention. He likes her more than she could have hoped. When he phones her, she listens to his broken accent and how he pronounces her name. It's all music to her ears and a balm to her soul.

He was made redundant a few months ago and is working freelance. But it is not going well. It doesn't keep them from meeting to have a drink and go out for a meal. One weekend, she manages to meet him in Margate.

'Oh Darling, it is so nice to see you. I can visit you in your room for an hour or two, but then I must rush home again. I have to meet friends at our local pub tonight.'

After he drops her off at the quaint bed- and- breakfast where she booked in for the weekend, she dresses warmly before she walks to the shops where she buys food. Kiki savours the deliciousness of what she is doing: she escaped the House of Curry for an entire weekend! She has a room to herself and the prospect of seeing Kurt. As she walks along the edge of the ocean, she takes pictures and marvels at the fact that France is just across the strip of water. This feels good, being here in the United Kingdom. She is privileged to experience this.

Having someone special in her life makes her even more determined to change her current situation. She puts her name on the Au Pair website. Within days she receives a call from Alice from London. Alice's current au pair will leave in June, and she needs someone to take over then. Alice is an author and sounds genuinely nice.

They decide to meet in London as soon as Kiki has a free day.

Later, when she arrives back home from Margate and finds that the family is not home, she acts a little out of character. When she goes upstairs, she finds her bed crumpled and the room in a mess; someone's belongings are strewn everywhere. She phones Shona. The invasion and lack of consideration, horrifies Kiki.

'Hi Shona. I arrived home to find someone had moved into my room. What is going on? May I use my room, or should I wait till you return?'

'Oh Kiki, we are in Canterbury for the day. We should be back soon. Vasal stayed in your room for the weekend. He will not mind if you place his belongings on the floor in a corner of the room.'

Oh, this is great! Her neat and tidy room is in a mess. She experiences one of her hot flushes and the horrible accompanying feeling of desperation. She gets these attacks more frequently nowadays and she must often rip off her cardigan or coat only to put it back on again within minutes after she cooled off.

She fumes while she changes the sheets. She puts Vasal's clothes on the floor in the corner of the room and then proceeds to unpack her weekend case. Vasal is a lovely man - an artist and a photographer and she doesn't mind that he stayed in her room and slept in her bed. If only they had thought to tell her about it.......

'I will work for you until the end of June, but then I plan to leave. I hope this suit you.' She stands in the family bedroom's doorway. Normally she gets an invitation to sit on their bed or to slip in under the cover while Shona works on her laptop. But tonight, even if they were to ask her, she has no intention of stepping over the threshold.

'Yes, Kiki, it seems as if we aren't getting on anymore. If that is what you want to do, I'll start looking on the website for a replacement for you.'

They glare at each other for a moment before Kiki turns on her heels and shuts the bedroom door firmly behind her.

The next morning, she receives a call from a distraught, crying Shona. She phones Kiki from her place of work. She says she is upset about their deteriorating relationship and wants to apologise for her part about it.

'I am so sorry, Kiki; I never meant to hurt you. You know you are part of our family, and you know we care about you. We never meant to make you feel uncomfortable. I should have asked you first if Vasal could sleep in your bed. Please forgive me.'

'I am guilty too, Shona. I am so sorry: I overreacted.' Kiki almost feels pity for her, but she feels confused - she is not thinking straight anymore. Her world has become so small, without security nets, and no walls or moats to protect her. She is also feeling sad after saying goodbye to

Kurt at the station in Margate. She has no idea when they will meet again. He told her that he might soon return to Iceland.

'You can visit me while I am there my darling. I am going to help my brothers to build a family holiday home. As soon as the first room is ready, you can come to stay with me for a while. Iceland is so beautiful in summer. My marriage is such a mess and I need to get out. There is no work for me here my darling.'

It scares Kiki to think that the only person who cares for her might leave her soon. But who knows what might happen in future? In the meantime, until then, she must take care of herself. The only way she can imagine something changing is if she shuffles the chess pieces of her life, hoping to find a new game plan. She dares not become dependent on any one person at this stage of her life.

Her only hope now is that she and Alice will get on when they meet. She would have committed immediately to Alice, but to complicate matters she receives a call from the recruiting agency. They inform her that she is on their short list to go for an interview in Aberdeen, Scotland.

'Are you sure that they are interested in me?' Straining to hear Allison's voice above the noise of the children's TV program and ignoring Lika, who is tugging at her arm, wanting something to eat, she struggles to maintain a calm voice. She hopes she sounds professional.

'Aberdeen in not just down the road, you know……' The truth of the matter is, she does not know where Aberdeen is, how she will get there, or what she will tell Shona where she was going to.

'Yes, they are extremely interested in you. The position is to sell apartments to retirees and your sales experience in South Africa matches very well with their requirements.'

She is thrilled. Her mind goes into overdrive. This is her opportunity to prove herself. Oh, she can't wait to tell Keith that she will work in Scotland. Soon she will buy her own car and live in her own apartment. She will dress nicely and enjoy the respect of normal people again. Perhaps Kurt will come to stay with her in Aberdeen. Surely, he will find a job there.

As she cooks rice for Lika, she feels a surge of optimism run through her body. It makes her feel lightheaded. If she gets this position, she will not have to work as an au pair for Alice's daughter.

A little while later when Shanti visits her, they watch in dismay as Lika and Sian have an altercation. There is an angry red scratch on Sian's arm and Kiki must calm Lika, who does not understand what he has done wrong. He sits on Kiki's lap, and she holds him close against her body for a long time.

'Shanti, something has happened, and I need your help. But please, you must promise me that you will not tell Shona where I am going, or what I plan to do.' Kiki has Shanti's full attention, and she tells her everything. She

knows about Kurt and her job applications. Although
Shanti wishes her well, she does not want her to leave
because they support each other daily. Recently she
helped Kiki to apply for her National Insurance number, a
process she did not know how to approach.

'I understand, Kiki. No, don't let her know where you
are going. Tell her that you are going to Wales to help
Keith move to his new home. Should you tell them that
you are going for a job interview, you will immediately lose
your job. Let them know that I will take care of Lika while
you are away; that way there will be fewer problems.'

As she speaks, her burka slips off her shiny black hair
and her beautiful, serious eyes meet Kiki's concerned gaze.
Although she is still feeling nervous, she is more prepared
now to formulate an action plan, and to get to Scotland in
time for her life- changing interview.

The following day she puts Lika in his buggy and they
walk to the station where she buys a train ticket for her
journey. She will take the train from Gillingham to St
Pancras International. From Euston Station she will travel
to Edinburgh, and then she will take a train for the last leg
of the journey to Aberdeen. From the station to the
Premier Inn, where the interview will take place, she will
take a taxi. Kiki reads up on interview technique tips on
the internet and makes extensive notes about the
company for which she may soon be working. It is easy to
imagine herself sitting across from the interviewers. She
has invested a lot of money in this interview and there's a

lot at stake. She is convinced that her time to escape has arrived.

Kurt is impressed with her endeavours but from what Kiki can gather, he is planning his own escape from the UK and from his dead marriage much sooner than she imagined.

On Saturday, she goes to the shops to search for an appropriate outfit for the interview. Kiki buys a charcoal suit with a matching black shirt. In a charity shop she finds black shoes that complete the outfit. She buys a small overnight suitcase with wheels that will come in handy for future travels. Since she is paranoid about this trip, she hides her purchases in the back of her wardrobe. Her stress levels are sky-high. She counts the days and hours before she must embark on her journey.

'Who is your best friend, Lika?' she asks the little boy. He sits next to her as he watches his favourite TV program.

'Mr. Tumble is my best friend.' Kiki smiles and pulls him closer to her. Her mobile phone rings and her heart beats faster when she sees Kurt's name appear on the screen.

'My darling, my plane leaves for Iceland tomorrow at two o'clock.'

She is so shocked; her brain goes numb. 'But how can you do that? I am leaving for my interview tomorrow! Are we not going to say goodbye? Do you realize we may never see each other again? Could you not wait to leave until after my interview, until I have returned, so that we could at least see each other one more time?' Her thoughts and words jump around in her confused mind like Mr. Tumble, Lika's friend.

'The ticket was cheap. It was available for tomorrow, and I have packed everything already. I signed my divorce papers yesterday. It has become unbearable here. Get the job; you can do it. I believe in you.'

She is in shock; her hands shake. When she gets a chance to speak, her voice sounds strange and unfamiliar to her. 'I will be on a train to Scotland, while you are flying to Iceland.'

Her life is looking like a scene from a movie. It reminds her of Doctor Zhivago, leaving his beloved Lara behind...... The words in her mouth become thick, and all she can muster is: 'Good luck. I hope you travel well.'

So much then for her beautiful, newfound feelings of love. All gone - so much happiness in such a short time. She should not depend on anyone for support; this is about her, and her alone and she must stay focused and be strong and brave.

When she tells Shanti that Kurt is leaving the following day, she shakes her head. 'What did I tell you, Kiki? Never trust a man. Can you see why I dislike men? They are only interested in themselves. No Kiki. Do your own thing and you will not get hurt. Be careful, be incredibly careful.'

'This is different Shanti; this is not an arranged marriage, like the one your parents forced you into. This is love; this is about two people who care for each other.' She is determined to show Shanti how wrong she is.

After the interview, when she steps out of the taxi on her way to Aberdeen station, she barely has enough money to pay the taxi driver. She had a problem withdrawing cash at the hotel, where she stayed overnight. She knew there was enough money to cover her withdrawal, but her debit card would not work.

The interview seemed to have gone well, but she found it disconcerting that they held interviews on two consecutive days. How many applicants were there on their short list? It seemed like a long list to her, and she might have wasted all her time and effort on this venture.

It is freezing here in Aberdeen station and her hands shake as she puts her card into the cash machine. Again, no luck. She curses herself for not withdrawing cash before she embarked on her journey. This means that she has no money to buy refreshments on her return trip to Gillingham. All she has with her is a bottle of water she filled at the hotel before she left. After all the tension of the interview, the stress of getting to Aberdeen, the realization that Kurt has now left the UK, she feels deflated. She is close to despair.

As the train speeds along, she obsesses about food and notices what the other commuters consume. Kiki craves the packet of crisps that the girl seated opposite her is devouring. Her tummy rumbles which make her feel extremely uncomfortable. She cannot remember when last in her life she was so hungry and envious of other people's food.

The family is still awake when she pulls her small case into the house that she had left the previous morning. They are sitting in their bedroom. She stands in the doorway, still wearing her coat with her bag hanging over her shoulder.

'How did it go with the move? Is it a nice place where Keith is going to stay? I hope you did not have to work too hard.' They are kind and genuinely interested in her.

She lies and tells them about the imaginary move.

And then, like the strike from a guillotine, Shona executes a deadly blow: 'Kiki, while you were away, we found a replacement for you. Our new au pair will start here on the seventh of June.'

'But, Shona, I told you I will leave at the end of the month. You have moved the goal posts by three weeks.'

'Oh Kiki, if you have any problems in finding another position, I know of a care home where you can easily find a job. Just let me know if I may help you.'

When she finally lies down on her bed, she is tired, shocked and sad. But as she drifts off to sleep, she tells herself: *don't worry, what must be, must be.*

The next day she phones Alice and tells her about her interview in Aberdeen and that she hopes to soon be appointed as an estate agent. She tells her she would not hold it against her if she employed someone else because she realizes that her au pair is leaving on the sixteenth of June. Kiki knows she has put all her eggs into one basket, but there is always another option, one which she still does not want to consider....

Trying to cover her bases, she sends Keith an email to ask him if she can stay with him in Wales for a few weeks, should she be homeless and jobless. 'I am sorry, but my new place is too small for two,' is his response.

Shanti has been feeding her lately. She had noticed that Kiki was losing weight, as she did not eat enough. The heavily spiced food was too much for her. Shanti brings her home baked naan bread, or a plate of western food that she prepares for her and Sian in her kitchen. Some evenings Kiki visits her in her room. They tentatively discuss the possibility of sharing a flat in the future. That could only happen if Kiki finds an estate agent job in Gillingham.

The days pass and the longer she waits, the more she realises she will not be invited to a second interview. Another week passes without a phone call and now she is convinced she is not going to live in Scotland after all.

She does not have the heart for England anymore. Kiki feels sick - the hot flushes are more frequent, her heart beats too fast, her mouth stays dry. At the surgery, she admits to the Indian doctor she feels paranoid. The safety of her passport and bank card becomes a concern for her and she worries that she might get trapped in the House of Curry forever.

'If you have a problem, take your things and go to stay in a Bed and Breakfast,' he says, staring at her with his huge, brown eyes.

Yes sure, as if an au pair can afford to do that. Kiki realizes that he can't understand her predicament.

She needs to plan urgently, as there is not much time before the new au pair's arrival. One evening she overhears a Skype conversation between Shona and the new au pair. It does not sound positive; it's almost as if the Spanish lady can't afford a plane ticket.

Mm, that does not sound good. Kiki is now more determined than ever to leave before the seventh of June.

Kurt regularly contacts her on Skype from white, icy places. Often though, he can't speak freely since his brother is also in the room. It seems as if his brother is restricting the regularity of their brief contact. She realizes that though her heart is aching, she might have to get over him soon. But she will need time and energy to deal with the pain. Either way, it now feels as if the only spark of happiness she experienced in the UK was brief, and permanently over.

One evening, feeling desperate, she opens her laptop, and googles 'cheap plane tickets to Cape Town, South Africa.' After some research, she finds what she is looking for. She could travel the way she came, via Istanbul. After buying a single ticket to Cape Town, she would still have enough money to survive for a few months before finding work. If she stays with her youngest daughter, she will be fine. People in their town will still remember her.

Yes, that is what she will do. She will go home. She writes on her Facebook page wall: *'I am coming home. Table Mountain, I will see you soon.'*

Her youngest daughter is elated. 'Your room is ready for you Mom. You can stay with us for as long as you wish.'

It shocked Kurt to hear she was throwing in the towel. 'But my darling, you were so positive you would get the job in Scotland! Well, you can always visit me from South Africa. Once you are there, we can arrange something.'

'Yes, since you left, the UK is not the same.'

'Shona, I have decided to return to South Africa on the seventh of June.' Shona shuts her laptop and gasps for breath. She has a good heart and means well. They each have a unique way of dealing with matters in their adopted countries.

'Really? Oh, Kiki! Are you sure you are doing the right thing? Will you return to the UK?'

'No, I will never come back. Living here is too hard for me. I have had enough of this experience.'

Rashid does his best to convince her to stay in the UK. He advises her that in the long run children always do their own thing. He thinks she is too attached to her family, and it is time that she stands on her own two feet. She shuts her ears and closes her heart to his words. How would he know how it feels to give up your home, your life, your privacy? He has a wife, a son, a good job and a home. Even though his wife owns a car, she does not yet have her driving licence and now her 'driving instructor' is deserting her.

'No, Rashid, I will not stay any longer. And no, I shall never come back, never!' She stares out of the window, looking at the street where the cars are parked tightly in front of similar homes. She ignores his pleading look.

In South Africa we have double automated garages, and each house looks different. She bites her lip; afraid her thoughts might become spoken words.

A few days later, Shona tells her they have problems with the new au pair's arrival date. 'Would it be possible for you to postpone your departure date? Please, Kiki?'

'No, I am sorry. You said I should leave on the seventh and I have already bought my ticket.' She is adamant that she will not stay in this country one day longer than she needs to. No, she is going home; she is going home...

She is getting more and more excited about the prospect of returning to South Africa. So much for her dream, her new life in the UK where she could earn pounds and slowly make a life for herself as had been suggested by her husband.

'Yes, life is very tough here. One has to really want to live here.' If she had expected any understanding or sympathy from Keith, she was mistaken. She finds she has nothing more to tell him.

She packs her painting materials, ornaments, notebooks and pictures into a box. Wrapped in brown paper and addressed to her daughter's home, she takes her time walking down the street, her shoulders straining from the weight of the precious box.

'This will cost twenty-four pounds.' Kiki stares at the Pakistani man who works at the post office.

'What! How much?' She struggles to hide her dismay. That amount is more that the value of the contents of the box. She carries the heavy box home again. Whatever she can't fit into her suitcase, she will give to Shanti. Maybe she will leave the pictures and ornaments in her room for the next au pair, whoever she may be.

Her case is packed and ready well in advance. She weighs it on the bathroom scale and repacks it until she is satisfied that what she leaves behind is of lesser value than what she wants to take home. She shows Lika the suitcase resting on the chair in her room.

'Lika, I am leaving soon. I am going to my home.' She needs him to understand this simple message - she loves him dearly, and she is sad to leave. But he is young, and she can't expect him to grasp the inevitable. They have become close and have an intuitive understanding of each other.

On the last Saturday before she leaves, it is the Sweeps Festival in Rochester. She takes pictures of the festivities and of the cathedral. She loves these celebrations, and the thought of leaving this behind makes her sad. There are groups of musicians, people dressed as chimney sweeps, Morris Dancers, many food stalls and groups of people milling around. Is she really going to give this up? She experiences another hot flush and rips off her sheepskin coat, only to put it on again after a few minutes.

At the pub where she goes for a drink, she drinks too much wine. It is late when she finally returns home. All the lights are off. As she unlocks the front door, Vasal, sleeping on the couch, wakes up. She walks towards him and puts her freezing hand into his. He pulls her close and holds her tightly. They do not speak and after a few minutes, she leaves to go to her bedroom. Still fully dressed, she quickly falls asleep on her bed.

A letter arrives from Scotland the day before she leaves.

'We have received many applications and unfortunately, this time you have not been successful.' She also receives her National Insurance Number through the post and puts the document inside her laptop bag. *What will I do with a National Insurance Number while living in South Africa?*

Vasal will stay with the family until they have sorted out their au pair predicament. On her last evening there, he and Shona cook Biryani for dinner. Shanti and Sian come to the house to enjoy her last supper with them.

I will miss all of this. Maybe another time, another place, another life. It could have all been so different. I have been so blessed by these amazing people.

.

Before the taxi arrives to take her to Gatwick Airport, Vasal carries her luggage down the steep staircase. It is as if Lika suddenly realizes what is happening.

'No, no, do not leave!' he cries while throwing himself on the floor. Vasal and Kiki look helplessly at each other. She picks up Lika from the floor and holds him tightly, her eyes full of tears. Will she ever see Vasal again? This kind and gentle soul has been so good to her; he has shown her his heart is bigger than the pettiness of daily troubles. How will Rashid and Shona cope without her and how will the new au pair ever understand them all?

Vasal carries her case to the waiting taxi, and she hands him the sobbing boy, who reluctantly releases his grip on her arms. It is time to be strong. She walks past the blue Mazda parked in front of the house. *How long will it stand there before someone drives it again?*

As the taxi drives away, she checks her handbag once more. She must be certain that her plane ticket and passport are in her bag. When she feels the texture of the green book underneath her fingers, she smiles. She sits back in the car seat. She has escaped from the House of Curry. But her life is so much richer now; she can smell spices on her hair and clothes. She hopes the smell will last for an awfully long time.

Chapter 11

THE TUNNEL

She has become an experienced traveller. She flees from the plane; her small case chases her ankles like a puppy on a lead. Her family waits for her at Cape Town International arrivals and she doesn't want to waste one minute while going through customs. They have prepared a room for her in their home. They have taken the day off work and obviously Kiki's grandson did not go to school today.

She was reversing her steps and crawling through the hole, which had now become a tunnel. Here she is. Her feet are on South African soil again. Ten months ago, when she was so eager to join her husband in England, she could not have imagined she would feel so relieved and emotional being back in South Africa.

Last night she had spent six hours in transit at Ataturk Airport in Istanbul. When she first heard the flamboyant sounds of Sotho and Xhosa voices, she knew that she was slowly, inch by inch, moving closer to her destination. The loudness of the group of South Africans gathered in the departure hall had no boundaries. Somewhat embarrassed, she was drawn to them like a moth to a candle.

'We are insurance brokers and were awarded a cruise by our company. We are on our way home after having a fantastic time. Here, look at my pictures!' Kiki ignored the disapproving looks of fellow travellers and moved closer to her compatriot's mobile phone. She looked at the pictures of the woman's holiday on a cruise liner.

"So, tell me about you. Where have you been? Were you on holiday in Turkey?' a member of the group asks her.

'No, I stayed in England for ten months. But unfortunately, things didn't work out for me and my husband and now I am returning to South Africa. I worked as an au pair for an Indian family. I've had enough of that kind of life.'

She could see that the woman, who had quickly translated her story into Xhosa for her friends, did not know what she was talking about. That she - a white woman - worked as a servant, was totally incomprehensible to them.

But what *did* matter to Kiki was that she could talk to someone who was from South Africa. The weight of the last few months' experiences had pulled her body out of alignment, and she felt disorientated.

She realized she had betrayed herself, but she had to flee the damp, sinking island. At the same time, though she sensed she was closing a door to her destiny. *It does not matter; nothing else matters other than my urgency to get home,* she argued with herself.

I cannot handle life in the UK anymore. Everything changed when Kurt left.

At Gatwick Airport they had talked on the phone. She was close to tears, and he also sounded miserable. Her frustration at Keith's desertion further fuelled her determination to get away from the country that spat her out like a piece of chewing gum. It relieved her she had made it to Istanbul. From there it was straight home, sharing a flight with a boisterous group of insurance brokers.

When the plane finally touched down on the tarmac in Cape Town, she shared the relief of the girl seated next to her. She had worked for two years as an au pair in Belgium. Last night, as the plane flew over Africa, she had shared details of her ordeal with Kiki. Realizing they were home finally made them both emotional.

And, finally, here she is rushing through customs at Cape Town International Airport. Her passport carries a stamp stating that she is home. She relaxes her grip on the precious document and drops it with reckless abandon into her handbag. For months she had been paranoid about her possessions: her bank card, her passport, her mobile phone, a train ticket. Worrying that something could happen to her, she obsessed about all things small. Now, she couldn't care less!

When she arrives at the carousel, her polka dot suitcase waits for her. Knowing she is so close to her family makes her emotional and she must swallow hard to contain her tears. Before she can compose herself, her family appears in front of her. She kisses her daughter first, then her son-in-law, and then her grandson. Each greeting becomes a sweet embrace, melting her resolve not to cry. *But then, why shouldn't she cry?*

She can't stop looking at her beautiful daughter's face. From the front seat of Elizabeth, their pride and joy, a 1984 Mercedes, she eagerly admires views of a wet and rainy Cape Town. Seconds later, she turns her head to take another look at her daughter and grandson who are nestling closely on the rear seat.

He has changed a lot, she thinks. She can't resist the impulse to take another look at them. It has been exactly ten months since she last saw her grandson. She wonders about her other grandchildren; how will it feel to see and hold them again? For that privilege, she will have to wait a few days.

'Children aren't allowed to travel in a car without a booster seat in the UK.' For a moment she is reminded of Lika and Vasal. How will they cope on the first day of her absence?

'We have the same law here, Mom. He is not supposed to stand on the seat. When we notice a traffic officer, we tell him to sit, and he complies.'

They all laugh, knowing it is not an acceptable practice, but done in the name of a 'peaceful trip.' They have so much to share, and they briefly touch here and there, but she does not want to encumber them with her tales of woe at this moment. She weighs her words and thinks twice before she speaks.

They drive beneath the shadow of Du Toits Kloof Mountain Pass. Not only was she on her way to her daughter's house, but she was also returning to the town that she had left when she and Wessel got divorced so many years ago. She realizes she has not prepared herself for a life without a car, a house, a job, and a life in the same town where she is a member of a growing family.

They stop for a drink at the hotel where she spent the first night of her honeymoon as a nineteen-year-old bride. Standing on the veranda, she has the first sip of South African dry white wine. It's raining and the majestic cliffs loom close to them. It seems as if she can touch the mountain with her hand. Vibrant waterfalls crash like shards of broken glass onto the rocks, hundreds of meters below them.

'England has many beautiful places, but it is sights like these that I missed most.' She points towards the rough boulders of the majestic mountains. They watch an eagle twirl in the rain. The ruggedness, the naked beauty, takes her breath away.

'This is what I missed,' she repeats and turns to face her daughter who embraces her. 'Tomorrow morning you will have to get up early,' says her daughter with a smile. 'I want to spoil you with a pedicure and a facial at my salon. We also have an appointment with Amy, my hairdresser friend, who will cut and colour your hair.'

They placed strategically ornaments and pictures from her old life throughout the house. She steps into her new room. In the wardrobe, clothes she gave away before she left are hanging, waiting for her to wear again. Kiki recognises the duvet on the double bed, the duvet that was hers and Keith's when they still lived in Cape Town.

Regardless of what may happen in future, she has a room in her daughter's house. The room tells her that she is loved and welcome. The last time she was here, she and Keith were still together. She banishes thoughts of him; he is not welcome here. *I am back home. Stay in your white Wales while I'll live in my rainbow country.*

On her first morning back in South Africa she relaxes on her daughter's salon bed. She receives the first of a series of nonsurgical facelifts. She feels the tension leave her shoulders and when she looks at the 'before' pictures of her face that her daughter took earlier, she notices the tiredness in her eyes.

Amy cuts her hair noticeably short. 'There is no style. Your mother's hair needs a proper shape. With low lights added, she will look fabulous!'

So much for my Polish hairdressers' styling, Kiki thinks. She tries to recognize herself in the ornate mirrors of the trendy salon. To hear them communicate in Afrikaans is like music to her ears. They draw her into their conversation and when asked about her life in the UK, she shares titbits about her adventures as a single woman.

Hopefully, her son-in-law will sort out her hot flushes. He greets her at his doctor's surgery with a warm hug and a big smile. She tells him about the debilitating hot flushes and explains how it makes her feel as if she can't breathe.

'Mom, I will prescribe you a hormonal gel. If you rub it on your arm each day you should soon feel better.'

'Is it not risky to use hormones at my age? That is what the doctor at the NHS told me.'

He smiles and assures her she will be fine. There is no NHS in South Africa, and she must pay for the script at the pharmacy. Within a few days she notices a difference in the intensity and frequency of the debilitating attacks. She sleeps better and slowly she regains her energy. Life seems easier and she feels more hopeful.

One morning when she wakes up, the Boland mountains are covered in snow. Winter has begun. She takes pictures of the Karoo Botanical Garden and the neighbouring golf course to send to Kurt.

'Can I play golf there when I visit you one day?' Kurt sounds intrigued.

'Of course. The golf course is just across the road from where we live. I'll also send pictures of the wine festival in

Rawsonville. We went there this weekend. I went for a drive through the vineyards, sitting on a wagon pulled by a tractor. I wish you could have been there. It was so lovely sitting in the sunshine under big umbrellas!'

She can't believe it, but she drives a car again, even though it's Elizabeth, their old Mercedes Benz. She meets her daughter in town, and they go to the Cave, a popular restaurant where they sit under the ancient blue gum trees in the courtyard.

'Cheers Mom! It is fantastic to have you back. Please remember that we want you to stay with us – that is, if that is what you want to do. Our home is your home. Tomorrow evening we have a function at the golf club, and we bought a ticket for you to accompany us. Oh, I am so happy! My mother has returned from the cold. There is only one thing you must promise me: never take Keith back into your life. He hurt you so much and though we were great friends, I will never trust him with you again.'

Kiki inhales the fresh Boland air. The smell of eucalyptus blends with the aroma of the fruity wine in her glass. Her head is spinning already; it is intoxicating. Shortly they will drive to meet her eldest daughter and three grandchildren who live on an export grape farm in the district.

'Wow Mom! You are so thin!' she exclaims where they greet in the hallway of their farmhouse.

'It happens when you're on an Indian diet,' Kiki laughs.

She hugs her two youngest grandchildren. 'Now that they each have their own Kindle, they want to read at every moment,' says her eldest daughter. She leads the way to the veranda. They sit on the comfortable loungers next to the sparkling pool. She serves espresso in tiny hand painted cups. Kiki cherishes the rich aroma of the coffee. A tractor drives through the vineyard close to the house. She sits back and closes her eyes for a moment.

Her eldest granddaughter has grown into a tall, gangly teenager. It is obvious though that she can't wait to get back to her Kindle and she excuses herself after a brief chat.

'Mom, I am so happy you are back. I can really do with your help. I can't cope with my work plus driving the children to their after-school activities. '

'I would love to help you. Until I find a job, I will be available. Just let me know when you need me.'

'If you could help me on Tuesday afternoon, I'd be delighted. I have a consultation in Cape Town, and I won't be back in time to collect the children from school.'

At the golf club prize giving, she meets one of the lawyers she knew from her estate agent days. 'I recently returned from the United Kingdom. I stayed there for almost a year, but now I am looking for a job in town,' Kiki tells him. He holds her hand while he listens intently. The gong goes to announce dinner and he must return to the table where his golf partners wait for him to join them.

'Make an appointment with my secretary on Monday. We need to have a chat. Who knows, I might have work for you.'

On Monday morning she makes an appointment to meet him at his office. But he keeps her waiting for fifteen minutes; he 'forgot' about their arrangement. The position he has in mind is with his friend, who is currently away on a hunting trip in the Karoo. He will contact Kiki next week after his return.

But, in her heart of hearts, she knows she doesn't want to be a debt collector. Chasing targets on a phone isn't something that interests her. But beggars can't be choosers, and anything is better than nothing. She must start somewhere......

Lizelle, her friend from their school days, phones her and offers her a plane ticket to visit her and her husband in Port Elizabeth. The generous offer overcomes Kiki, and she can't refuse her gift. She still has not been to visit her mother, but the thought of seeing her lying on a mattress on the floor is unpalatable and she keeps making excuses. When she returns from her visit to Lizelle, she will go to see her mother.

One evening after dinner she receives a Skype call from Kurt. He says he misses her and would she please come to visit him in Iceland. Her daughter is shocked when she tells her about this development. Not only was she going to visit Lizelle so soon after her return, but now she is considering a six week visit to Iceland!

'Oh Mom, I don't want you to leave so soon, but you know what, you must do whatever makes you happy. Visit Kurt before you start to work. Regard it as another adventure and when you return from Iceland, you'll know what to do.'

'I am not sure if it will be possible for me to go. First, I'll have to find out the price of a plane ticket, how to get a visa and then see what the requirements for a deposit are, prior to visiting Iceland. I'll go to a travel agency tomorrow for more information and only then I'll be in a position to make a decision.'

On her way to the travel agency, she visits the manager of a local estate agency. Apparently, they have an opening for a receptionist. She does not want to work solely for commission again, but maybe this position might develop into something from which both she and the company may benefit.

She can see the manager is impressed with her resume. Kiki already achieved the government requirement NQF5 certification – the manager is still studying for it! She suspects that the company is not doing very well. The property market is still as dead as when she and Keith threw in the towel months ago. It is easy to imagine herself working in an office again, dressed nicely, meeting clients, visiting properties for sale, doing valuations, preparing portfolios. Oh, she could do that! How would she love to do that again!

The travel agent provides her with all the relevant information for a flight to Iceland and that evening she e-mails Kurt the details. 'You need to send me an invitation to visit you. I will get all the other required documentation in place. My family offered to put the deposit down on my behalf. I will have to go to Cape Town for an interview at the Icelandic embassy.'

'My brother says you must come as a normal tourist. That way, you won't need an invitation letter from me.' She is a bit taken aback at this remark. What does he mean?

'But I **am** a normal tourist! As a South African wanting to visit Iceland I need a Schengen visa. All right then. I'll ask the travel agent to mail you all the requirements. '

She tries to stay calm, but she knows his brother has a different opinion. A few times when she had phoned or Skyped Kurt, he could not talk because his brother was also in the room. It makes her sad because she can feel the distance and lack of communication influence her relationship with Kurt.

It seems Kurt and his younger brother are working extremely hard at building the house. On Skype, he shows her how the building grows. She can see how thin Kurt is now. He looks tired and gaunt but seems happy to be away from the UK. But it does seem as if his oldest brother is in control of his life and the building operations.

The next day she walks to the shopping mall on the outskirts of town. She perspires as she walks past the school where her children used to study. They had warned her about the safety of walking on her own, even on a bright, sunny day. On her return home she feels tired and annoyed that she had to walk so far.

As she unlocks the front door of the house, the two cats run towards her to welcome her. Kiki puts her bag and shopping on the bed in her spacious room. A group of cleaners gather outside on the street corner where they wait for their bus. She listens to their banter in Xhosa, their mother tongue. The sound of their laughter and their cheerful voices is in stark contrast to her loneliness. Her family will want her to stay with them for as long as she wishes, but it does not feel right for her. A young couple needs privacy and their own space. She does not have many choices yet, and her intentions are to find a job and then eventually, once she earns again, she will rent an apartment. Then she will buy a car and slowly get back on her feet.

Later her daughter arrives home from work and with her she brings light into the house. She wants to know all the details of Kiki's visit to the travel agent.

'I have flight dates now, but I will have to make an appointment to go to the Embassy. Kurt wants me to be with him by the end of their summer when it is not too cold yet. I think I will have to assist them with cooking and cleaning while they build their house. I worry I will be sad when I return from the visit, but who knows what might happen in the future.'

'Mom, go! Enjoy your life! Have you decided yet when you are going to visit Lizelle in Port Elizabeth? I think you should fly next week. Stay there for ten days and after your return you can sort out the visit to Iceland. And when you have returned from Kurt, you can look for a job in town. My, suddenly, you have so many options!'

'I'm really not looking forward to leaving you so soon, but I would like to see Lizelle. I think a good chat about the old days will mean a lot to us both.'

Kurt has received the information the travel agent sent him, but his brother insists she come as a 'normal' tourist. She is defeated. What a pity. She really wanted to add Iceland to her traveling resume. *How hard can it be to write an invitation letter?*

When they leave on Saturday morning to visit her family in Cape Town, she also takes her packed case ready for her visit to Port Elizabeth. Her son-in-law will take her to the airport on Monday afternoon and Lizelle will meet her at the airport in Port Elizabeth.

She is torn between sitting with her son-in-law on the veranda at the barbeque and wanting to watch her grandchildren play. It is so lovely to be here with her loved ones; she must pinch herself. While sitting next to the roaring fire, they drink red wine and for dinner they have snoek, sweet potatoes, bread, and salad.

Her family encourages her to talk about her life in England and she tries her best not to get too emotional or bitter about Keith and how things turned out between them.

Her daughter comments on how much she has changed since Keith and she separated. Kiki is pleased to hear her comments. Unnoticed, her brain opens new pathways, pointing towards her life of independence.

Tonight, she sleeps in the same house whence she left for the UK. Barely ten months ago, she was so desperate to get away, to find a hole through the wall. She wanted to be with her husband in the UK more than anything in the world. And now she was back in South Africa trying to pick up the pieces she had left on this side of the wall. The difference this time is that this time she is now on her own and without many options. Each time Keith creeps into her thoughts, she gets upset, and she must remind herself that she is better off without him.

When she boards the plane for Port Elizabeth, she feels a sense of achievement. She is doing her own thing on this side of the wall. She can and will make the best of her circumstances. Who knows what life still has in store for her?

When she and Lizelle greet each other at the airport, it is as if they have never been apart. They have known each other since they were five years old. Lizelle has always been a good friend who kept their relationship going. It feels strange, though, to be here with her and Alec, her husband. The last time she was here for a visit, Keith was by her side. After supper she excuses herself and goes to her room. She wants to read her emails. She feels a bit disorientated and somehow her loneliness is more tangible than it was when she was with her family.

The next afternoon they go for a walk on the white, sandy beach. It is famous for its rock formations carved over millions of years by drifting sand and moving tides. Tourists and naturalists from all over the world come to view this part of the country.

Slowly, almost painfully, Lizelle extracts her life's story bit by bit. She asks Kiki many questions. Why did she get divorced from Wessel? What happened then…. Why this? Why that and before long, Kiki shares details of her life in an open and intimate way.

Later they play tennis and after Lizelle has beaten her convincingly, Lizelle takes Kiki to a friend's house to show her a beautiful mosaic pathway. She accompanies Lizelle to her ladies' monthly tea group and on Sunday friends come over for tea and scones at their house. This is a typical period in Lizelle's routine. They have lived in this seaside village for more than a decade.

She notices Lizette's frustration at the fact that Alec is still employed at the municipality. Though Alec has often said he would retire soon, he never does! Lizette has many hobbies and interests to keep herself busy. She plays tennis, visits her friends and they frequently travel to

Gauteng to stay with their children. Kiki wonders if this is the type of life she would like to live, should she be offered the opportunity.

Returning from another walk on the beach, Kiki goes to her room to read her emails. It does not seem as if Kurt or his brother will ever grasp the requirements for a South African to obtain a visa for Iceland. Gradually she comes to terms with the fact that she might not go there. It also dawns on her there exists a vast chasm between her and the rest of the world.

What am I going to do here in South Africa? Wherever I go, I am reminded of Keith and our life together. We had good times, but we also had terrible times. Telling Lizelle about their problems during his alcoholic period has refreshed memories it forced her to face.

One evening after dinner, Lizelle, Alec, and Kiki sit in the lounge chatting and drinking coffee. Alec tells her about his work at the council. He works in an advisory position, but he encounters so many problems and feels concerned about South Africa's future. Their son lives in Australia and if it depended on Alec, he and Lizelle would emigrate. Lizelle's knitting needles make clicking sounds as she knits another jersey. The frown on her face tells Kiki she is annoyed. Emigration is not an option for her.

'Why don't you return to England, Kiki? How long will it take you to get British citizenship? I don't want to influence you, but you know, if I were you, I would seriously consider going back. At least when you work there you earn pounds. You will be surprised to see how quickly eighteen months pass. Once you got Permanent Residency, you can decide what you want to do next.'

Both Lizelle and Kiki stare at Alec in dismay. This is crazy! How can he make such a suggestion? Has he any idea how hard it is to live there on her own without a home or any family? Only a man with a degree in engineering could be so hard and unsympathetic!

Patiently she explains her hopes and dreams of life possibilities in South Africa. He may be more practical than she is, but she must work hard to convince him.

That night, after their conversation, she struggles to fall asleep. She tosses and turns on the bed. The steely grip of reality forms a tangible band around her head. Her heart beats too fast, and she has a panic attack. She resists the urge to flee. Her inner resolve takes over. Alec is right. What is she doing here? She has been given a great opportunity and she's throwing it away. Yes, it is fantastic to be here in her beautiful country with her family and friends. But realistically it is going to be hard to live without credit, medical aid, a car, and a home.

Keith has only one thing to offer her and maybe she should grab it and use it to her advantage. Only recently, she sent him an e- mail to formally request, a divorce. But surely, he will understand and wait for just another eighteen months. In fact, he had never replied to her message when she asked him to make their separation official.

The following morning Lizelle continues to teach Kiki how to master Sudoku. She has never enjoyed figures and Lizelle has always beaten her at any board game.

'I think Alec is right, you know, Lizelle. Perhaps I should return to the UK. At least I will have a goal then. Think about it - I will have a British passport. That will enable me to travel without this blasted Schengen visa. Also, with the right attitude, I can turn my time there into an exciting experience. There is still so much I would like to see in England and Europe. And to be honest with you, I feel so much better now that I don't get these debilitating hot flushes anymore. '

'You are much braver than me, my dear friend. After all you have been through! I can't picture you going through all of that again. Why don't you just give life a chance here in South Africa? You've hardly recovered from your ordeal and now you want to run away again. Don't listen to Alec, please, Kiki.'

'No, please! Don't think that he can influence me. I won't allow that to happen. It is my life and only I will make my decisions. But do you know what? Somewhere, deep in my heart I feel like such a coward having returned so soon. I needed to be here with my people for a while. I had to touch them again; feel their breath on my neck and the warm touch of their hands in mine. But maybe I should return and complete my task?'

She cannot believe that it is her speaking. Is she crazy or what? How will she explain this to her children? She has not even been back for three weeks and here she sits talking about returning to the UK. This time it will be even harder. There is no Keith to go to, no rented apartment, no car, television, no coffee machine waiting for her. When she goes again it will be only her and her polka dot suitcase, going who knows where.

It takes a few days after her return to Cape Town for her to summon up the courage to break the news of her new plans. However, before she can bring herself to do that, she contacts the estate agent and the lawyer one more time. Neither of them has a position for her now.

'Is it because you feel there are more opportunities for you in the UK that you want to return?' They sit in the kitchen, her photos run on 'slide show' on her laptop. Their favourite music plays loudly in the background. Her daughter is cooking dinner. Kiki cherishes their togetherness, their easy companionship.

'Yes, I feel there is more potential for me there.'

She is not completely truthful. Sure, statistically, because there are so many more people living there, the chances should be better that something good will happen to her. But more importantly, she must rid herself of the remains of the old Kiki; the one who left here with a husband and returned with her tail between her legs. She felt defeated because he had left her high and dry. If she returns one day, she wants to do so as a strong, victorious woman.

By the time she put her profile on the Au pair website she feels optimistic that she will return to England within the next month. She expects it to be difficult to find a position from South Africa, but to her surprise she receives three offers for employment within the first week. The interested families are from Clacton, Harlow and Newark. These are places that she has never heard of. The third offer seems to be the best one, but the second enquiry is equally as good and may be the one she should accept. But, since her word is her word, she commits to the first one. So, she will earn silver pounds in future in Newark, working for a young mother with two small girls. They agree on a date for Kiki to arrive at Heathrow Airport. Her new boss's mother will collect her there and then drive her to her daughter's home in Newark.

The travel agent is surprised when she wants to buy a plane ticket to England and not travel to Iceland. No, she's had a change of heart. She is going to fly from Cape Town to Heathrow Airport, London.

This is a different tunnel to climb through. It is not a hole anymore. She has discovered a way to go back and forth, and she can return, as and when she has the funds, the desire, or the time to do so. Is she stronger now? Can she do it better this time?

Again, it is hard to pack her whole life into a polka dot suitcase. One small piece of hand luggage, a brand-new laptop, and a handbag – that is all she can take on the plane with her. When she struggles to close her bursting case, she must leave more items behind: shoes, jewellery, winter clothes and scarves. It will be summer when she arrives, but when the seasons change again, she will have to buy new clothes.

She spends her last weekend in Cape Town with her family. They will take her to the airport on Monday afternoon. She is freer of possessions than ever. She has learnt her lessons. It is not anyone's lesson, but only hers. She needs to experience healing and acquire peace of mind and vision. To achieve this, she needs to be free of material 'things.'

Her six-year-old granddaughter cries as they drive closer to the airport. Kiki holds back her own tears. Her grandson holds her hand tightly and possessively.

She bids goodbye to the family at the car parked at the designated 'Drop and Go' area. She finds a trolley, puts her belongings inside, and pushes it towards the Departures Hall. Dressed for the South African winter, she realises that her black boots and thick trousers will bother her as she nears the humidity of Dubai airport. But as they go along, she will discard the layers of clothing till she feels comfortable.

She notices the entrance to a hole that leads to a tunnel. She turns around and takes one last look at her family where they are still sitting in their car. They have done what they could and brought her here to the entrance of the tunnel. One last wave of the hand and she turns around sharply. She must do this. Only she can do it. Her heart beats fast, way too fast. She sighs, then she takes a deep breath before she dives in, headfirst.

Chapter 12

A CELL FOR A ROOM

Alice McDonald's Skype mantra reads: *Don't make a promise you can't keep.* Kiki's reads: *'A tear and a smile'.* She was thinking of Kahlil Gibran because she loves the idea of simultaneously smiling and crying. Alice certainly can't mean what she proclaims there, because it is not true. 'Making a promise' and 'keeping it', is not part of Alice's true-life mantra. To this day, she still owes Kiki half of her last month's wages.

Never in her life had she been so happy to meet someone as she was on the day when she met Alice. Her wild bunch of red, curly hair signalled louder than any bouquet of red roses could have. Appearing out of the crowd at Heathrow Arrivals, waving her crutch as if in a biblical vision, she became Kiki's saviour.

It was not really a crowd, but at that moment Kiki thought it resembled a huge gathering of strangers. They waved placards bearing different handwritten names. She looked and looked but did not see a placard with her name being waved around. The panic she had tried to suppress for so many hours while the plane flew across Europe from Dubai to London had valid reason to manifest itself now.

She felt cold sweat running down her armpits and the familiar pin pricks on her lips were very noticeable. She had heard Alice's broad Scottish accent on the phone when they discussed their meeting 'arrangement,' but she did not know what she looked like. So, whom was she hoping to meet?

Going through customs took forever. There were many people queueing and to make matters worse, it was humid and hot in the large hall. A young girl waiting close to Kiki in the queue fainted, and paramedics squeezed into the line to assist her. Kiki had no idea what she would do, or where she would go, if Alice weren't there to meet her.

Finally, she stacked her luggage on a trolley. This time she was prepared for the inconvenience and had her pound ready. She had kept it in her wallet while she was in South Africa, making sure it would be available for a trolley at the airport. But where was Alice?

Then, to her great relief, she heard someone call her: 'Hiya Kiki! Here I am!'

She wondered how on earth Alice recognized her, but it did not matter now. Soon she learns that Alice is a 'horse person' and had hurt her leg when she fell off a horse a few weeks ago. Alice is thin and tall, and has freckles spread over her face; she is a true 'ginger.' It surprised Kiki that someone would come to an airport wearing jeans, a nondescript tee shirt and flip- flops. She wondered if her daughter, her future boss, resembles her.

After putting Kiki's luggage in Alice's car, they drive away from the airport and soon approach the highway, going toward Newark. It will take almost two hours to get there. Now that Kiki is safe, she relaxes. Knowing that she is going somewhere where she was needed means a lot to her. Alice drives fast, but she handles the car like a professional driver.

They get on well, and Kiki enjoys their conversation. When Alice tells her about her 'yummy daughter,' something alerts her antennae. She needs to gather all the information she can about her new work before they arrive in Newark.

By the time they are halfway to their destination, Alice knows about Keith and the reason that Kiki temporarily returned to South Africa. She also understands why she is here now, driving with Alice in the UK. They might become friends, but Kiki stays cautious. She reminds herself that while she works for Alice's daughter, caution comes first.

'Cathy is absolutely gorgeous! You must see her body! If only I could have a figure like hers! Even though she is the mother of two daughters, she still looks like a teenager. She spends a lot of time at the gym. She is preparing for a bodybuilding competition in August. I am so proud of her. She is also training to become a carer; she is especially interested in palliative care work.'

'Her boyfriend is a personal trainer. Don't be concerned Kiki, they separated recently and only see each other when he comes to visit the girls. The older girl,

Annie, is two- and- a half years old. Alan is not her Daddy, but he treats her as if she were his own daughter. Gorgeous Bea is only nine months old. She is such a calm baby. When she is tired, Cathy puts her in the cot with her bottle and she goes to sleep by herself.'

'Body builders eat little; they live on protein drinks and vegetables like sweet potatoes. In August, Cathy and Alan will go to the Philippines for a holiday and then you and I and the girls will visit my family in Scotland.'

All this information makes Kiki's head spin, and a picture emerges slowly. She hopes it differs from what she imagines; there is a possibility that she will soon be on a protein shake diet.

The car speeds past yellow canola fields that seem to wave at them. They are now in Lincolnshire. It is a very rural region, and she looks forward to seeing Newark for the first time. But, to her dismay they turn into a small, built up neighbourhood, signposted 'Apple Blossom.' It seems as if a developer built dozens of homes amongst the canola fields, ensuring that no shops or facilities are in proximity.

'How far is it from their house to the town? Is there a bus service close to the house?' Kiki tries to figure out how she will get to town, but Alice doesn't know; she has only been here once since Cathy moved from London. Alice pulls up next to a black Camry parked in front of a terraced home. It relieved Kiki her long journey is over – at least for today.

'This is Cathy's car. My Cathy likes speed, and she needs to drive a big and strong car. Oh, come on! Let's go inside. Meet my yummy girl and my gorgeous babies.'

Kiki grabs her bag with her wallet and passport as she gets out of the car. It seems as if her other luggage will be left in the unlocked car. She trusts that it will be safe but feels concerned leaving it there unattended.

A pretty, petite woman wearing denim shorts opens the front door. Her bleached hair is tied into a ponytail. *So, this then, is 'Yummy Mummy...*

'Kiki meet Cathy. Cathy, this is Kiki. And here is Bea.' Cathy offers Kiki a limp hand. From her hip, clinging to her like a tiny wallaby, a black- haired baby grins at Kiki, revealing one huge front tooth. Cathy points at the chubby blond girl, sitting on a potty on the floor of the tiny lounge. 'Say hello to Kiki, Annie!'

A sofa, coffee table and huge TV take up most of the room. Toys are strewn all over the floor.

Cathy offers to make coffee; a gesture which Kiki accepts gratefully. In the kitchen, a sink filled with dirty dishes awaits them. Alice rinses two mugs under a running tap. It gives Kiki the opportunity to take stock of the kitchen. There is no table, only a baby's highchair. The counters are full of equipment and utensils. Fridge magnets cover the fridge door from top to bottom. *Should she even give Cathy the fridge magnet of the South African flag she bought at Cape Town Airport?* She wonders if it someone will notice it amongst all the others.

168

Annie has finished her business. It does not seem as if her mother or her granny is going to try to wipe her bottom or put on her trousers.

Between sips of coffee, Kiki tries to concentrate on the mother and daughter's conversation. They seem awfully close, but she feels tired after the long flight, the lack of sleep, and the drive here, and she can't focus on their conversation or attempt to understand their strange dialects.

'The previous au pair did nothing to stimulate the girls. She ate a lot and watched TV all day while sitting here on the couch. In the end I had to ask her to leave. She had the audacity to ask me for a letter of recommendation! Can you believe it?'

Cathy looks at Kiki to find out if Kiki understands the severity of the girl's actions. Kiki asks to be excused. She fetches her luggage from Alice's car. It is cool, but her South African winter outfit is too warm for this weather.

'Let me show you your room.' Cathy leads the way. There are safety gates at the bottom and the top of the stairs. Kiki struggles to open them. Cathy shows her the tiny, shared bathroom. She notices there is no mirror against the wall. *At least there is a shower*, she thinks. Within the next hour, she finds out that it does not function properly.

'This is where the girls sleep.' Kiki peeks into a bedroom furnished with a cot, a child's bed, a dresser, and a pitched tent in the one corner.

'This is my room, and here, next to mine, is yours. I am afraid it is quite small.'

'That's all right, as long as I have a bed and space to store my clothes.'

Can a room be any smaller? She squeezes a few belongings into the tiny wardrobe and leaves the rest of her clothes in her suitcase. From the bedroom window, which is adorned with broken vertical blinds, she can see the backyard where toys decorate the weed infested lawn. Further away in the distance, she notices pastures and green fields with trees spread out forlornly like sprouts in a vegetable patch.

She places her painting materials, her hair dryer and make-up on the windowsill. Her suitcase will have to serve as a side table. Maybe she will ask Cathy to buy her a reading lamp.

Inexplicably, the size of the room does not upset her. She senses the beginning of the next episode of her life in this room. Strangely, victory hangs like the smell of fresh flowers in the cubicle and she senses that she must be here right now. This is something she must do; it is preparation for things to come.

It will take a while to get used to being in England again. It is summer and gets dark only at about ten o'clock in the evening.

The broken vertical blinds hanging like loose cotton threads are disturbed by the early evening breeze. It makes a gentle noise. *I must not let Keith know where and under what circumstances I live now.* At least she is not a captive in beautiful Wales. She misses her family already, but she feels full, as if she had eaten a good meal that would last for a while.

She wakes up to the sound of a crying baby. She reaches for her mobile phone lying on the makeshift bedside table beside her. It is only six o'clock and her alarm is set for seven. She tries to sleep again but the baby's crying intensifies, and it does not seem as if she will be attended to. Kiki wonders how long before the older baby will wake up too because of the noise.

There is no point in trying to sleep again. She gets up, still wearing her pyjamas and she tiptoes to the babies' room. In passing, she peeks into Cathy's room. She seems to be fast asleep, ignorant of her baby's desperate cries.

When Bea notices her, she immediately stops to cry. Kiki is rewarded with a toothy smile. The baby is irresistible, and Kiki can't help falling in love with her. When she picks her up, she realizes the baby is soaked from head to toe. She finds a nappy and searches for dry clothes in the chest of drawers. The drawer is so full that it is hard to find something appropriate. The baby hangs from her hip as she struggles to open the safety gates. She changes Bea on the couch in the lounge.

In the kitchen she opens and then abruptly closes each cupboard. *Where is the porridge?* The lack of order frustrates Kiki. *There is absolutely no logic!* It seems as if anything goes everywhere. *How do people live like this? Are my standards too high, or am I expecting too much from a twenty-three-year-old mother of two young children?*

Well, since she is here, she will try to add value to their lives. As soon as she has a free moment, she will rearrange the kitchen cupboards. That way, she will see what food, utensils and so on there are in the house.

More surprises wait for Kiki. They use the downstairs toilet for storage. *What a waste!*

Bea is hungry and enjoys her porridge. Kiki looks for something to eat. She finds bread and cheese in the fridge. She will ask Cathy to buy her muesli and yogurt, her preferred breakfast.

She puts Bea on the floor and opens the cupboard beneath the stairs. This is where the toys are kept, and last night she noticed Cathy push various items into the cramped space. A pile of dolls and prams tumbles down and cascades onto the floor. Annie is now also awake and eats her breakfast while she sits on Kiki's lap.

Cathy finally arrives in the lounge. Kiki is desperate to go to the bathroom. She wants to brush her teeth and get dressed. This is going to be a long day. She is tired already.

'I have to train at the gym at ten o'clock. When I return, we can go to Tesco to do a food shop. Please make a list of groceries you need. I am on a protein diet and mostly drink shakes. The girls enjoy fish fingers or chips.' Kiki shuts her mouth; unable to keep her eyes off Cathy's short outfit.

Annie does not get on with Bea. The war starts as soon as their mother's black Camry leaves the driveway. They argue about toys and Annie pulls Bea's hair. Kiki is not ready to be a judge and disciplinarian at such brief notice. All she knows is that the nine-month-old baby can't protect herself from her older sister. It is her responsibility to keep her safe from bodily harm.

These fights happen repeatedly and by the time their mother returns, Kiki is shattered. Though outwardly calm, she is on tenterhooks. Annie refuses to dress and fetches the potty. She then carries it to the back door and throws the urine outside onto the cement in the yard. Minutes later, Bea crawls through the wet patch. Kiki picks up the wet baby and looks in dismay at her wet and now smelly shirt!

Oh, my word, this is difficult! She expected the care of two small girls to be difficult, but in her wildest dreams, she could not have anticipated this. Their mother is away most of the time, and when she is at home, she occupies herself by sending texts on her mobile phone. Though they do not live in the same house, Cathy and Alan are constantly contacting each other. Kiki wonders when she will meet Alan.

After they had done the shopping, Cathy leaves her and the girls at home. She will be back home after another practice session at the gym.

Maybe she should bath the girls before Cathy returns. Kiki quickly realizes that bath time is another obstacle course. Annie nearly drowns Bea, and soon the bathroom floor is covered in water. She dresses them both in their pyjamas, their bedroom is a mess, and she realises that Bea's cot smells of urine. Kiki changes the sheets, and she sorts their drawers out in the morning.

Despite their agreement that Kiki will only work till five o'clock. Cathy arrives home at seven. When she finally sits down on the bed in her cubicle, she realizes she did not have a moment's rest for the entire day.

She opens her laptop and reads her emails. There is one from Kurt who is still shocked that she has returned to the UK. There are also a few messages on her internet dating website. She enjoys the messages from Kit. He is one of the original friends that she 'met' while she was in Gillingham. They stopped chatting for a few weeks after she returned to South Africa. Then, one day, he surprised her: 'Hello South Africa. Are you there?' She replies to his mail in the tentative hope that they might meet one day.

Despite her fatigue, she paints an image of a woman she saw on a magazine cover. While she draws the dimensions and focuses on the positioning of her features, she starts to relax. The vertical blinds sway lightly in the breeze. Tension escapes from her body like the air from a party balloon. It is hard to stop drawing because she finds it exciting to see the shape of the woman's face develop. When she hears Cathy come up the stairs, she quickly switches off the light. This lack of privacy makes her cringe. She feels oppressed in the tiny room and stretches out sleepily on top of the duvet.

Is it any wonder the previous au pair sat on the couch all day long? If I find it difficult to manage the two girls' fighting and living in this small untidy, disorganized home, so far from any shop or convenience, how would an eighteen-year-old girl who still misses her own mother, be able to cope?

Before she falls asleep, she tries to compartmentalize the events of the last few days. She left South Africa, her friends and family in order to complete the task she felt obliged to finish in the UK. In eighteen months, she may apply for Indefinite Leave to Remain. She needs to provide six original documents to prove that she and her husband are living together. These letters must be spread over two years and must come from at least three unique sources.

She gets mad at Keith when she thinks about the situation in which she finds herself. Ultimately, the less she thinks of him, the better are her chances of healing. He did promise, though that he will do what he can to assist her with her application. Only time will tell if he will, or not. There is no point in worrying about it right now. All she can do at this stage is to be aware of the requirements to succeed.

Clearly, she has chosen the worst job of the three prospects. She must make it work, though. Maybe she could help this small family. Maybe, once the children get to know her and accept her as their caregiver, they will become more compliant.

Then, also, it is obvious that Cathy is unhappy about her and Alan's separation. That they are texting each other all the time shows they are still pretty much joined at the hip. At her age, she should still be partying and dating, and it must be hard for her to raise two little girls.

Kiki also has administrative things to worry about. Soon her tablets will run out. She must register at the nearest NHS surgery. Her driving license must be changed from South African to a British one before the end of the month. She has no idea where to go or how to arrange that. She must also change her postal address at her bank.

The next day she mentions to Cathy that she has a dilemma and to her surprise Cathy offers to help her. She brings an application form from the closest surgery for Kiki to complete. To deliver it to the surgery, she must walk three miles to Apple Blossom village. She gets a doctor's appointment, and to her relief, she is registered with the NHS again.

In the afternoon, Cathy takes her to Newark where she applies for her driver's license. Within days she receives her UK driver's license through the post. What a relief! One afternoon, while Cathy has a tanning session in town, she goes to a branch of her bank and changes her postal address. Now she is ready to focus on her next mission. She must find a way to get to town on her day off.

She asks the Google God for a bus timetable from Apple Blossom to the city. On Saturday morning at eleven o'clock, a bus will arrive at the main road, opposite the estate where they live.

Early on Saturday morning, she dresses with care. Kiki puts her wallet, the house keys, and her notebook in her bag. She walks to the bus stop like a woman on a mission with her back towards the slight breeze. As she peers down the road to see if the bus is coming yet, she resents this waiting with a passion. Brushing her damp hood off her face with her gloved hand, she remembers how spoilt she used to be. Never has she had to make use of public transport. Standing there in the elements, waiting for a bus that might or might not appear, she is desperate to get to town. She needs to do something for herself, something pleasurable.

She has read about the historical castle and cathedral in town, and if she can come home later this afternoon with the knowledge that she had seen something special, she will feel so much better. Maybe there is a

Wetherspoon's. Who knows, she might even meet people and make friends.

After waiting for an hour, her optimism is delivered a immense blow. There is still no bus on the horizon, and she must throw in the towel. She walks home with a heavy heart and stiff legs. Cathy is not home; she probably whizzed past her with her eyes on her mobile phone without noticing Kiki waiting at the bus stop. Kiki goes to her cell-like room, changes into leggings and a tee-shirt and sits cross- legged on her bed. The intriguing lady from the magazine cover calls her and she continues with the painting.

There are three major sports events in the world today that she is interested in - the ladies single final tennis match at Wimbledon, the Durban July in South Africa, and the finals for the Curry Cup where the best rugby teams in the provinces compete for the prestigious trophy. She knows her family will be glued to the TV, and it seems so unfair that she is here on her own today.

Keith will be somewhere in Wales, certainly not thinking of her. Why should she even spare him a thought? Luckily, there are other lonely people in this world and as it happens, Kit texts her during the long afternoon. Now and then, she puts down her paintbrush to text a reply.

Cathy's voice sounds excited when she bursts through the front door.

'Let's put all the boxes on the floor in the kitchen. Your mattress can lean against the wall behind the couch in the lounge. That way it won't take up too much space.'

A man's deep voice confirms Kiki's suspicion that Alan is moving in with them. The rest of the afternoon she is stuck in her bedroom as they carry stuff up the stairs to the already overfilled main bedroom. Eventually she must go to the bathroom. The passage has become a danger zone, blocked with cases, black garbage bags and piles of clothes.

'Oh, hi Kiki, this is Alan. He is moving in with us.'

'Hiya Kiki! I hope you'll be happy here with us.' His dialect is hard to follow, and she just smiles at him and lowers her eyes to avoid contact with him.

He is tall, dark and handsome. Kiki also recognises a bringer of trouble. She knows Alice does not approve of him and though she can only guess why; she gives him a chance and waits to see what happens next.

There is a commotion going on in the small house, and she tries hard to stay out of the way. When she goes to the bathroom again, she notices that the body builder put the mirror, bought for her by Cathy, against the wall above the hand basin. He did not consider anyone other than himself when he knocked on the nail. When she stands on tiptoe, she can barely see the crown of her head.

The following day, the family seems content and happy. The girls now have a daddy in their home, and

Cathy's smile is huge and contagious. In the afternoon, they ask Kiki if she wants to accompany them to Lincoln for a visit.

'We can visit the cathedral and then we'll show you the old part of town. It is quite a steep hill to walk, you'll see.' Cathy wears a mini dress with impossibly high killer heels. The looks on people's faces when they notice her are a mixture of admiration and surprise. Kiki feels dowdy dressed in her practical jeans and flat shoes as they ascend the steep hill towards the cathedral.

Another week looms ahead of her. Motivating herself feels like an ongoing battle. The medical problem she had previously, when her heart beat irregularly and too fast, has started again. She often despairs and wonders what she is doing here in the UK. She tries her best to bring peace to the fighting girls, but she gets very distressed and is at her wits' end how to manage the situation. It is a relief to be able to text with Kit in the evenings and then gossip about the day's events and 'Yummy Mummy's' activities.

One day Cathy had an appointment for a photo shoot which brings her home late in the evening. Prior to her leaving, the risqué outfits that she planned to take with her lay spread out on her bed. The couple had a huge argument the night before, and maybe Alan had valid concerns about the true purpose of the costumes.

In the mornings, the kitchen looks like a war zone; bottles with protein drinks and containers of fried sweet potatoes cover the counters. The downstairs bathroom is now even less accessible, filled with bodybuilding equipment.

She makes an inner vow not to push herself too hard. It is hard not to lose her patience when Annie, once again, throws the contents of her potty on the doorstep and Bea crawls through the mess.

Alice sends her an email to say that Cathy is thrilled to have Kiki there, and that she also told the 'world' on Facebook that she never wants Kiki to leave. It is also evident that Alice does not know that Allan has moved back into the house with them.

There are many weeds on the small lawn at the back of the house. Kiki sits on the grass and weeds while the girls play there; she weeds when she brings the laundry in from the washing line; she weeds while they have lunch in the warm summer sun; she weeds regularly and decides to stay there until she rids the lawn from all the intruders. Kiki uses scissors to trim the edges of the beds and put the clippings and weeds into the bin to throw away with the garbage.

The girls and Kiki make up a game where they knock on the gate and call out: 'Is anyone home?' She and Annie are creating a bond, but this lasts only until her mother arrives home.

In the evening, when Kiki lies on her bed and listens to the sounds of the night owl, she often thinks of Keith and her losses, and struggles to envision a future for herself. She has made a few new internet friends, and they give her a fragile sense of value. She learns how to communicate, how to flirt, how to express herself, how to reach out. Clearly there are thousands of lonely people craving human contact. After having these deep thoughts, she feels better, knowing that she can reach out and 'touch' someone who is as lonely as she is.

One Saturday morning she boards a bus to Lincoln. The bus drives through rural Lincolnshire and eventually she disembarks in town. It is a beautiful historical town, and she takes pictures of the river from the bridge. She asks a Japanese tourist to take her picture as she poses against a wall next to the cathedral.

Her plan is to build a life for herself in the UK, but it can only take shape once she uses her memories as building blocks; each block must be cemented tighter and closer to the heart of this unfamiliar country. When she walks downhill towards the bus station, she spots a café with tables outside on the pavement. She spoils herself with a meal and a glass of wine. She wants the world to notice her; so that she can partake in a life that others take for granted.

It is time to send Kit a message and to tell him that she wishes he were here with her today to experience this beautiful town, perched on a hilltop like a bird on a nest of eggs. He replies and says that unfortunately his helicopter is in for a service. It makes her smile, but she realizes they are physically too far apart to even dream that they could meet.

When she arrives home, Cathy is wailing and lamenting like a widow who has lost her husband in a war. 'Alan left us! He took his clothes and bags and now the children are confused again.'

'Why? What has happened?' It becomes clear that they had a huge fight while Kiki was out. She finds it hard to believe that Alan has so little staying power. Perhaps he will take the mattress and the boxes that are stored in the small living room shortly. When Kiki hears Cathy's sobs through their shared wall during the night, her heart breaks for her. For a moment she thinks that her own plight is not so difficult, and she gives gratitude for the life lessons she has already learnt.

Cathy bounces back surprisingly fast. She has a friend who also resembles a bodybuilder. At first, they meet in the park under the guise of 'taking the girls to the park', but soon he visits her inside the house.

Kiki looks forward to the weekend because the girls will visit Alan's parents and the house should be quiet and peaceful. On Saturday morning, she walks to Apple Blossom to buy a newspaper. It is a long and lonely walk past the canola fields, and she experiences a bout of homesickness. She must remind herself to live 'one day at a time' and that 'today is the only day she has.' She buys a chocolate and a bottle of red wine to take home.

Cathy decides to enjoy her newfound freedom, and in the evening, she leaves the house floating on a waft of perfume. While staggering on her precariously high heels; she tugs at her short dress to cover her bum.

'Alan is with the boys tonight. He does not have to know that I am going out,' she tells Kiki.

There is not a lot of food in the fridge, but Kiki eats some of the cottage pie that she had cooked the night before. Lying in bed, she chats online with a few of her internet friends and then turns off the light to face another lonely night. When she wakes up a few hours later to a banging sound and muffled noises, she realizes that the time has finally come to find another position. She must leave this house as soon as she can.

It is already midday when Cathy emerges from her room. 'I was very drunk last night. Did you hear anything, perhaps?' Cathy's mascara streaks her face, and her hair extensions are coming loose.

'No, I heard nothing. Why do you ask?' Kiki lies. She is embarrassed on Cathy's behalf. Cathy does not have to know that when she went to the toilet in the early morning hours, she had seen her lying on the bed with a naked man, the door ajar and both oblivious to the world. She also doesn't have to know that she heard the front door closing and a car leaving the complex a little while later. Kiki also doesn't want her to know yet she plans to escape from her life as soon as possible.

As a start she mails her previous contacts to find out if they have found an au pair in the meantime. To Kiki's relief, Karin has found no one yet and after a Skype interview, she invites her to join their family in Essex. The household comprises of Karin, her husband, her son, their toddler, and her mother, who lives with them. Kiki says she will first read her requirements to see if she thought she would manage the work required of her. 'I won't enslave you,' says Karin. The house is big and old, and Kiki would have the whole attic to herself. There is also a little car available to use for errands or excursions during free time.

'I am moving to Clacton,' she tells Kit.

'That is awfully close to Southend-On-Sea.'

'Really? All I know is that it is in the East of England.'

She does not want him to know that she had Googled the area and realized that she was going to live about an hour's drive from him.

'If you look on Trainline.com, you will see which trains to take to get there. Have you told the Yummy Mummy yet that you are leaving?'

'Yes, I have. She asked if there was anything that she could do to make me change my mind.'

'And is there?'

'No, I am afraid not. I am so sorry for the girls. They crave their mother's company, and they only see her when she puts them in bed. Hopefully, they will find an au pair less sensitive and caring than I am; one who just does her job and has no desire for a social life.'

Alice has not paid her wages for the last two weeks, and when she enquires about it, she tells her that she would pay it at the end of the month, 'as per usual.'

The next day, Cathy drives her to the station to buy her train ticket to Clacton. The two naked children, sitting in their car seats, aren't quiet for a single moment. Their mother texts messages as she drives. Kiki says a silent prayer of gratitude that it won't be her ongoing task to assist this family.

It is even more difficult this time to close the polka dot suitcase. She owns more summer clothes and shoes now than when she arrived a month ago from South Africa. She leaves two pairs of trousers in the wardrobe. Since losing weight, she now wears a size ten. Once she takes her paintings off the walls, the room looks naked and forlorn.

Luckily, she had kept the number for a taxi driver that she had found on one of her walks to Apple Blossom. She won't rely on Cathy to take her to the station tomorrow. Whenever she must travel to a new destination, she needs to be in complete control. Only she knows where the opening of the hole is.

Chapter 13

THE ATTIC

Today she will travel with dignity, slowly an gracefully. Not like the day she travelled from Wales to Gillingham and fell on the stairs, hurting herself. Despite her caution, it's a daunting task to handle two suitcases, a laptop, and a handbag. It filled her with trepidation for this journey from Newark to Clacton.

Fortunately, British railways are reliable, and if she makes no mistakes, it should all work out according to her printed schedule.

Before the taxi arrives to take her to the station, she tidies her room and washes the dishes. She leaves the children in Alec's care and hopes he'll manage on his own. Cathy left the house early this morning, dressed in her carer's uniform.

At Newark station, Kiki boards a peculiar- looking train, comprising of only four coaches. Too soon, the first leg of her journey is over. She joins other commuters standing in the shade of billboards. She shifts her weight from one leg to the other. Finally, the train to London King Cross arrives. As she boards the train, she scrapes her shin against her suitcase, and blood streams onto her shoes. She tries to stem the blood with a tissue. Not realizing that one could reserve a seat on this train, she stands for one and a half hours in an overcrowded coach. Travelling on the underground proves a nightmare. Where there is no lift, she carries her suitcase to the top of the stairs, then leaves it there to fetch her other luggage at the bottom of the stairs.

She boards a train at Liverpool Street Station, destined for Thorpe-le-Soken. There she changes trains once more. By now, she is perspiring and hydrated.

It seems Kit has devoted his time to her today, and soon he knows exactly where she travelling to. He is her companion, guiding and encouraging her by text. 'Why did you choose the hottest day of summer to travel?'

When she finally disembarks at Clacton, she looks out for Karin. Surely, she will be waiting for her. Once again, she manages her luggage on her own. Finally, her strength deserts her; she is depleted, physically and mentally. She is almost close to tears as she stands on the empty station waiting for her new boss. Her eyes scan the empty road once more. She hopes she does not appear too forlorn and tired. She does not want Karen to regret her decision to employ an older au pair. Once again, she looks up and down the road to see if there is a car turning onto the station road.

Ten minutes pass and she notices a woman walking towards her. Where is her car? Certainly, she cannot expect Kiki to walk to their home with all this luggage!

'Hi, I'm Karin. Here, let me carry your laptop.'

Kiki should be grateful for the help offered. Maybe she would have been more pleased if Karen offered to pull her heavy suitcase. The sidewalk is bumpy and uneven. While she prays the wheels of the case will not break, she wonders which is heavier - her heart, or her luggage?

By the time they reach the old, listed home, Karin has told her they moved to Clacton a few months ago, and there is still a lot of work to do on the property. The heating bills for this winter were exorbitant, and next winter they will not use central heating at all. To reduce the costs, they plan to install wood burners in the kitchen, lounge, and main bedroom. The windows of the house, built in the 1500's, are single glazing, but new council regulations might force them to change it to double.

All these red flags. Kiki stores them in her 'read later' file. She can't imagine what it will be like in winter on the hottest day in summer.

There is indeed a lot of work still to be done in the garden. Robert, Karin's husband, and Lea, her mother, have a tea break. They sit at the kitchen table. They have been working in the garden since early this morning. The farm style kitchen is enormous, and at a quick glance, it required hard work to keep it clean and tidy.

'Sorry, but how does one pronounce your name again?' Robert is an attractive man. He is dressed in work clothes and comes across as confident and sincere.

'I know, I know!' Kiki laughs. 'It sounds more difficult than it really is. You can call me Kiki. On my passport, I am someone else, but to be honest, I dislike being called that. When I realize someone is going to struggle with the Afrikaans pronunciation, I don't mind.

Karen disappears into the recesses of the house. She instructs James and Ella to come to the kitchen. Soon, they join the grownups in the kitchen. Kiki is pleasantly surprised by their friendliness and warm hugs. What a change from the Yummy Mummy, the Body Builder and the two girls in Newark! This is her new family - a proper family. They even own a dog!

'This is Tiger, he has been in our family for many years.' Karen points at the sleeping dog on the floor. Kiki realises that despite his old age, he is much loved.

'We rescued him when he was still young; he is often in pain because of his bad hips.'

'Karen, did you tell Kiki how Ella stabbed you with her fork in your face?' Robert asks.

She looks at Karen's face for longer than would be polite. There is a large bruise on her one cheek bone. Her blonde hair and large blue eyes compliment her sumptuous mouth. Kiki struggles to follow Robert's Essex

accent, but she tells herself that she will soon get used to
it.

'Oh, I remember when I had a cataract operation a few
years ago, my cheek was blue, and later it turned to
purple. It was so embarrassing!' Kiki realises it will take a
while for them to get used to her accent, so she speaks
slowly and clearly.

The boy sounds quite 'posh.' Ella, who is going to be
her primary charge, does not say much. Kiki steals glances
at her beautiful features, her gorgeous mouth and lovely
hair. She notices they all have generous mouths which
apparently derive from Lea, their grandmother.

She understands the importance of her and Lea's
future relationship. She has a good feeling about her. Lea
points to the slightly chaotic utility room: 'It is all a terrible
mess, but I hope to tidy it after the weekend. I iron in the
kitchen.'

Kiki notices a clothes rail and a steam iron attached to
a pump stand. The room is full of boxes, piles of laundry,
books, and ornaments.

'Karen, show Kiki the rest of the house while I take her
luggage to her room. She is probably tired and needs a
rest.' She is thankful that Robert will carry her cases up the
steep staircase. Her legs feel weak and wobbly, and she
has reached the end of her energy quota for the day.

'And here is the attic! This is your space.' By now she is
confused and cannot remember how they got there. The

house is enormous and like all old houses,
disjointed. There are different levels, with eaves and nooks
and crannies.

So, this is her room then – an inviting space, with a
pale green carpet covering the floor. There is a desk with a
swivel chair, a wardrobe, dressing table, two comfortable
chairs, a bookshelf, a dresser, and a monk's bed in the
corner. Wow, quite an improvement on her 'cupboard' in
Newark. The modern bathroom is on the same level as her
room, but to reach it, she must cross a landing. She
realises she must be careful on the steep staircases,
especially the one that leads from the bedroom section to
the bathroom. The uneven old wooden floorboards feel
like the waves of the ocean beneath her weary feet.

'Our previous au pair put her bed in this corner. Move
the furniture. I thought you might like the desk here by the
window, so when you paint or write, you can enjoy
the views of the paddocks and the garden. I washed the
lace curtains today, but once I have put them up again,
you will have total privacy.'

When she wakes up the next morning, she expects to
hear the usual Sunday morning sounds of a family of five.
She strains her ears, but the house is unnaturally
quiet. She needs breakfast and goes downstairs to the
kitchen. The children sit in the living room. James plays
computer games. Ella sits snugly on a chair, drinking from
her bottle. They look up and smile at Kiki.

'Wow, the house is so quiet. I am not used to this. My grandchildren are much noisier than you guys! Where are your parents?'

'Mom is sleeping, Dad is busy in the garden, and Nanny is in her room. We are going to church later, so I suppose we should get ready. Come Ella, let's wake Mommy.'

Ella glares at Kiki with a 'don't you dare touch me' look and clings to her brother's hand. Kiki realizes it will take hard work to become her friend.

It takes a while to find the coffee and cups in the strange kitchen. She cannot open any of the lower cupboard doors. There are locks on each door.

'Here! Use these magnets. We keep the bottom doors locked to prevent Ella from getting to the detergents and cleaning stuff. It is such a nuisance, and sometimes the magnets get lost, or are left inside a cupboard.' James has an infectious grin, and Kiki decides she likes him.

Back in her room, she hangs the pictures she painted in Newark. It will take a while to feel like home, but she is pleased there is potential to put down her stamp. She has few possessions and belongings, and it must stay that way, but she might just walk to the nearest town this morning to buy more work clothes.

By the time she is finally dressed, and on her way to town, the family drive past her in their minivan on their way back from church. They wave at her. She does not know how far she must walk, but Lea told her that it is a comfortable walk. Yesterday, Karin showed her the Golf she will drive once they insured her as a driver. She hopes it will happen sooner than later.

On the horizon, scattered like thorn trees in the Lowveld, she notices many wind farms in the ocean. It seems to be a popular holiday town. Many older people stroll on the pavements. Though unimpressed with the quality of clothing in the charity shops, she finds a few shirts and trousers that will come in handy. Before returning home, she buys a newspaper and chocolates.

She opens the gate to the peaceful scene of Robert and Lea working in the garden. Karin cleans the kitchen, and the children sit in the living room where they watch a movie.

'I left a plate of food for you in the fridge. Please help yourself whenever you are hungry.'

She goes outside to sit in the garden where she reads her newspaper and observes the family. She needs to find out how they interact and relate to each other. When the children come outside to play on the trampoline, she notices James is an adept football player. Ella does her own thing. She plays with her outdoor toys, and often sits on the trampoline, enjoying the movement of the swaying base.

When Karin goes to work on Monday morning, Kiki is left with a toddler whom she hardly knows, a kitchen stacked with dirty dishes, heaps of dirty laundry, and a heaviness in her limbs and heart. When it is time to dress Ella, Kiki takes her to her bedroom. There is no changing table, and she places the screaming toddler on the carpet. It is difficult to choose her dress for the day; they are all so pretty.

Kiki spends the day watching the toddler play in the garden. She tries to connect with her unobtrusively. Kiki cannot expect Ella to accept her immediately, but she knows that eventually their bond will grow. Maybe, one day, when she leaves here, the little girl will miss her.

The washing line is very tall, and she must stretch to reach the top. It is lovely to be outside, and hanging the laundry is a great excuse to be in the sun. At the far end of the property, next to the cottage, she finds an abandoned lounger. She carries it to the front garden where she needs a retreat. Ella and Kiki eat lunch there, before it is time for Ella to go to her bedroom for her afternoon nap.

After school, James arrives home on his bicycle. Kiki is eager to see how he spends his time at home. By now, she is exhausted. All the juggling between Ella, the laundry, and her attempts to bring order to the house, has taken its toll. It is a great relief when Lea tells her at five o'clock that her work is done for the day. Wow! This is different from her previous jobs. Lea is taking over from her. She relaxes on the lounger in the garden and watches the children play on the trampoline.

She jumps when her mobile phone buzzes with a text message. 'Would you like to go out with me tonight? I'll pick you up at eight. Kit. *Typical of an accountant. Straight to the point*…. She is surprised and delighted, but also shocked. She decides to act cool and not to reveal her feelings.

'Send me a text me when you are outside and I'll come to your car,' she replies.

Rushing through the kitchen on her way to the attic, she informs Lea that she won't eat dinner with the family as she is going out on a date.

In less than an hour she washes her hair, changes into one outfit she bought at the charity shop and refreshes her make up. She is satisfied with the appearance of the woman smiling back at her in the mirror.

She recognises Kit immediately. When she opens the gate, she sees him where he stands next to his green sports car, wearing the same hat she had noticed on his internet dating profile. It feels as if she has known him for a long time. He has done his homework and knows more about the local area than she does.

They drive to Frinton-on Sea, where Kit parks his car before they go for a walk on the beach. They have drinks at an Italian restaurant before they order dinner. How wonderful to have a friend interested in her. She tells him about her family in South Africa and the lovely attic room in which she now lives. He explains the reason he was in a hurry to meet her; at the end of the week, he will go on holiday to Spain for fourteen days.

At the end of a rather long, but exciting day, she feels as if she achieved a lot. Not only has she survived her first workday without incident, but she also went on her first date since she had returned to the UK. It is a pity Kit must go to Spain now, but she is flattered that he drove here to meet her. All she must do, while he is away for the next two weeks, is keep herself occupied and stay busy. They made no promises to each other, and she has no guarantee they will ever see each other again. Obviously, they will keep texting each other while he is away. She looks forward to hearing from him again.

But, as the days go by, there are no texts from Spain. She struggles to stay focused on her new work. She needs someone to speak to, someone who is interested in her. Without contact, she feels less grounded and more insignificant. *Perhaps he does not have international roaming on his phone?* His lack of contact needs a justification; she feels frustrated.

James is clearly addicted to his computer games, and when he sits in the lounge for days on end without communicating with his family, his mother locks his laptop away. He approaches Kiki, crying and begging for sympathy, but she does not get involved.

Lea becomes her confidante. She is kind and considerate, the cog that keeps the household running smoothly. When there is a supply shortage in the house, she gets into her little car and drives to the shops to buy groceries. She does a lot of personal online shopping, and they joke when the doorbell rings once again with another delivery for Mrs. Potter.

After the summer school break, Ella will go to two different church play groups during the week. Karin accompanies Kiki to each group so she can see where they are hosted. It is the last week before term ends and for the next six weeks there won't be any groups.

Finally, she is insured to drive the little car. With a mixture of trepidation and excitement, she takes her first drive into the unfamiliar Essex countryside. Karen gives her a Satnav, but she does not know how to use it and prefers to study a map before she ventures out into the unknown.

Slowly, she puts her roots down. One Saturday she drives to the shops to buy canvasses and paint. In a charity shop, she finds CDs that she thinks she might enjoy.

In the evening, she reads about the requirements to get Indefinite Leave to Remain. She worries about how she will obtain six letters sent to her and Keith's 'joint' address, spread over two years, from unique sources. Her nights are often disturbed and sleepless. She admonishes herself; there is still plenty of time, and she must just deal with the things she can manage now. Not expecting Keith to be too concerned since there is no real advantage for him, she realizes she will have to do this by herself. She did not return to the UK for nothing, and it is imperative that she makes a success of this life-changing project.

The long, hot, days take a physical toll on Kiki. She is surprised how the English summer can transform her pale winter skin into a healthy shade of brown. Although she feels disappointed that Kit forgot about her so quickly, she realizes that her energy and future do not lie with him.

Her duties start at eight in the morning when she tidies the kitchen, makes the beds, and cleans the bedrooms. Once Ella is awake, she feeds and changes her. The rest of the morning she entertains her and plays with her. After lunch, it's time for Ella's nap. Only then, while she sleeps, Kiki performs all the other household tasks. Some mornings they walk to the park with Ella in the buggy, and Ella plays on the swings. The garden at home has much more to offer than the park, and the route there is not scenic, but it is a change to their daily routine.

'Butterfly! Bird!' Kiki points out items to Ella; she wonders why she does not talk yet. To put her to sleep in the afternoons, Kiki sings Afrikaans lullabies to Ella. The songs are catching, and Ella cannot resist the magic. She lies in Kiki's arms and sings along till she finally gives in and falls asleep.

One evening, James comes outside to where Kiki is resting on her lounger. He holds his soccer ball in his outstretched hands. His bright smile is irresistible. 'Please Kiki, will you play ball with me on the trampoline?'

Her first instinct is to make an excuse: *I am too old to play on a trampoline. I might hurt myself and then I won't be able to work. I won't be a challenge for you.* These thoughts go through her mind, but she throws caution to the wind. She warms up first, unaccustomed to the movement of the swaying trampoline beneath her feet. The exercise and fun will be good for her. She and James will establish a bond this way.

Soon, playing soccer on the trampoline becomes a daily event. Kiki throws or kicks the ball, and James defends. Even though James pushes his luck and begs her to play during her work hours, she makes him understand that her duties come first. Ella joins them and often gets in the way of the ball. When they leave the trampoline after a practice session to go back inside for dinner, panting and sweaty, an eerie silence settles over the garden.

'Hours after I arrived in Barcelona, I was pick pocketed. What a shock to find that my phone was stolen! I am waiting for my new phone, but in the meantime, it is such a hassle. Would you like to go out for dinner on Wednesday evening? Then I can tell you about my holiday.'

So, that explains it - Kit's silence and the lack of communication. His attention had spoilt her. This was the companion who had helped her adjust to her new life. And then, his silence. It is as if a weight has been lifted off her shoulders. It's good to know what had happened.

Kit surprises her again with the amount of research he's done about the area. They drive to the Naze in his open sports car. Hand in hand, they stroll on the top of the hill. From there ferries, crossing the grey ocean en route to Europe are visible. They stop to read inscriptions on the footpaths, showing where, during the Second World War, defence shelters were built to protect the coast from a potential invasion. Inside one of the musty smelling shelters, Kit draws her close and kisses her. The kiss does not last long. Other ramblers inquisitively peering into the dark crevices of a bygone era soon joined them.

They eat dinner in a local pub where they learn about each other. When she shares her past with him and tells him how she and Keith became separated, she becomes emotional again. Before she can control herself, tears run down her cheeks. To her surprise, Kit, too, tears up when he shares snippets of information about his wife, who had died of cancer fourteen years ago. It shocks her that anybody can still mourn for someone so intensely after such a long time.

Soon it is the weekend, and she has an urge to drive to the Naze again. This time she takes her camera with her so that she can take pictures of the scenery and the war shelters.

In the afternoon while she sits in the attic, she paints, and listens to music. Though she is content, a growing sense of loneliness plagues her. It dawns on her that Kit is her 'Wednesday man.' It seems as if he is terribly busy during the weekends – Wimbledon, dining parties, birthday celebrations, all the occasions 'normal' people attend. Perhaps he doesn't intend to share this part of his life with her, as if it were off limits. The irony is that she is busy during the week, but when she needs company during the weekend, she feels lonely. Though her new family kindly invites her to accompany them on outings, she realizes she must create her own social circle.

James often mentions their previous au pair. Nobody in the family seems to have liked her. Kiki's wish is to add value to their lives: to help Lea with her chores, to see if she can be a friend to James, to love Ella and help her get through the 'terrible two's' stage. Maybe her grown up attitude will create a positive vibe in the family that will last for a long time.

One evening she and Kurt have a Skype 'argument.' Kurt looks exhausted from all the physical labour while building the family's' holiday home. Kiki blames his condition on his controlling brother and then Kurt becomes defensive.

'All I do is work, work, work! I do nothing for enjoyment; I never take time to rest. Can't you please come to visit me here in Iceland?'

Hopefully, this time, Kurt and his brother will understand that a Schengen Visa is a requirement for South African travellers.

'Oh! That would be nice. I'd love to come! Let's see what I can do to arrange a visit. Next week the family is going to Italy for a week's holiday. Maybe I'll ask for a few extra days' leave. I'll contact the Icelandic embassy in London to find out how it all works.' Kurt is satisfied with her approach, and they end the call with optimism in their hearts.

The letter from the Icelandic authorities arrives within days and Kiki forwards it to Kurt. Nothing has changed since she enquired about the requirements while she was in South Africa. His brother's approach, too, is the same. She understands that this lack of comprehension and sympathy towards her situation is the final curtain at a cheap matinee, drawn over their fragile relationship.

The house becomes a hive of activity while the family packs their van for their trip to Italy. After they leave and the house becomes strangely quiet, Tiger lies down in the kitchen's corner, already awaiting the family's return. Lea and Kiki have a whole week to rest and do whatever they please. The summer weather entices her to go outside on most days. She reads and paints a lot, enjoying the peace and quiet.

'Why don't you invite Kit to join you here for dinner one evening, Kiki?' Lea surprises her with this suggestion. 'I might just stay in my room, and then he can spend the night with you in the attic.'

Kiki finds it hard to believe Lea's generosity. When she tells Kit about Lea's invitation, he is delighted with the prospect of the visit.

Finally, she has time to tidy James's bedroom properly. It takes hours to move the furniture and sort out his toys and clothes. When Lea sees the changes that Kiki made to the room, she decides they must drive to

Colchester to buy new bedding and curtains. Lea is her co-pilot and directs Kiki to drive confidently through roundabout after roundabout.

Their purchases complete, they drive to Sainsbury where Lea buys groceries. She puts a bottle of Rose and a bottle of red wine into the trolley. 'You said Kit drinks Rose. Well, let's hope he enjoys this one. Now, let's find the ingredients for your meal.' Kiki plans to cook lamb's liver and onions with mash for Kit, a dish he enjoys.

But, the night before their planned rendezvous, she wakes up in the middle of the night feeling disorientated; her heart beats irregularly, her body is damp with perspiration. The tiny bed on which she sleeps is tucked away in a corner, far from the window. *Is this why she is panicking, why she can't breathe?* She is fully awake when she hears the familiar buzz of a text message on her mobile phone.

'I can't sleep. I am in the kitchen making a cup of tea. In a few hours I will leave to spend the day with you.' This is a coincidence. Kit is also awake. She wonders if he is apprehensive, or is he just overly excited?

'I'm awake too. But do you know what? I've been thinking about things, and I've realised that I'm not entirely happy about your visit,' she blurts out. 'Perhaps we need more time before we spend a romantic night together.'

Everything in her mind and body has shut down. How can she allow a man to spend time in her space, listen to her music, see her art, if he is not prepared to show her where he lives or share his family with her? Kiki realizes she has been way too harsh and unrealistic. Though she knows she is protecting herself, she is also aspiring towards more than a causal relationship. Ideally, she would like a person to take her into the palm of his hand to hold her there, safely and securely.

Kit is so shocked by her change of heart; he promptly arranges to go on holiday to the Isle of Wight. Lea is also surprised, but wisely, does not pass judgement or make comments. The two women enjoy the liver and onions for dinner. The bottle of Rose stays in the fridge for weeks and weeks until one evening, visiting friends of the family enjoy it.

'Kiki, would you like to visit Cambridge tomorrow? You can drop me at a restaurant, and I'll wait for you while you explore the beautiful town.'

'Oh, yes, what a lovely idea. Do you know the way there though?'

'Some of the way I know very well.' Lea fetches her large map book and Kiki studies the route to get an idea of where she will be driving.

Kiki is thrilled but feels slightly apprehensive about the long drive. But the fact that Lea will sit next to her with the map book, plus Google God's instructions on her mobile phone, gives her confidence. Lea is an excellent navigator, and they arrive in Cambridge without any incident. Kiki leaves Lea at a coffee shop where she will wait for her. Not knowing where to start, she blindly follows a small group of tourists who lead the way. They frequently stop in their tracks to stare at the marvellous historical buildings. Kiki feels as if she is in a fairy tale. Light falls like gold dust on her, and she is lightheaded. She takes many pictures of beautiful old buildings with her camera.

For an au pair, a ride on a punt costs the equivalent of three days' work, but she can't miss the opportunity. A student wearing a bowler hat steers the punt expertly down the river. The punt drifts past university buildings and glides beneath the Bridge of Sighs. The young man explains how old windows were protected from bomb raids during the Second World War. Time passes way too fast, and she finally rushes back to the restaurant where Lea waits.

When they return home, Kiki downloads the pictures she took on her laptop. She paints a picture of a restaurant on the water's edge, close to where she rented the punt. It was a good day; one she will always treasure. Though she was on her own, she did not feel lonely, but instead, rather proud of herself.

Lea and Kiki drive to James' new school to collect his school uniform. Shortly after they arrive home, Lea tells Kiki that Karin had called her. The family is enjoying the break so much that they decided to stay another week in Italy.

'What about James' school? Is this a wise decision? A new school, plus a new year?'

Lea shrugs her shoulders. 'I don't agree with this one bit, Kiki. It is not a good way to start a new year. Please remind me on Monday that I must let the school know that James will join them later. Oh, James's soccer...... I also have to phone the club.'

Kiki relishes the bonus free time she receives. She reads in the sun on the lounger for hours. Kit and she text each other regularly, but he is still confused about her sudden change of heart. They agree to meet again when he returns from his trip, but she is very aware of the fact that she has disappointed him.

The day before the family's return, she cleans the whole house. When the van stops and parks in the driveway, the sound of children's chatter sounds like music to Kiki's ears. Once the van is unpacked, Robert presents the bargains they had bought at the Italian flea markets. He carries a double bed to the attic and places it against the wall.

'This is yours Kiki. We just need a piece of wood to fix the base, then you can sleep on this lovely, antique bed.'

The cans of red wine that Robert had bought at various cellars are stacked in the guest toilet. A lovely chandelier is temporarily placed on the top of the fridge; when he has time, Robert will hang it in the kitchen. Kiki knows the family well enough to realize that the suitcases, filled with holiday clothes, have been put down in the bedrooms, where they will stay untouched until she unpacks them.

James comes running outside to look for Kiki where she and Ella are standing in the vegetable garden.

'Oh, Kiki, thank you for changing my room. It's lovely. I am so happy!'

He hugs her, tears of gratitude stream down his face.

'It is a great pleasure James, I really enjoyed doing it.' Such a little thing to make him so happy. Her heart is happy too. She is pleased they have returned safely and can now resume their normal day-to-day life.

One morning, at five thirty, her phone rings and wakes her. Her brothers' name appears on the screen. Her mother had died during the night. She was ninety-four years old and suffered from dementia. Though Kiki has been expecting the call for a long time, she is unprepared for the grief crashing down on her like a tidal wave that threatens to drown her.

Lea suggests that she takes the day off, but Kiki prefers to keep busy. Every now and then the realization that her wonderful, wise, intelligent mother, is not on this earth anymore, punches her in her stomach. Like a ghost, she moves around the house, trying not to attract too much attention to herself. She informs her friends of her loss and soon texts arrive, one after the other. These texts carry her through the day as she cries, cleans, and mourns in turn.

The family sends her flowers with a handwritten card that comforts her greatly; 'Dear Kiki, when you look at these beautiful flowers, know that is what we see in you.'

After work, Claude, her friend from a neighbouring town, persuades her to accompany him for a walk on the beach. It is good to talk to someone who cares. He stops in his tracks every hundred meters, looks at her and says: 'A hug!' He then wraps her in his teddy bear-like arms.

'When are you leaving for the funeral, Kiki?'

'I'm not going Claude. I said my goodbyes when I left the country. I'll visit South Africa in October when it is my granddaughter's birthday. I'll write a letter that my daughter will read at the funeral. That way I'll still be present.'

'Kiki, I am serious. You should re-consider this. One day you could be sorry that you didn't go. Please, allow me to give you the money to buy a plane ticket.'

'No, Claude. Thank you very much. I have enough money. I just don't feel I should go.' His generosity and caring astounds her.

On the day of the funeral in South Africa, she works till lunch time. She then drives to the beach where she sits in the car, meditating and thinking of her mother. Later, when she phones her children to enquire about the funeral, she can't reach them. She makes five different phone calls, each one in vain.

Somehow, in the days after the funeral, it's easier to feel her mother's presence. She often hears her speak to her; urging Kiki to stay positive, never to give up - her words of wisdom play like a tape recording in her head. 'Come, my girl. A person must give and give, till you have nothing more, and then you give even more.'

Still, life becomes a struggle. Lea asks her one day if something is the matter. 'You don't look happy. What's worrying you?'

Maybe she is still mourning her mother's death. A change of scenery might lift her mood. A bank holiday follows this weekend, and she decides to visit Brighton for a few days. She can't afford to become depressed. She has saved enough money for her Indefinite Leave to Remain application, which is still a few months away. Should she want to fly to South Africa, she can afford a plane ticket. If she is careful with her savings, she can squeeze a little holiday out of the few pounds in her bank account. That evening, she searches on the internet for Bed and Breakfasts in Brighton. She must also figure out how to get there by train.

To her surprise, Kurt contacts her to tell her that he has returned to the UK for business. Initially she ignores his attempts to meet her, as she feels resentful that he did not tell her in advance that he was coming, but eventually she relents and tells him about her weekend plans.

'Can I meet you in Brighton? I'll join you there.'

'No, sorry, this is something I want to do for myself.'

'Please, I really want to spend some time with you Kiki. Certainly, you could do with some company.'

'You have to believe me. I don't want to complicate my life and I need time on my own to rest and think.' She is determined not to get distracted by his presence. What is the point? She is on a mission to find the road signals directing her to her own destination. Kiki doesn't need moments of relief or mere hours of distraction. She wants a life of her own and Kurt hasn't been part of it for a while now.

The scenery from London to Brighton differs greatly from the East of England. She enjoys being out by herself, away from the attic and the busy household.

Though it is December, and she must wrap up in her warmest clothes, she does what tourists do. She visits the Brighton Pavilion, where she walks around for hours. In the evening she goes to a pub where she drinks two glasses of wine while enjoying her meal. Looking around her at the punters who look so connected, she wonders where she belongs? What is she really doing here? When she returns to the pokey room, she feels scared and nervous. Sleep evades her and she paints till early in the morning before she finally falls asleep.

This is an adventure. How many other people could do what I am doing right now? You are brave, strong and courageous, she tells herself when she wakes up the next morning.

Kiki enjoys her visit to Brighton and wishes that she could live in a more cosmopolitan environment. People dress differently here, and she enjoys the variety of interesting faces wherever she goes. *If only she could get a position as an estate agent! Why is it so difficult to be employed in this country?*

When she leaves Brighton the following day, she retraces her steps on the subway to Liverpool Street Station and from there she takes a train home, to Clacton. With determination, she takes control of her destiny. Kiki can't wait for things to happen to her; she will have to make them happen. Maybe, tomorrow her life will become easier.

Chapter 14

ESCAPE FROM THE ATTIC

The English Christmas is subtly catching Kiki in its snowy net, no matter how hard she tries to resist it. They brought the Christmas decorations down from the loft to be put up in the house. Karin disappears for an entire day; nobody knows where she's gone. She arrives home in the evening, walking from the train station while pushing a shopping trolley overflowing with gifts and wrapping paper. They learn she went to Colchester to do her Christmas shopping.

Beautiful Great Granny and her South African partner of many years, Mike, arrive from Italy for the holidays. They will stay in the cottage at the back of the garden. She brings with her a waft of expensive perfume and a reminder that age is just a number. Kiki tries her best to ensure that Ella is on her best behaviour. In the afternoon, Great Granny cooks dinner in the family's kitchen. Lea says that Great Grandma is a Cordon Bleu cook. She is in control of the Christmas lunch menu, and everybody looks forward to the traditional feast.

Mike is a decorator and handyperson, and Robert asks him to varnish all the wood inside the house. Kiki enjoys his presence in the house during the day. Although he has lived in the UK for many years, his accent is undeniably South African. Unfortunately, he does not speak Afrikaans. They laugh at how things have changed in their country of birth.

'Ha Kiki, look at you and me! We are doing work here as if we are ordinary laborers. What has become of the world? Everything has changed.'

'I know what you're saying. If my colleagues had to see me now! Me, the businesswoman! What a far cry from the days when I wore skirts and high heels to work...... Oh my, how I miss the thrill of negotiating a deal. Nothing gave me greater pleasure than a successful sale, a happy seller and a delighted buyer. And now? Now I'm happy when Ella goes to sleep without resistance. Ha, ha!'

Lea hints that a painting of the children will make a wonderful Christmas gift for Karin and Robert. Kiki takes a picture of them posing in their new Christmas outfits and starts sketching the photo on a big canvas. In the evening she sits in the attic where she listens to music while working on the painting that should resemble James and Ella. To her dismay, it does not look like them at all! She covers her first attempt with paint. She tries again and again, but it only gets worse. It's a disaster, but she persists. Her reputation as an artist is at stake. Recently Karin commissioned her to paint a scene of Canterbury. It was a thrill to see the vanilla sky develop until she felt satisfied with the result. But now she can hardly recognize the people in the painting. Eventually she must admit defeat. It's too hard to replicate people she knows.

Like a typical older brother, James is often hard on his little sister. 'Ella is like a clean piece of paper, James. This is how she arrived on this earth. It is up to us and the way we handle her, how she is going to turn out one day as a grownup. If we treat her with love and respect, she will absorb that love and become a gorgeous, caring person.'

James stares at Kiki with his huge, blue eyes. She sees he understands her on a deep level and for the next few weeks she notices a change in his attitude.

One evening Robert comes to her room where she is sitting painting on her bed.

'Kiki, we are so happy to have you here with us. We are still unused to someone like you in our home. Our previous au pairs were young and never stayed very long. One of them left after the first week! But you, you are different. Like a Zen figure, you bring peace to our lives.'

Kiki feels flattered and is happy to hear that her presence and actions have a positive effect. She knows Lea enjoys her friendship. But Lea can also sense her frustration. Kiki suspects Lea realizes that after eight months it is time for Kiki to test her wings.

So, it delighted her when a well-known estate agency in Colchester invites her for an interview. Claude offers to take her there on Saturday afternoon in his car.

She prepares well for the interview. She reads about the groups' policies and history. It helps to memorize a few facts and figures, but she is nervous when Claude drops her off at their head office on the main road. He waits for her in a nearby coffee shop.

'How did it go?' he enquires when she meets up with him after the interview. They enjoy a glass of wine at an Italian restaurant.

'It went very well. Howard thinks I am well suited to their office in Woodbridge. He is going to get in touch with the office manager who will contact me to arrange an interview.'

'Well, Kiki, that is fantastic news. Woodbridge is a lovely place. Why don't we drive there tomorrow so that when they call you, you will at least have seen the place?'

The office is closed on Sundays, which suits her. She stands at the window and peers into the depths of the smart- looking office. It is easy to imagine herself sitting at the desk. She pictures a client sitting opposite her, putting in an offer to purchase a lovely home.

'I wonder where I'll live. I'll have to buy a car. What about furniture; a bed, a wardrobe?' She realizes she is running ahead of herself, but, at the same time it feels as if she is close to achieving one of her dreams.

'Kiki don't worry about those things now. I'll bring you here for the interview. I'll plan my schedule to accommodate the interview time.'

'Oh, thank you, Claude. I'm sure I can drive here by myself. I must explain to Karin where I'm going. I would prefer to get the job before I let on that I'm looking for another position.'

She asks Karen if she can have Wednesday afternoon off, after she gets the phone call inviting her to meet David at the Woodbridge office. She assumes they think Claude is taking her out on a special date.

Kiki knows she looks the part when she walks into the office. She wears her black outfit, which suits her so well. She replies to David's questions with confidence and enthusiasm. This is her opportunity to shine and prove that she knows her profession through and through. She believes she would be an asset to their business. She leaves her referees' details with David and after the interview she is full of hope for the future.

But days become a week with no feedback. After two weeks of torture and still no call from the company, she sends David an e-mail. She thanks him for his time, but asks, 'Have they decided regarding the position yet?'

The following day she receives a reply: 'Unfortunately they have appointed someone with local property knowledge.'

What could it be? Is it because she must still get Indefinite Leave to Remain? Is it because she doesn't own a car yet? Is she too old? Perhaps they don't like her accent?

That's it then. So much for her dreams of becoming an independent woman, living her own 'real' life. The telephonic interview she had for a position as sales agent in Portsmouth also went south. She is stuck in the attic. The eaves close in on her, making it hard to breathe. She allows herself the luxury of a good cry; she may relieve herself of futile hope and her faith in a better future.

Later that evening she opens the au pair website that has been dormant for seven months. The site still has her profile, and she unhides it.

Christmas is in a couple of days and the thought of being on her own and separated from her family accentuates her loneliness. It is summer in South Africa and her family will spend their holidays on the beach. That scenario is far removed from her life in England. Should anyone enquire about a typical Christmas spent during summer, her explanation won't be understood. She is lucky though to spend her first proper British Christmas with a caring family.

'Please, please come to stay in Margate and spend Christmas day with me. The house will be handed over to the new owner early in the New Year, and now I am stuck here on my own. On the twenty sixth of December, friends from Iceland will come to stay with me. If you come tomorrow, we can spend a few days together.' Kurt sounds quite desperate to see her.

Oh, what the heck! Why am I punishing myself like this? Kurt is not a stranger to her after all, and does she really have to be here with all the family and their friends? The last thing she needs now is to be hurt again, but she suspects the feelings she had for Kurt are dead and buried. So, if she keeps her head, she should be safe. It might even help her to conclude this unfinished chapter with Kurt.

But, when the train arrives in Margate, and it is the same Kurt whom she saw over a year ago who meets her at the station, she can't help but feel emotional. He uses the same after shave she loved, and the smell brings happy memories to her mind. They get on well, but the trust, the spark, is gone. They go to buy food for their Christmas lunch. He introduces her as an old friend at his old local pub. In the evening they listen and dance to music in the half empty apartment. They talk a lot and share events of the time when they had been separated.

On Christmas morning Kurt goes to the pub where he meets his friends for a drink. Kiki stays at the apartment to wait for him. Their Christmas lunch becomes dry and tasteless and when he finally arrives home, he is clearly tipsy. Kiki is not amused and realises she has made a terrible mistake coming to Margate to be with him.

She also finds out too late that in the UK no trains run on Boxing Day. Kurt is in a state. He must get rid of Kiki before he goes to the airport to collect his friends from Iceland. Kiki is amused at his reaction and decides to stay calm. 'If you drop me at a hotel in town, I will somehow find a way to get home. Don't worry about me.'

Not knowing how to get out of her predicament, she texts Claude, her trusty friend. Luckily, he is at his son's house about an hour's drive from Margate and he offers to pick her up. Kurt drops her off at the hotel and she must wait for three hours for Claude to arrive on his white horse. It is with great relief that she greets him. They spend the day driving around in Kent, enjoying the sights and scenery. They have lunch in a quaint historical pub. A day that started so horribly becomes memorable; she will save the pictures she has taken on her laptop.

'Have you arrived safely?' Kurt's text comes shortly after she arrives home, but she doesn't reply. He does not deserve an answer. Not now, or ever again. When she walks into her room and sees they covered her bed with gifts, she feels guilty and sad. She must admit she made a huge mistake going to Margate. Though it was an experience, it was not a good one.

Between now and New Year, her mind stays busy. Her main thoughts concern where she would like to live and work. She is free to go anywhere in the UK. Should an employer call her, she will arrive on their doorstep within days or maybe, weeks. She is confident that she now knows what she does **not** want to do. She should know how to trust her instincts; they will warn her if a position is not suitable.

Early in January 2014, a few potential employers on the au pair website contacted her. She considers each opportunity carefully. One family has too many children; another does not offer a separate bathroom; one pays too little and offers no free weekends. One position is on a farm, and she would have to care for horses as well. Luckily, nothing is pushing her out of the attic; it is her decision alone, and she will only take it once she is ready.

It seems as if Keith's future in Wales is also on the line. He has not achieved his sales targets and he might soon be hunting for a new position. She feels extraordinarily little when she hears his news; her main concern is that if his financial position is bad, it could affect her application for Permanent Residency.

Finally, she makes up her mind. *I will take the position in Brighton. Working for a single mom with one little boy of three years old – how hard can that be?*

Chapter 15

A RIVER IN FRONT OF HER

She can sense Claude's trepidation; it matches her own. They are approaching her new home in Brighton. He has been against this move, right from the start. She remembers how they sat in her attic room on many Sunday evenings. His stockinged feet stretched out on the worn green carpet. She sat on the office chair, pulled up next to him, her aching, chilblain toes nestling against the pillow. They needed heat to ease the pain.

They discussed the pros and cons of her potential move to Brighton for the umpteenth time. 'Whatever I have to say will not convince you to stay,' he says with a sigh and just a flicker of a smile on his serious face.

He is right, of course. She has decided, and nothing he says will convince her to stay. She feels she has done her bit in Clacton, and it is time to move on. 'I need a fresh experience, Claude. Seven months of hard work in this house – it's more than I can endure. Just look at this town: it's a place few people have heard of, and nothing will happen here to entice me to stay. It is time to escape from the attic; I want to see and visit places, push myself out of my comfort zone.'

He had heard this speech before and couldn't contradict or convince her. She will miss his friendship. They had returned that afternoon from yet another lovely drive in the countryside. He had shown her Colchester, derelict castles and buildings in Suffolk and the harbour in Ipswich.

'If this does not work out, I will simply do another search on my trusty Au Pair website.' Claude shook his head and reached for the cookie jar.

She can't believe she has talked herself into this situation but would love to say to him one day: *I told you it was going to work out. If I hadn't taken the opportunity, I would never have sold so many paintings to all those quaint and queer, arty people in Brighton.*

Then, finally, the dreaded moment arrived. The family waved goodbye from their front porch and shut the front door on her – Ella did not understand that this 'goodbye' differed from any other. Her two-year-old charge will miss her as much as Kiki will miss the child. She feels like a snail without its shell, leaving the warmth and comfort of the family who showed her so much love.

Claude's car is overflowing with her possessions. The zip of the polka dot suitcase would hardly close. A box full of paints and brushes, an easel, a bag of summer clothes, a couple of canvasses, the CD player the family gave her as a farewell and birthday gift – all evidence of settling down, putting down roots during her eight months stay.

As they drive along the 'scenic route', they chat, albeit without their usual enthusiasm. They talk about the exotic Mona, who is driving Claude wild with anticipation, but who stays elusive. Over time, they've learnt to trust each other. Claude is the one person she knows who would patiently listen to her thoughts and dreams; they are at peace in each other's company.

The sun shines brightly on the white cliffs of Brighton as they approach the town.

'I like the hilliness of the area. It reminds me of Durbanville Hills, an area outside Cape Town where there are many wine farms and cellars. I thought that all of England is flat, like the East.'

Her gaze shifts from the mediocre homes, stuck like tufts of wool on a hill, to the glare of the shimmering sun on the flat ocean. Not knowing whether she liked what she sees, or if she is disappointed in her new neighbourhood, she tries to identify landmarks. There is a park close to the beach, and she knows instinctively that is where she will have to take her new charge, frequently and regularly.

Maria greets them at the front door of the modest bungalow. She looks different from the pictures Kiki had seen of her on her au pair profile. They cut her hair noticeably short in a spiky style, which enhances her serious looking eyes.

'Bring your luggage inside, and then I'll show you the house. We're just having our lunch.'

Kiki glimpses a petite, dark- haired girl sitting at the kitchen table. Claude unpacks the car, and soon the front bedroom is full of her belongings. The room is larger than she expected, and it delights her when she sees there is a double bed.

She tries to shake off the feeling of dread that is slowing down her movements, making her appear stilted, like a rigid, automated toy. She notices the boy's room is adjacent to hers and the family bathroom is next to his room. *I'll constantly be aware of him, whether he is awake or asleep.* From the hall, a staircase leads to an upstairs room, which she assumes is Maria's bedroom.

Once Claude has put all her belongings in her room, Maria appears again. She takes Kiki to the kitchen, where she finally meets Henry. He is still seated in his highchair next to the table.

'Henry, this is Kiki.' The boy is beautiful. His dark eyes, hair and complexion differs from his mothers' light appearance. Henry does not look pleased to see her and squirms.

'Meet my friend, Tilly. We are going to a party tonight.' Kiki is taken aback. Are they really going to leave her with the boy on the first night of her stay?

Pointing to the room beneath the staircase, Maria says: 'My lodger, Guy, stays in that room. He is a carer and works odd hours. He is sleeping now, so we try to keep the house as quiet as possible.'

Poor Guy, Kiki thinks. *It must be awfully hard to sleep during the day enduring a noisy toddler in this small house.*

An apprehensive-looking Claude waits for her at the front door. Kiki tells Maria they are going to the shop to buy supplies for her. Maria has already pointed out her allotted storage space in the fridge. There is also a shelf in a cupboard in the kitchen that she may use. Kiki is excited about the fact that from now on she may decide what she wants to eat.

Claude finds a shopping mall at the Brighton Marina and soon she puts milk, muesli, yogurt, fruit, bread, red bush tea, margarine, salad and two prepared meals into a basket. She grabs a bottle of South African red wine off a display shelf, and Claude shows her the extension lead he thinks she will need. It will provide enough space for the plugs for her lamp, computer, mobile phone charger and the baby monitor. She is feeling more spaced out by the minute and wonders if there is still enough time to change her mind and drive back to Clacton with Claude.

At the till, she reaches for her wallet. Claude stands in front of her: 'Kiki, I want to pay for this - just to get you started.'

She knows him well enough not to argue with him but to accept his offer with gratitude. Her eyes fill with tears – caused by a mixture of sadness, joy, and gratefulness. Will she ever have a friend like him again? She hugs him, wiping her tears as fast as they appear with the back of her hand. 'Thank you so much, Claude.'

Kiki unlocks the front door for the first time with the key that Maria has given her. She attached her South African key ring to the key and wonders how many times she will use it to come and go through this door. Claude carries her groceries to the kitchen. Finally, there is no more reason for him to stay longer. He must return to Clacton and will have to leave her on her own in this unfamiliar house with a strange family.

One last wave of hands and Claude drives away in his white car. She realises that this was her choice and now it is up to her to make it work. *I can do it. This is different, but it is what I need to do now,* she tells herself.

She unpacks her groceries in the kitchen. The previous au pair left salt, some spices, Basmati rice and a half empty bottle of coffee in the allotted space. According to Maria, she left after one week's stay because she was inattentive to Henry's needs.

'I came home unexpectedly. He was crying while she was playing guitar with her headphones covering her ears, oblivious to Henry's distress.'

Kiki pulls a face. *That is not right,* she thinks. She is surprised to hear there was an au pair, working here during the period when she and Maria were discussing her proposed move to Brighton. She wonders what would have happened to her if the girl had not been caught out? Would Maria have informed her that she was no longer required when she had already resigned from the job in Clacton?

Maria points to a black notebook lying on the kitchen table. 'I write my monthly schedule in advance in this book. That way you will know what I'll be doing each day. I know my program a year in advance. It might change though, since I didn't qualify for the senior position that I applied for. That might mean that my one weekday shift could change to Saturdays.'

Kiki doesn't comment but can't help to wonder how it would affect her plans to find extra work to supplement her income. A different book lying on the kitchen table is used by the au pair to write comments regarding Henry's daily activities.

It will be in my interest to read this, she thinks. Her stomach feels tight.

'I had such a awful experience with an au pair who stayed here for five months. After him, the Hungarian stayed for a week. He ate a lot.'

Mm, it seems there is a pattern here. When the unsuitable au pair leaves, Maria's friend, April, steps in to help. She lives an hours' drive away and does not mind taking care of Henry.

Kiki reaches for a tissue in her pocket. The cold she's been fighting for a few days is getting worse. What terrible timing! How can she possibly get sick now? She has taken decongestant tablets for a week already, but the coughing is getting more persistent and though she hates to admit it, she doesn't feel great.

Maria wants to shower Henry before they leave. Conveniently, a bus going to Brighton's town centre stops about fifty yards from their house every fifteen minutes. Tonight, the two women won't take the red car parked in the driveway, as drinking and driving is not an option.

She observes as the two women shower the boy. Wrapped in a towel, his mother carries him to the lounge, where she puts him down on the carpet. The lounge is warm and sunny. Kiki notices toys, DVDs, nappies and wipes placed around the room. It is obvious life in this house revolves around the boy.

While the women get ready upstairs, Kiki takes a stack of flash cards and shows them to the boy. She is impressed at his intelligence and when he wants to repeat the exercise; they play the game again.

'How do I look?' asks Maria as she enters the lounge. She is wearing a black outfit while her modern hair style, accompanied by a big smile, completes the picture of a young woman going out to a party. Surprisingly, she is prepared to leave Kiki, a newcomer, to her home, with her precious boy, just hours after her arrival in Brighton.

'You look great,' Kiki says. 'Henry and I are friends already. Please relax and enjoy your evening. We'll be fine.'

'The monitor in Henry's room is switched on. He should be ready for bed at a quarter to eight. Here is his sleeping bag. Place him in it, switch the music on in his room and leave him in his cot.'

If it works like that, I don't mind babysitting on a Saturday night, Kiki thinks. Shortly after they have left, she receives the first text message: 'How is my little boy doing? Is he alright?'

'Yes, he is fine,' Kiki replies. 'We're playing on the drums in the lounge.'

She's impressed with the boy's loving nature. 'I need a cuddle,' he often says and comes to sit next to her; his short arms circle her neck like a warm, woollen scarf. She returns the hug and knows she and Henry will be all right. He'll soon love her and vice versa.

Soon, the second text arrives. 'Is my little boy happy?'

'Yes. He is sleeping and I am unpacking my belongings.'

She places three canvas paintings above the bed on top of the headboard. She places the painting of the red rose on the bookshelf and hangs her scarves over the curtain rod. The room appears more welcoming than before. She must ignore the other au pairs' distress, unhappiness, worries and sadness which hang from the walls, just like bats hanging on trees in the dark.

Still, she struggles to shake off the feeling of unease. The child's regular, heavy breathing on the monitor reminds her that she is trapped once again, just in a different time and place.

Tomorrow will be her sixty-fourth birthday. How is it possible that she is doing this?

She sleeps fitfully; the strange room and her constant dry cough wake her up at brief intervals. She becomes aware of the dog's uncut nails scratching the bare wooden floor as he wanders aimlessly across the entrance hall to the front door and then back to the lounge again. Like the boy, he seems to accept newcomers to the home without judgement. She hears the couple when they arrive home, but she forces herself to stay calm and in a state of sleep.

When the ring of her mobile phone wakes her on Sunday morning, she has slept for just a few hours. It is Lizelle, her friend from South Africa, who wishes her a happy birthday.

'Are you still sleeping?' she enquires. Kiki is surprised to hear how hoarse her own voice became during the night. *How wonderful to be remembered on my birthday! But, Lizelle obviously has no idea that the time difference between the two countries is two hours!*

When the call ends and she drift off to sleep again, she imagines the start of the day at the house in Clacton. *How I wish I could be there now,* she thinks. That was her home for eight months and here she is now, feeling sick and alone on her birthday. But she knows that door is shut, not because the family would not take her back, but because she had made the choice to move on.

Too soon the baby monitor announces that Henry is awake. It is seven o'clock, and she soon learns that she can set her alarm according to his waking time. Fortunately, it is Sunday, and she hears Tilly and the boy playing in the lounge. Later, the sounds of people preparing to go out make her feel more relaxed. Then, eventually the front door slams and the house is quiet. Now it is she and the dog alone in the strange house, his sharp, uncut nails scratching continuously on the wooden floor.

She spends the day in bed – reading her e-mails, reminiscing and feeling sorry for herself. It is her birthday, and yes, Maria brought her a card, and yes, she received sixteen friends' congratulations on Face Book plus another twelve text messages from friends and phone calls from her family in South Africa. But she realizes the one person she had hoped would contact her, has forgotten her special day. Not only has Keith chosen to ignore her birthday, but this date also marks the day they last saw each other, and their first year of separation. *After twelve years of marriage, it does not matter to him that it's his wife's birthday. It should not matter to me, but it really hurts,* she thinks.

Her chest feels tight and her muscles ache. Her daughter, who is a General Practitioner, says she should get antibiotics, but heaven knows, how will she get to a doctor to ask for a prescription?

The red car leaves the driveway early on Monday morning. Kiki gets up at seven to be ready before the boy wakes up. But he beats her, and she must do her ablutions and dress in front of him. Tomorrow she will have to wake up earlier!

She realizes it is going to be an exceedingly long day and her heart is filled with dread. The boy is not in a napping routine which means he is her constant companion from the second he opens his eyes. He is also used to entertainment on tap and demands her attention all the time. The first text from Maria also arrives at seven o'clock: 'How is my little boy doing today?'

Guy, the boarder, is talkative and kind and directs her towards the doctor's surgery. If she does not act soon, she will get quite sick. Kiki dresses Henry for the cold and snowy outdoors: a duffle coat, boots, gloves, and a warm cap. She puts him in his buggy and with a determined tread she pushes him up a steep hill, past the park, towards the shopping centre. The strain of this effort makes her heart bounce out of her chest. After every fifty meters of pushing, she must stop to take a rest. Though she does not expect to get an appointment with a doctor today, she plans to get an application form to join the NHS in Brighton. Once she has completed the forms at home, she will hand them in tomorrow. To her delight, a doctor can see her within half an hour. Henry plays contentedly in the reception area. Kiki watches him with one eye while she keeps the other eye fixed on the electronic board displaying patients' names.

'You sound South African,' says the handsome doctor. 'What brought you to Brighton?'

She points towards Henry. 'I'm here to look after this little boy. I'm his au pair.' She doesn't want to explain or talk too much. She is here now; the past is the past, and she doesn't think the doctor is really interested in more details other than her short explanation. The doctor hands her a prescription for penicillin and they go to the pharmacy to wait for the medicine to be dispensed.

The outcome of the morning relieved her; she feels lighter. They spend the cold, rainy afternoon in the lounge while they watch TV and play with Henry's toys. Tomorrow she will feel better and hopefully soon she will be in control of her life again. She decides to make this job work - she wants to succeed.

When Maria arrives home, she makes it clear that she is unhappy with Kiki. 'What did you do today?' she asks. There is a sharp frown between her dark brown eyes.

Kiki tells her about her major achievement of the day; how well her son behaved at the surgery, and how lucky she was to get antibiotics. It takes a moment to fully comprehend how dismayed Maria is.

'A doctors' surgery is not a place for a child,' she scolds. 'Did you go to the park at all? Did you take the dog for a walk?'

'No Maria, I could only manage to get to the doctor today. In my current condition, it was difficult enough to push the buggy up the steep hill.'

The second these words slip out of Kiki's mouth; she knows she made a terrible mistake. In Maria's eyes, she will be regarded as weak. The reality of what is expected of her hits her through waves of nausea caused by her phlegm-filled head. She read in the diary of the two daily excursions to the park or the beach. Of course, failure to do that is unthinkable. She is worse than the girl who practised her guitar!

'Why did you not let me know that you weren't feeling well enough to take him to the park?' she enquires disapprovingly. 'I would've let my friend come to take him out. This boy has so much energy, if you don't let him get rid of it, he won't go to sleep at his usual time at night.'

Kiki is shocked. She is at a loss for words. It is hard to think straight when one's head is filled with phlegm. Finally, she blurts out: 'I am sorry Maria. I am too sick now. Tomorrow I'll be feeling much better.'

'No, I'll ask April to take him to the park tomorrow. I will still pay you, though.'

This comment shocks Kiki. Of course, Maria must pay her. She did not say she wasn't going to take him to the park the next day. She will take him, but if Maria wants to ask her friend for help, that's fine. Maria has no understanding or sympathy for Kiki, that much is clear.

'I must tell you now that I am going for a weeks' holiday in May and then I'm definitely not going to pay you.'

But that is not fair, Kiki thinks. *It isn't my fault that you're going on leave.* As a businesswoman, she has learnt to express her feelings, but still, she hates conflict. All she knows is that she must tell Maria that she thought this was unfair - that is how South Africans do it; they don't beat about the bush.

'This will not work for us, is it?' Maria's piercing eyes go through Kiki like a double-edged sword.

Kiki tends to agree. *No, this will not work.* But she must play for time. She needs to position herself carefully before she makes her next move.

'I am sure we can work it out, Maria. It is still early days, and we will and can make it work.' She realizes she is skating on thin ice. The last thing she needs now is to be homeless. She will start to look for another position on the website as soon as she is free.

That evening she phones Robert telling him how much she misses them all, and that her heart is sad. They are genuinely concerned about her. 'You sound as if you're in distress. Remember, you are welcome to return anytime. We are here to help you.'

When she goes to sleep that night, she is full of resolve: tomorrow she will feel better, and she is convinced that she wants to experience life in Brighton.

Yes, she must find an extra job, but eventually it will all work out.

Henry and Kiki walk to the park the next morning and within minutes of their arrival, it rains. They rush back home and as they enter the lounge; the sun breaks through the windows to light up the dark room.

April arrives in the afternoon to take Henry to the beach. When they return home after hours spent outside, Henry cries from the cold; his trousers and shoes are wet. Kiki admonishes April in her mind but dares not say a word. How could she make the little boy feel so miserable?

On her fifth day in Brighton, she writes in Henri's daily activities diary: 'You were happy when you woke up at seven o'clock. You followed me around the house until I was dressed. We played with your wooden train set until we left home to go to Happy Days Play School. Even though you were shy initially when we arrived at your new play group, you still had loads of fun. I put you in your cot when we arrived home and you fell asleep within minutes. After forty minutes I had to wake you up.'

That night, on his way to bed, Henry gives Kiki a spontaneous hug. Before she could prevent it, he kisses her full on her mouth. She intuitively knows the innocent gesture will be the final nail in her coffin; it sealed her fate in this house.

'I am so Sorry Maria. I did not invite that kiss!'

'You should have turned your face away!'

'I am so sorry, it happened before I could prevent it.'

April arrives again the next afternoon and takes Henry and the dog to the park. Again, they stay away for hours. Time, accentuated by the Brighton bus arriving in front of the house at fifteen minutes intervals, passes slowly for Kiki.

When Maria arrives home late in the evening Henry is sleeping. Kiki is in her room doing research; she is looking for a new position on the internet. Things might move fast for her. Penny contacted her this afternoon after she noticed Kiki's profile on Great Au pairs. She feels that Kiki is the right person to be their son's au pair. Penny might be the angel sent to rescue her, but Kiki is concerned about the paltry remuneration. They agree to stay in touch as Kiki does not want to close the only chance beckoning to her now.

The following morning, Kiki takes Henry to town on the bus. The boy is as excited as Kiki. Henry gets up from his seat and she must hold the buggy with one hand while keeping him firmly in one place with the other.

They must meet Angel, Maria's friend, at the bus stop opposite the Ferris wheel. From there they'll walk to the Thursday play group, which is held at a church nearby. After getting off the bus, Kiki worries they might not be at the right meeting place. Eventually Angel arrives, pushing her daughter, who sits snugly in her buggy. They walk together in the lovely sunshine, and Kiki feels happy to have met Angel and her daughter.

Kiki finds that the play group is terribly busy, with too few toys for the number of children. Henry has a great time. He cries once when his friend eats pretzels without sharing with him. He desperately wants one and, against his mother's orders, Kiki allows him to have one pretzel.

As soon as Maria arrives home from work, she confronts Kiki where she is preparing her supper in the kitchen. 'This is definitely not going to work for us. I think you must leave as soon as possible.'

'But Maria, we have not even given this a proper chance,' she protests. 'Henry and I get on so well....'

'My son gets on well with everybody,' she counters. 'It is you and I that I am not happy about. Our relationship will not work. By the way, did Henry eat anything at the playgroup today?'

'No, he didn't eat any of the food they served the other children. But, yes, he had one pretzel...' The look on Maria's face is like a victorious solicitor's face in a difficult court case: 'I rest my case,' it says.

The blood drains from Kiki's face. Never has she had to admit defeat in a new job; never. There is nothing more to say or do. She is thrown out unceremoniously; she is told that she must leave. Her time in Brighton is over, finished, done.

'Will you please take the dog for a walk?' Maria asks. 'I want to spend time with my son, and I'll take him out for a while. Oh yes, will you still be available to take him to the Nursery school at eight o'clock tomorrow morning?'

'Of course,' Kiki says. She puts the dog on his leash and closes the door behind them; the key with the South African emblem clutched tightly in her white fingers. They walk up the hill and the further they go, the harder she finds it to hold back her tears. She resists the urge to cry. Tonight, she is going to have a Skype interview with Penny, and she wants to look at her best.

The interview goes well. She also meets Anna, the Polish au pair, who puts Kiki at ease. They agree Penny will fetch her on Saturday. She will stay in the spare room for two weeks until Anna returns to Poland. Then Kiki will move into the bigger room upstairs and work for the family.

The following morning, Kiki takes Henry to his nursery school. Maria had instructed her to leave the buggy with Henry still sitting in it, with the assistant. He is not happy when she leaves, but Kiki turns on her heels and trudges up the hill towards the house. Today is her free day, and she has no plans to sit and mope at the house.

She dresses with care to make sure that she is warm and comfortable. She puts her camera in her bag and takes the bus to Brighton. A return ticket costs four pounds and sixty pence. She must be careful with her money as she does not know if she will get paid for this week or when, in the future, she will earn again.

While the bus races through the streets of Brighton, she texts Maria: 'If you pay my wages tonight, I will leave tomorrow.' She is trying to make sure she will get paid, but she realises she is skating on thin ice. If Penny can't collect her tomorrow, she might end up on the street.

When she gets off the bus at the carousel, radiant sunbeams reflecting on the ocean illuminate the white wheel. She notices many tourists and decides to also act like one today. She would have loved to have lived in Brighton. All her senses are piqued by being here.

She walks on the promenade and takes many pictures. She stands on the pier for a while to listen to the roar of the ocean as the waves tug the pebbles back and forth. *Why am I so drawn to Brighton, just to have had my dreams shattered? It feels as if the universe mocks me, making a fool of me.* She tries hard but can't decipher the message of the moving stones.

Penny texts her as she walks in the town centre. Her husband, Ben, wants to Skype her later. She texts back to say she will only be available at three o'clock. She buys food for lunch and dinner, realizing too late that she still has a few eggs left at the house that she could have eaten.

The interview with Ben is brief and to the point: 'I was just wondering how long you intend to stay with my family before you move to another job? Why are you leaving Brighton so soon?'

Her mouth is dry, but she tries to stay calm: 'There are no guarantees with this type of work; some situations work, and others don't. This one was just all wrong for both Maria and me.' He seems satisfied with her reply and when Penny speaks to her again, she says she will pick her up on Saturday after Stan has returned home from his skiing trip.

She is saved! She has somewhere to go to. The pay is not what she desires, but once she is settled, she will look for an extra cleaning job. Penny told her they knew a few estate agents and she might look for a Saturday viewing job with one of them.

Penny texts her again with a change of plan. She will collect Kiki on Sunday and not on Saturday. Despite her trepidation, she asks Maria if she can stay for another day. 'We invited friends to stay over on Saturday evening and the room will be occupied.'

So that was that then. Her heart beats so fast, and she feels the icy grip of panic as it clutches at her. *What could be the worst thing that might happen to me?* she asks herself. *I can sleep in a Bed and Breakfast and have a great time on my own.*

When she tells Claude about her predicament, he offers to drive from Essex to take her to Ascot. She thanks him but declines the offer. Penny, however, must have a sixth sense. She sends Kiki another text saying that should she have a problem staying for another night, she will collect her on Saturday, albeit later in the afternoon. Kiki is relieved; she realises she came remarkably close to being homeless.

She sleeps fitfully; half packed, half removed from her situation; she puts on a protective shield. On her Face Book page, she posts a poem she wrote about homelessness. Her friends read between the lines, and do not know what to think or say. She knows nobody can help her, but it is encouraging to know there are people who take an interest in her safety and wellbeing. She has one other safety net too, but she will keep that as a last resort.

There is a river in front of me. I can't go over it, I can't go under it, I've got to go through it. She is on a bear hunt, just like in the book she always read to Ella.

Finally, it is Kiki's last morning in Brighton. She gets up and completes her packing. One of Maria's friends rings the doorbell. There is a bounce in the woman's step, and she carries a gigantic bouquet in her arms, like a prize. Minutes after she walks into the house, she hangs the washing, clears the dishes, and dresses Henry.

Soon they leave to take Henry to his swimming lesson. On her way out, Maria hands Kiki the money she owed her. She prays she will be gone before they return.

The tenant, wearing a striped dressing gown, appears from his room. They go to the kitchen where they make coffee. 'I am so fed up with the noise in this house,' he complains. 'I pay my rent, and all I ask is some peace and quiet. It was so different when you looked after Henry, at least he was much more peaceful.'

She eagerly laps up his positive comments. Her self-esteem has been dealt a blow, and she wonders how it is possible that Maria couldn't see how good she would have been for her son.

'Last night Maria told me she will probably regret the fact that she let me go,' she tells Guy. 'Actually, she is doing me a huge favour. I would've left myself, but in my own time, when I was ready. Somehow, Penny is ready for me, and even though the current au pair is still there, at least I have a place to stay.'

The day drags on. She closes her cases and puts all her luggage in the entrance hall. She sweeps the room, takes the dog for a walk, feeds him, makes a cup of tea, goes to the bathroom multiple times, and it is still not five o'clock. Later, she stacks her belongings outside in front of the door. She leaves the door open and then later, moves it even further away from the house, towards the gate.

Guy returns from a visit to town and keeps her company until Penny finally arrives. She parks her luxurious car in front of the house. Kiki puts the house key, stripped now of the South African token, in Guy's outstretched hand. He will hand it to Maria.

'Let's stay in touch.'

'Yes, let's be friends,' she repeats, knowing that it won't happen. Their contact was too brief and for Kiki, an experience that she would rather forget.

Chapter 16

A SAFETY NET

'It wasn't easy to find this place,' says Penny as they drive away from Maria's house. 'I was fine until Brighton because I often come here to work. But then I struggled to find the route from the beach road.' She points to the map lying on the floor next to Kiki's feet. It surprised Kiki that she drives without satellite navigation.

Whatever Penny has to say, Kiki wants to leave Brighton as quickly as possible. *Please dear Lord, help me get away from this house.* Unlike the biblical Lot's wife, she refuses to look behind her as the speeding car leaves the town. She doesn't intend to turn into a pillar of salt.

Even though she knows she should feel safe in Penny's presence, stiff fingers persist in clutching at her heart. She still doesn't believe that anyone was going to stay over at Maria's house tonight, but it doesn't make any difference now.

She explains to Penny what has happened since they last spoke and why she is so relieved that Penny could fetch her today. Kiki glances at Penny's lovely face and admires her beautiful eyes and hair. She feels privileged to be in her company. This, then, is what her Angel looks like.

She must push aside the nagging thought that jumps into her head like a tin toy soldier. Yes, she won't be earning enough, but Penny tells her she will have plenty of time to earn an extra income.

'Anna works as a cleaner for a couple on Saturdays. She takes a train to the station and walks from there to their house.'

'When I noticed your profile on the au pair website, I thought it was too good to be true, finding someone like you. I've often thought I would like to have an older person as our au pair - someone who can spoil me too. I work awfully hard to provide for Stan. He is a gifted gymnast and holds a double scholarship. And do you know what, Kiki? We aren't pushing him; he has so much drive, he is pushing himself. I am a bit concerned about his reaction when I tell him that I appointed a new au pair while Anna is still with us. They get on very well. When I told him Anna had to leave soon, he said: 'Why does Anna have to leave? I don't want her to leave.' I had to explain that Anna's year in the United Kingdom was over and that she was looking forward to continuing with her life in Poland.'

From what Kiki understands, it will be her job to drive Stan to school in the morning. When she returns home, she must clean the house according to a weekly roster, cook Stan's lunch and do the laundry before she must fetch him at school in the afternoon. In the evening, Penny will take him to the gym to practice. Then, the next day, they will follow the same routine. Kiki hears the whispering voice in her head again: *And you will only get eighty pounds per week for doing all this.*

'Ben finds it hard to believe that you are "for real". He says you are such an eloquent person and that makes him wonder how you could do this work and find yourself in your current position. You might have some explaining to do.'

'I understand.' Kiki looks straight ahead at the busy road. She feels tired and isn't in the mood to explain herself again. Where should she start? How do you explain your journey to a secure man, a managing director of a company, who has, according to his wife, 'only numbers' in his head? Oh, well, she will just take it as it comes. Normally she isn't shy and if she must look him in the eye and expose the nitty-gritty of her life, then that is what she will do. If that is what is required for her to survive, she will share the reason why, at her age, she is an au pair. More than anything else, she will have to prove her inner strength to herself.

But I am going to earn only eighty pounds a week, and I must stay in the spare room until Anna leaves. Who knows when that will be?' repeats the little voice. *But if this opportunity had not arisen and Penny hadn't fetched me today, I might have to return to the attic in Clacton.*

That would be an easy outcome, an escape. But did she really want to retrace her steps? She could run straight into the loving arms of the family, help them with their day-to-day living, be part of their laid-back, friendly existence. Though she had worked too hard physically, she had never felt resentful about her remuneration. Maybe, just maybe, something better is waiting for her.

Penny turns right at a roundabout, and then, after another right turn, she drives into a housing estate boasting large, double story homes. Kiki realizes that they have reached their destination. This is home.

'Let's go inside to meet the others before we bring your luggage in.' Penny opens the car door and walks towards the house's entrance. Kiki follows her example when she sees Penny take her boots off and walks on her socks towards a door to her right. Kiki's first impression of the dining room, an open plan area with the kitchen, is that it is huge.

She can smell food cooking and realizes how hungry she is. Feeling too nervous, she had eaten little today at Maria's home. The sight of a table laid with plates and utensils, combined with the smell of lasagne cooking in the oven, overwhelms her, and she hardly notices Anna who is looking inside the oven.

The oven in the modern kitchen looks like an old-fashioned Aga to Kiki. Penny mentions it stays on all year, winter and summer, day, and night. There are many cupboards and there is a drinks fridge that resembles something you would find in a shop. In the garden there is a shed that Ben uses as his office. The sight of a trampoline in the yard brings memories of summer in Clacton when James and Kiki had played soccer.

'Let me introduce you to Ben. Ben! Here is Kiki.' A dark-haired man appears in the doorway of the lounge. His outstretched hand grasps hers firmly, but not too hard. She looks into his eyes to see what she can find there, but he does not give away anything. She is relieved that his accent is understandable.

'Here I am,' she says with a broad smile. 'This is me, Kiki. As you can see, I am an actual person.' Her attempt at humour fails. He just looks at her without commenting and when Penny suggests they go upstairs to meet Stan, she is relieved.

She follows Penny upstairs to the bedroom area where they enter a typical teenager's bedroom. There is no sign of the boy, and she is surprised when Penny opens the doors of the wardrobe. There, crouched on the floor, amongst rows of sport shoes, sits a boy, his face covered with both his hands.

'Hi Stan. Look who is here. Please darling, Kiki wants to meet you.' Penny sits down on the bed and indicates that Kiki should join her. She does not know what is happening here but realises this is an unique situation. They wait for a reaction from Stan, and Kiki holds her breath. She has grandchildren of the same age and there is not a chance

that they would react like this. She has no idea what to
expect next, and when he finally drops his hands to reveal
his face, she is pleasantly surprised. His eyes are large and
dark. He has a full mouth and a lovely smile. For the first
time since she's arrived here, Kiki feels slightly optimistic.

'Darling, Kiki has four grown- up children. They are all
successful in their work and sport. You will see, she
understands what it takes to excel in what one does.'

It is as if his mother must impress on him the fact that
Kiki will cope, whatever demands or requirements he
might have. Kiki would never have expected this approach
to work with a young boy, but surprisingly, he looks at her
with approval. She grasps for the right words to say,
knowing that whatever she says next is going to make or
break her future relationship with the boy.

'Yes, Stan. I have grandchildren of your age. They also
swim and run and are gymnasts.' She rambles on, not sure
if his eyes are just scanning her face for future reference,
or if he is taking in what she says. His mother decides that
they have had a breakthrough and that they can leave him
sitting in his wardrobe. They go on a tour through the rest
of the house.

'Here is Anna's room.' It is a pleasing area, furnished
with a double bed, a small couch, and a clothes rail. The
modern bathroom has a shower behind a glass wall. She
knows she will enjoy living in this room, but until Anna
leaves, she will have to stay in the guest room, next to
Stan's bedroom. It is a small room with hardly any space to

unpack her belongings. The bathroom that she will have to share with Stan is right next to his parent's bedroom. The house is large, and she feels disoriented as Penny opens and closes the doors of one room after another. 'This is where Stan chills out. This is our lounge, and here is our second lounge. We hardly ever use the conservatory. In summer it is too hot, and in winter it is much too cold. '

But it still must be cleaned regularly, she thinks but says nothing. Her heart feels heavy and cold. Finally, it is time for dinner, and they all sit at the table. Even Stan has questions about South Africa, and she must choose her words carefully. She does not want to show negativity but feels that she should rather impress them with the fact that she is happy to live in the United Kingdom.

After they finish the meal, Penny asks her to explain to Ben why she was in her current position. 'Please, Kiki, not that Ben doesn't like you, he just needs to know the events that led up to you being here.'

The glass of red wine that Ben gave her to accompany the meal gives her enough courage to share an abbreviated version of what happened to her and Keith in South Africa, their move to England, their stay in Norfolk and Wales, how she ended up in Gillingham, why she returned to South Africa and why she returned to England again after six weeks. She tells him about her stay in Clacton and the reason she left to go to Brighton.

It is her own very personal story, and it hurts her to discuss it in so much detail. But she perseveres as she realises, she must prove herself to this man. To think she must bare her soul for the position as an au pair that will only pay pocket money! If it were for a professional position in a corporate situation, she might have felt more compelled. This feels absurd and it irks her, but who is she to complain? Tonight, she will have met her basic needs: she will have a bed to sleep in, a roof over her head and food in her stomach. These are the people God sent to rescue her for the moment, and she must accept the offer.

Having Sunday morning breakfast in the kitchen is an excellent opportunity to absorb the mood in the house. She needs to learn more about the family. Like a ballet dancer, Penny darts between the oven and the sink; she touches here, cleans there, while simultaneously cooking bacon and eggs for Stan. When Ben and his friends return from their weekly football match, she starts all over again.

Beth, Penny's mother, arrives for a visit. Kiki was told that she is a keen ballroom dancer and should Kiki want to, she could join her group. Who knows, she might then gain a social life of her own. Beth's husband is older than her, Penny tells her.

'Take note, Kiki,' says Penny. 'Because he is a "moaner", Beth does her own thing. He has no right to complain since he's had his chances and wasted them!'

It soon becomes clear to Kiki she must also share her life story with Beth. For a second time within twelve hours, she relentlessly trudges across her heart, wearing muddy boots. When Beth has had her fill of Kiki's story, she says: 'Don't you have to Skype one of your children or do something in your room?'

Kik removes herself from their Sunday family gathering and goes to the small bedroom. Maybe she will find solace on the keyboard of her laptop.

She wakes up early on Monday morning and gets up at seven thirty. It is her first school run with Stan and Anna and since it is still ten minutes before they leave, she goes upstairs to the bathroom to clean her teeth. But, as she comes down the stairs again, she hears a car leave the premises. She opens the front door and watches in dismay as the blue car reverses out of the driveway. Her first lesson in life with Stan is the military precision with which everything regarding his regime is performed. She waves furiously: Anna might notice her. Luckily, she does, and she stops the car so that Kiki can get in. She opens her notebook to make notes of the route to the school. Anna drives with confidence and the car speeds along the busy road. Stan is in a grim mood and there is little conversation between him and Anna.

Kiki looks forward to a cup of tea when they arrive home, but Anna is set in her ways and starts with her usual Monday routine. 'I always wait for Penny and Ben to get up before I start with the cleaning. But today we are lucky. They have left and we can begin now.'

She fetches a vacuum cleaner from the storeroom below the staircase, carries it upstairs to the main bedroom and efficiently vacuums the room, the bathroom, and the passage. The machine is not without fault and she uses tape to stick the different suction heads to the pipe. It is obvious to Kiki that she has done this unrewarding task many times over.

Kiki observes Anna as she works, but she is most interested in the loft room. She watches as Anna skirts a mop around a suitcase placed on the bathroom floor. She wonders how long it will be before Anna packs her belongings into that case.

She thinks the conservatory is very dusty, but Anna doesn't spend a lot of time there. 'Once a month, a little dusting will be good…. The family hardly ever come here; I don't know why they even have this room….' Her Polish accent comes through when she doesn't concentrate and a few grammatical errors every now and then, make her even more endearing. 'In the beginning I did a lot more, but now, just enough.' Although Anna took English lessons and expresses herself well, her grammar is not fluent, and Kiki must concentrate hard to follow her.

Once Anna has mopped the kitchen floors, she is satisfied she has done her job. She can now go to her room to read her e-mails. It is only ten thirty, and she is free for the rest of the day. Later, they will make Stan's dinner and fetch him from school. Stan will eat while they travel back from school. He must digest the meal before his evening gymnastics session.

Not knowing what to do for the rest of the day, she goes to her small room, opens her laptop, and reads her e-mails. There are other au pair jobs available, but none suits her. She has committed herself to being here and feels indebted to Penny. But why won't this chilly feeling around her heart leave and allow her peace to return?

At five o'clock they drive to Stan's school to collect him. It is not a difficult route, and she imagines herself driving the blue car with an uncommunicative teenager as her companion. When they arrive home, Stan glides out of the car, glances towards the back seat, and mumbles an instruction for Anna to bring his bag into the house. Shortly after their return, his mother arrives, and she takes him to his gymnastics lessons at the local gym.

It will be easy for Kiki to get her own dinner ready: she was told to 'just look in the fridge and find something to eat.' She escapes to the spare bedroom as soon as she can. She sits down on the bed to survey her scattered belongings. It is going to be extremely hard to stay positive about this job. She feels so uneasy. The uncertainty of when she will move to the 'au pair' bedroom, probably caused this feeling. Also, Ben seems extremely uncomfortable having her in the house. She has no idea how to get past this, since she has never in her entire life been treated with such suspicion and mistrust.

She picks up a half-completed painting and mixes some acrylic paint. She thinks with fondness of Lea who bought her a music centre, and she puts on one of her classical CDs.

She doesn't want to shower before Stan and Penny return from his practice session. He might need the bathroom. But, when they finally return, it takes him ages to quieten down. She changes into her pyjamas and gets into bed without taking a shower. When she wakes up in the middle of the night to visit the bathroom, she notices the main bedroom door is slightly ajar. She tries to be as quiet as a mouse.

After their school run the following morning, Anna takes Kiki to the shopping mall. The walk takes forty minutes and when they arrive there; it seems to be semi-deserted. There are shops like Next, Boots and restaurants, but she finds the place soulless and empty. Anna buys her a cup of coffee and Kiki makes use of the opportunity to find out as much as possible about the family and her future job requirements.

'There is one house rule that all au pairs have to adhere to,' Anna says as she puts her cup down on the table. 'We aren't allowed to invite visitors to the house.'

'I can understand that, but not even your girlfriends or other Polish au pairs?' Kiki asks in disbelief.

'No, not even my Polish friends.'

After their excursion, Anna starts with her Tuesday 'dusting' day. Kiki watches her as she moves from room to room, skirting around the items and objects, touching here and touching there.

'In the beginning I did a proper job, but since I realized they don't really notice my efforts, I'm not too meticulous anymore.'

Once Anna has done her chores, she disappears into her room again. Kiki is free to do what she wants. She feels disconnected from everything, her family, her friends, her past, her future. In the afternoon she walks to Tesco and Marks and Spencer. She enquires about casual jobs. Tesco doesn't have plans to employ casual workers and at Marks and Spencer, a friendly assistant directs her to their website. There is a position for a casual worker at their pastry department, but the hours clash directly with Stan's school collection time.

Penny visits her in her room while she paints flowers on a canvas. 'Would you mind having another chat with Ben? He is still concerned about how it is possible that someone like you works as an au pair. He also asks me why you don't return to your family in South Africa. I don't know what to say to convince him.'

'Why doesn't he phone my referees? I'll even give him the numbers of my employers in South Africa where I worked as an estate agent.'

Kiki isn't used to being scrutinized to this extent. If she'd applied for a job with thousands of pounds of remuneration each year, she would've understood. This job isn't that difficult, and should they have wanted to make sure that she was a skilful driver, for example, she would've understood. She had opened her personal life to them, and they had peered, to their heart's delight, into her bag of life's turmoil. Working in the corporate world, as they are, they should have some insight into her calibre of person. Penny can see from the expression on Kiki's face that she faces disapproval.

'You know I am happy with you, Kiki. It is Ben. I told you he is a black and white type of person, and he won't rest until he knows everything about you. That is just the way he is. Please come downstairs and speak with him. Promise me that you won't cry.' She looks pleadingly at Kiki. She puts her painting and brushes on the floor, being careful not to accidentally touch the white bedding with the brush.

Once again, she must face Ben, who looks dark and brooding as his brown eyes connect with hers. 'You would have done the same if you had to employ someone to look after your son,' he says and Kiki thinks: *What would I do to harm your thirteen-year-old son?*

'I think it will be a good idea if you phone my previous employers. They'll be happy to give me a character reference.' Ben hands her a pen, and a used envelope. She writes the numbers of Robert, Shona, and Maria on the back of the envelope. Her guess is that he will phone Maria first. He is inquisitive and struggles to place her.

'I just can't understand why you don't go back to your family in South Africa?'

'One day when I am ready, I probably will return, but until then, I'll do my own thing here in the UK. While I have the energy and health, I view this experience as an adventure. In a few months, I can apply for Further Leave to Remain. Why should I give up on my dream at this stage? Yes, I do realize that I am an unlikely au pair, but I know I have qualities that make me an excellent choice for this position.'

When she returns to her room, she can feel a panic attack approaching. What a difficult position she finds herself in! But right now, she doesn't have any options. Obviously, she owes Penny her loyalty. She fetched her in Brighton when she had her back against the wall and was nearly destitute.

She texts Robert and Shona to warn them about the imminent enquiries, and they both say that they are happy to sing her praises. Shona is concerned about her wellbeing and offers her help, should Kiki ever find herself in trouble.

'I just want you to know that Ben phoned Robert and Maria and he is now perfectly happy that you are who you say you are.' Penny stirs her coffee, and Kiki's eyes involuntarily follow the shimmering diamonds in her wedding ring. Instead of feeling relieved and pleased, she is humiliated and insulted. How is it possible that Maria has the power to make or break her?

For the next hour, they watch Stan training while they sit side by side on a hard wooden bench. Penny has committed herself to do this for six out of seven days. She doesn't mind because this is what her son wants to do, and she supports him one hundred percent. It reminded Kiki of how she used to do the same for her own children and she finds it easy to identify with her.

The following afternoon, she walks to the station to see how far it is from the house. On her way there, she notices a lovely park. Anna offers to show her where the doctor's surgery is the following day. Though Kiki tries hard to settle in, it seems like a long time before Anna will leave. The date has been moved forward since Penny and Ben must go away for a weekend in two weeks' time. Anna will stay until they return; obviously, they do not trust Kiki to manage in their absence. It is a long time to be without an income while staying in the small room, but hopefully it will all work out.

That evening, when she opens her Facebook page, there is a message from an ex-colleague in South Africa. 'Kiki, a friend of my brother's is looking for you. She has a job for you near London. Please contact her on the e-mail address I put below. I will also try to get a contact phone number for you.' Shortly after this message, a phone number stares at her on her mobile phone.

Not knowing what to expect, but more out of politeness, she contacts Debbie by e-mail. 'I've just joined a new family as their au-pair, but please tell me more about this position.' Not expecting much to happen that night, it surprises her when her phone rings minutes later.

'Hello, this is Debbie speaking.' To her delight, she also speaks Afrikaans, and Kiki relaxes. Should they overhear the conversation, they wouldn't understand a word. Debbie explains to her how she knows her South African friend, but Kiki is more interested in the available position.

'Sally is a new mom, and I helped her to establish a routine with the new baby. Unfortunately, I must leave next week. I'm on my way to Holland to help a family with their new baby that they're expecting by a surrogate mother. Sally needs a companion; someone to accompany her to the shops and help her with the baby. Her husband works late in the evenings and that worries her. They are prepared to pay you four hundred pounds per week.'

'Sorry! How much did you say?' Kiki can't believe her ears. Surely, that can't be right.

'The pay is four hundred pounds per week. They plan to go to Italy in June for two weeks' holiday, and then you can stay in the house to take care of their dogs. They have three dogs – two are lap dogs, but the third one is huge. I hope you like dogs?'

'Yes, I love dogs.' At this stage Kiki is prepared to live in the same house with a dangerous lion or a Bengal tiger, just like Pi did on his boat.

Still, she holds back and refuses to get excited. This sounds too good to be true, and the saying goes that when something seems too good to be true, it usually is. Kiki tells her that her daughter in South Africa is pregnant, and she has a few things to consider before she can commit herself. Also, if Debbie could first discuss things with Sally and her husband to tell them who Kiki is and to ensure that she is the right person for the position.

Soon after the call ends, she receives an e-mail with pictures attached of the baby and the dogs. Debbie also writes about Sally's plans to buy an embroidery machine to embroider baby's names on towels and blankets to generate income from home.

The biggest surprise of all is Debbie's offer to buy Kiki a return plane ticket to South Africa for a visit before she starts work for the family. This would be for a favour. Would Kiki please take baby clothes in her luggage to give to a friend in South Africa?

Kiki replies to her e-mail, saying it seems wonderful, but she needs time to think about the offer. She is in a predicament: once she tells Penny that she is going to accept another job, she can't expect to stay in their home much longer.

That night she has a problem sleeping, and she can hardly wait till the next morning to find out what will happen next. To her relief, as she wakes up, an e-mail from Debbie awaits her. Debbie confirms that the family has decided they want her to work for them. They also won't mind if she first goes to South Africa and then, on her return, she can start working for them.

'Penge is a town in a London Borough, and it takes only twenty minutes by train to get to London,' she reads on Wikipedia. Since she'd arrived in the UK, she had always wanted to live close to London.

When Penny knocks on her door a few hours later, she is still unprepared for her question: 'How do you feel about the work now Kiki? How did it go this week? Are you settling in?'

She can't stall one moment longer and realizes that this is the moment of truth. Kiki blurts out that she has been offered another job with good remuneration, and that she is considering it. She tells Penny that she feels bad leaving without a replacement for Anna and that she is prepared to stay until they find someone.

'That is brilliant news for you, Kiki. I won't stand in your way, and I am happy for you. Unfortunately, we can't offer you more. Please don't feel bad about going, I understand. You aren't indebted to me; I only did what I felt was right; I am sure you would've done the same. Also, I'll ask the agency, and they'll put me in touch with other au pairs wanting employment. Do what you feel is best for you.'

When Penny leaves the room, Kiki realizes with a shock that she put herself in a very awkward position. She firmly closed one door without knowing yet how far exactly the other door had opened. Certain things about Debbie's offer concerns her. The money the family offers is unrealistic, but then again it is close to London and for all Kiki knows, that is the rate for a nanny's job in the area. It makes little sense that somebody can offer a stranger a free return plane ticket to South Africa.

Before she has time to fret too much, she receives an e-mail from Debbie: 'Start packing. I'm sending a taxi to collect you later this afternoon.' Everything seems to be sorted: Debbie will leave for Holland on Wednesday and Kiki's flight to South Africa will probably leave on Sunday. She can leave her belongings at Sally and Donald's home. When she returns in a month, all will be fine.

She feels like a fugitive on the run and is so anxious that she can't eat. After packing her cases, she puts all her belongings in the hall by the front door. She tries to act normal while she waits in the kitchen with Anna and Penny for the taxi to arrive.

'Ben said all along that he could not see you staying here for long,' says Penny.

Kiki thinks, but keeps her thoughts to herself: *I am so thankful you helped me when I was in a dire situation. But your role in my life is completed and somewhere, one day, you'll be blessed for it. But I have to leave now.*

Finally, the taxi arrives, and she puts her two suitcases, her canvases, her music player and her box of art materials in the car's boot. She keeps her coat and handbag with her. Penny and Anna wave at her as the car pulls out of the driveway.

She prays silently: *Dear God, please let something good happen to me tomorrow! But now I need the entrance to my next hole. Please show me where to find it.*

Chapter 17

CLOSER TO HOME

'Here, please take my card with my details. Once you have settled into your new work, will you please let me know how you are doing?' The taxi driver is more than just interested in her life's story – he is intrigued!

They had talked all the way from Ascot to Penge. She needed to relieve herself of her burden, to tell someone about her recent experiences. She knew she seemed calm outward, but he didn't have to know how nervous she really was about her next position.

'Sure, I will,' she says, as she reaches for the card in his outstretched hand. Her eyes scan the road as they drive, searching for number 20 Blueberry Way. The homes all look the same to her, but she can recognize a well-to-do neighbourhood when she sees one.

He slows down in front of a house with yellow flowering shrubs bordering the walled lawn. They parked a blue Mercedes Benz in the street in front of the house.

'Here we are. This is your new home,' he says with satisfaction. He parks the taxi behind the Mercedes, gets out of the car and packs her belongings on the pavement.

She walks to the front door of the home and rings the doorbell. Debbie had said on the phone that she would pay the taxi fare. There are still many things that are unclear to Kiki, but here she is now, and she will soon find out how everything is supposed to work. She hears dogs bark inside the house, and then, seconds later, the front door opens.

'Hi, I am Kiki. Hello Debbie.'

Her dark hair is cut in a short style and though she is slightly overweight, she is dressed in a modern outfit. Kiki feels a wave of relief rush through her.

'Welcome Kiki. Come inside. Let me introduce you to Sally and the baby. Oh wait! I must pay for the taxi. Bring your luggage in. My, you have a lot of stuff!'

'Yes, I know! I try to travel lightly but I seem to have gained more than I meant to over the last few months.' Debbie pays the taxi driver, and he waves at Kiki as he drives away.

She steps inside the modern home and notices that the reception area is spacious and light, smelling like fresh carnations. The kitchen is open plan with a counter with five bar stools standing in a row. There is a separate lounge furnished with two purple couches, a TV, a baby's crib, and a changing table with packs of nappies and other baby paraphernalia lying on top of it. The attractive young woman, sitting on the couch holding a baby in her arms, must be Sally. Kiki takes off her boots before she steps onto the fluffy white carpet and walks towards Sally to introduce herself.

It will take a while for them to get acquainted—Sally is probably as intrigued with the idea of an au pair such as Kiki, as Kiki is about to work for a new mother with a young baby. Kiki had raised four children of her own, and assisted her daughters with their babies, but had never thought about caring for a baby as an *employee*.

'Here is the guest bathroom. If you wash your hands, you may hold the baby.' Debbie is a qualified nurse and has many years of experience with new-born babies. Kiki obeys Debbie's instruction and goes to the bathroom to wash her hands, thinking about the babies she had raised. She takes in her new surroundings. After her trip from Ascot, she does not feel particularly motherly, and she feels apprehensive about the new situation. Taking the baby into her arms, she thinks: *Oh dear, I hope we'll quickly develop a special bond.*

'Sally needs help, especially during the night. She struggles to cope without enough rest. She suffers from post-natal depression. But unfortunately, I must leave next week for my new assignment. Sally's partner often has to work until late at night and she doesn't enjoy being home alone with the baby. Though she wants to be a hands-on mother, and does most things for the baby herself, she needs you as her companion – to go with her to the shops and help her in the house.'

Kiki smiles. She is surprised at how much information Debbie divulges in front of Sally. It seems rather inappropriate. But the job description sounds easy enough. She thinks she could manage easily and even enjoy the position.

'We haven't yet told Donald that you were coming today.'

Oh, so there is conspiracy here....

'Tomorrow evening Sally and Donald are going out for dinner and then she'll tell him about the plans to employ you.'

Kiki is taken aback by this news and immediately turns to face Sally, who is sitting next to Debbie on the purple couch. Sally notices Kiki's concern and tries to put her at ease.

'I am sure he will agree Kiki. He feels bad about coming home so late every evening and I told him I won't be able to cope without assistance.'

Debbie adds: 'We think you should first go to South Africa for a month to visit your daughter. If you leave on Sunday, you'll be there before her baby's birth. I will pay for your return ticket if you do me a favour. I have some baby clothes that I need to send to my friend in Cape Town. I will arrange for them to be collected from you.'

Debbie speaks fast and with authority. It sounds to Kiki as if Debbie's plans have been worked out prior to her or Sally's knowledge or approval.

Many thoughts go through her brain; so much conflicting information: *I am going to South Africa now? A strange woman is going to pay for my plane ticket. I must be her courier. I am here now, but I am not quite welcome. Will Donald, whom I have not met yet, accept me? What will happen if I leave for South Africa and spend a month away? Will they still want me to work for them when I return? What if they see they can manage without me, and don't need me when I return?*

'But how will Sally cope for a month while I'm away?'

'Her mother has taken leave, and she will come to visit Sally every day to help her. They will need you once her mother returns to work. Kiki turns to face Sally to see if she agrees, but all she can see is a blank and vacant expression. This is becoming stranger and more bizarre, especially when Debbie instructs Kiki to hide behind the door when Donald comes home tonight. They don't expect him to come home early, but just in case…. Tomorrow Debbie plans to put Kiki up in a hotel, where she will stay until her flight to South Africa on Sunday.

The dog runs into the room. The gigantic animal raises his front legs and jumps effortlessly onto the purple couch. He makes himself comfortable next to her. *Oops, the dog jumped onto the couch!* she wants to say. It seems it is not a strange occurrence; the dog may lie on the couch. *Well, then it should not concern me.*

'Are you hungry?' Debbie is in control of the household. Kiki must give her credit; she is an operator and things seem to happen around her.

'We bought many frozen meals, so please help yourself to any of the dishes in the freezer. Let me see which flights are available to Cape Town on Sunday. Would you mind flying via Istanbul or Dubai? I know it is a longer journey, but the tickets are much cheaper than a direct flight.'

'Just a moment, Debbie. Can I tell you something? I am not sure if I want to stay for a month. I am not sure how many days I may be out of the country during the two years prior to my Indefinite Leave to Remain application. I spent six weeks in South Africa in 2013, and I think we should first find out about that specific regulation.'

The truth is that she would not be earning for an entire month, and at this stage this presents a huge worry to her. Debbie ignores Kiki's concerns, and she listens helplessly while Debbie buys a ticket for her on Turkish Air Lines. The flight departs on Sunday at twelve noon from Heathrow Airport via Ataturk airport in Istanbul, and will return exactly one month later, landing at Gatwick Airport.

'Sally, will you be able to collect Kiki at Gatwick when she returns? We'll take the bus and train to Heathrow on Sunday morning.'

Sally looks up from her mobile and nods. 'Sure, I'll fetch her at Gatwick. No problem.'

'I wonder Debbie…. What time will I have to leave if I must be at Heathrow at nine o'clock? I have no idea how the bus or trains work from here.'

All of this sounds wrong to her, but it seems she has lost control of her life and decision-making abilities.

'Oh, don't you worry about a thing. We will sort it all out closer to the time. Now, remember, you can sit here with me and the baby in the lounge until Donald comes home. He will probably arrive late and might go straight to bed. But should he pop in to see the baby, you must stand here behind the door. It is important that he doesn't see you tonight. Sally, I think it is time for you to have your bath now. Say good night to Poppy.'

Sally leaves the lounge to go upstairs for her bath. Debbie instructs Kiki to carry her case upstairs to the spacious double room, which is supposed to become her room once she returns from South Africa. She notices the en-suite bathroom is modern and has twin basins and a glass walled shower. The lights go on automatically when there is a movement in the bathroom.

'Now, unpack your suitcase. Put everything here on the bed. Let me see what you have. It is summer in South Africa now, so you will need light clothes while you are there. Here are the baby clothes I need you to deliver. Leave enough space for all of this. Here is an outfit you can give to your daughter's baby.'

Kiki obeys and does everything, just as she is told to do. Within days she's become an uncertain, insecure puppet. This woman is totally in control. Within less than twenty minutes, her suitcase is packed with summer clothes at the bottom and lots of baby clothes at the top. Her other possessions, which will be left here while she's away, lie underneath the double bed, and they hide the rest behind the wardrobe.

Still unsure how things will work the next day, she brushes her teeth and returns to the lounge where Debbie is feeding the baby. She stretches out on a purple couch. She feels uncomfortable about the fact that Donald might arrive any minute, knowing she was expected to hide behind the door.

She makes one more attempt: 'Why can't you just be open and honest and tell him what's really going on?'

'You have no idea how awkward this situation could become. Trust me, this is the only way we can handle this. You will soon understand. It is only until tomorrow. Tomorrow we'll put you in a hotel until Sunday when you go to the airport. By the time you return from South Africa, everything will be fine.'

As she drifts off into an uneasy sleep, she hears voices whispering and forces her eyes open. 'If you want to, you can go to sleep in the bedroom upstairs now. Sally has spoken to Donald, and he now knows you're here. You don't have to hide anymore.'

Still feeling unsure, she goes upstairs to climb into the double bed in the strange room that might become her bedroom in a month's time. She sleeps fitfully until she eventually realizes that it is a new day and that she must face it and its 'stranger than fiction' circumstances.

Donald looks like a replica of Keble doing a clothing advertisement. She meets him downstairs in the family room where he is seated on the purple couch next to Sally. He doesn't look as tough as Debbie had described him; he is friendly, and they talk about the baby, the dogs and the house.

Debbie invites Kiki to go to the shops with her, but she declines the invitation. She prefers to spend time with her future employers. She has little time to cement a relationship with them - some memories of their new au pair must be created in their minds, and she has only a few hours left to establish this. Tomorrow she'll leave for South Africa; something she still finds hard to comprehend and digest.

They talk a lot and become acquainted. She shows them her paintings and shares a bit about her background.

When Debbie returns from the shops, she insists they return to buy gifts to take for Kiki's grandchildren in South Africa. She is impressed at the ease with which Debbie finds her way around, travelling on the bus, and she frantically makes mental notes for when she returns to come and live here. Debbie tells her about the convenience of an Oyster card, something she hadn't known about. She should also apply for a concession as she's a pensioner, and that will entitle her to free travel on public transport in all the London Zones. Kiki is impressed with her knowledge and experience and hopes that she will soon become as confident as Debbie. On their return, they leave the bus at Bradley Street and from there it is a short stroll to the house.

Kiki is nervous about her forthcoming flight and asks Debbie again how she thinks they will make it in time to Heathrow three hours before the departure of her flight, using the bus and trains. With so little time to prepare for an unexpected journey, eight o'clock is just hours away.

'Stop worrying about the details. Once Sally and Donald leave for dinner tonight, we can discuss everything.'

When they get home, Kiki asks the Google God about the availability and cost of a taxi to Heathrow. If she gets a free return ticket to South Africa, the least she could do is to get herself to the airport. Why would she lay more stress on herself or Debbie unnecessarily?

'What do you think, Donald? Wouldn't it be better if I take a taxi to Heathrow tomorrow? I am genuinely concerned that I will be late because I don't know my way around the trains and buses yet ....'

'Of course, Kiki. It makes perfect sense. A taxi will cost about sixty pounds to Heathrow Airport, and I agree it is worth it.' Donald has come to sit with her at the kitchen counter while he waits for Sally to finish her preparations for their evening out.

Debbie runs out of the lounge towards the kitchen, where Kiki and Donald are holding the conversation. The baby is in her arms, and her overcoat flaps behind her like the wings of a bat.

'Are you crazy?' she shouts. 'What have I told you? Why don't you listen to me? I told you we'll sort it out later once they have left!'

Her attitude and demeanour alarms Kiki, but she tries to keep her composure. 'All I have done Debbie, is to enquire about hiring a taxi to take me to the airport. Please tell me what is wrong with that?'

'You've gone behind my back and ordered a taxi without my consent.' She glares at Kiki with hatred written all over her face. 'You tricked me. I can't believe how you stabbed me in the back!' she shouts in Afrikaans.

'Debbie! How dare you speak like that at my house? What is the matter with you? I think you should put the baby down so that we can talk.' Donald is furious. Debbie goes to the family room to put the baby in her crib.

More words bounce between Debbie and Donald, words that Kiki does not understand, nor the reason for them. Kiki flees to the bedroom upstairs. It is obvious that these two have had disagreements previously.

An hour ago, she received an e-mail from her son-in-law in South Africa: 'Be careful,' he cautions. 'One does not just read about these things in the newspapers; it can happen. When something is too good to be true, it probably is. Why would a stranger buy you a plane ticket and ask you to bring baby clothes in your suitcase? As much as we're happy about this unplanned visit, you would be wise to reconsider.'

Like a frozen Buddha, she stays seated on the bed for what feels like hours; not knowing what to think or do, waiting for the scenario to unfold, take its course, follow its road to a beginning or an end. She hears voices in the kitchen, sounding both angry and sharp. Then, there are footsteps coming up the carpeted staircase towards the room. Debbie comes into the room and stands in front of her, her legs apart and her hands on her hips. She glares at Kiki.

'So, there you have it! It is all your fault! He's thrown me out of the house. I have to leave now. You will probably also have to go. If only you hadn't taken things into your own hands, all would have gone according to plan. And this, after all I have done for them!'

Kiki just stares at her, realizing there's no point in saying anything. The harm has been done and there is no way of undoing it. Somehow, she has become a pawn in a bigger game and right now she doesn't understand what has happened or where she fits into the puzzle.

The front door closes with a bang. Kiki stays seated on the bed, feeling helpless and paralyzed. She waits for something to happen, but she doesn't know what will transpire. Eventually Donald comes to the room, and he sits down on the bed next to her.

'I am so sorry, Kiki. But this woman has overstayed her welcome. She and I have had a few arguments during her stay here. Tell me, do you really want to go to South Africa tomorrow? Because, if you want to, you *can* go and then work here on your return.'

'It is not that important Donald. I am concerned about this freebie; it just doesn't feel right to take stuff in my suitcase for a woman I don't know, and who has bought me the plane ticket. Something is wrong. If I arrive at the airport tomorrow, she might well have cancelled the ticket and then things will be very awkward for me. What do you want me to do Donald? Should I stay or go?'

'I would like you to stay. Sally will need you to help her with the baby. So, if it is okay with you, please don't leave now. I believe Debbie told you that we would pay you four hundred pounds per week. That is more than we can offer, but if you agree to work for half of that amount, we have a deal, and you can work on Monday.'

In the television room, Sally sits holding her baby. Tonight, will be the first night that she will be solely responsible for Poppy. Kiki does not know what to do, but she is exhausted after the ordeal of the last few weeks and soon falls asleep in her new double bed.

The tunnel doesn't entice her this time. Kiki can see now that there are many fake entrances. If her heart doesn't feel right, she must not be lured into entering it.

Chapter 18

FEAST OR FAMINE

Kiki has the best room in the house. It has an en-suite bathroom, but there are no built-in wardrobes. It should be the main bedroom, but the couple prefers to use the room facing the street. Through her window she has a view of the back garden. Though she can hear the traffic noise of the busy road, the cottage, which is separated by a wooden fence from the main house, muffles the sound at the end of the yard.

As she goes downstairs to the kitchen for the first time as an employee, she passes the couple's bedroom. They are still asleep. The three dogs run from their room to greet Kiki; they probably hope that she will feed them.

She hardly slept last night; it is possible that the unsettling events that had happened and everything else she'd experienced since she'd left the attic, traumatised her. This morning she is tired, and she feels relieved that she does not have to board a plane today. She needs to clear her head so that she will be strong when she starts to work tomorrow. This presents a challenge. Sally is a new mother who has abruptly lost her night nurse and must now attend to her baby's needs solo for the first time without Debbie.

'Good morning, Kiki. Have you helped yourself to some breakfast? I must go to the delicatessen in a few minutes to buy food for lunch. We're expecting family to come over for the day. Would you like to accompany me to the shop?'

Donald seems keen to get preparations for the day going, and Kiki would like to help where she can. This looks like a great opportunity to familiarise herself with the neighbourhood. She fetches her bag and follows Donald to his car.

'We are so glad you are here to help us, Kiki. I do a lot of entertaining for my work and having you here will make Sally feel less lonely. As you've probably heard, we plan to go to Italy in a few weeks and it will be a great help if you could look after the house and the dogs. Just so that you know, I phoned the references you gave me last night. I received an incredibly positive report from both. Robert said: "Our loss, your gain."

This news makes her heart feel lighter. Perhaps things will work out here. New babies sleep a lot. It is a nice house; she has a pleasant room and bathroom, and the pay is good. She makes mental notes of where they drive. There are a few other shops near the delicatessen. At least it is within walking distance from the house.

After they return to the home, she cleans the outside table, sweeps the patio, and collects the dog poo in the back garden. She stacks the dish washer and puts the laundry into the washing machine. Sally sits in the lounge, holding her baby in her arms. She seems to be tired and concerned, but there isn't much Kiki can do for her today. The visitors arrive and Donald introduces her to everyone. They sit outside in a semi-circle and watch Donald barbecue.

After lunch, she takes a walk. She needs to get exercise and fresh air; it will help her get rid of the excess adrenaline that has built up in her body. The neighbourhood is affluent – the cars parked in front of the beautiful homes look expensive. Her mobile phone rings it surprised her to see Keith's name appear on the screen.

'Hi, how are you? Where are you now?'

'Hi, I am fine, thanks. I'm taking a walk in my new neighbourhood; I want to locate the pub to buy a drink. I started a new position yesterday in Penge. Where are you?'

'I moved to Ireland last week, and I thought I should let you know where I am. I started a new job, but I have my doubts whether it is going to work out. The property industry is still dead. Salespeople at this project have been unsuccessful. How are you doing with your Indefinite Leave to Remain application? Just remember, when you're ready, I'll sign the required documents. And oh yes, on the day of your birthday, I was on holiday in the Canary Islands. I sent you a text, but I guess you probably didn't receive it.'

For the first time in a long while they have a proper conversation. She shares her experiences in Brighton and Ascot with him and tells him about her new position. When she asks him if he has anyone significant in his life, he confirms his girlfriend is from Wales. To Kiki's surprise, she finds she takes in this information without experiencing too much pain. Maybe her healing has started subtly without her noticing the changes. Finally, she can think of the past without bitterness or self-pity. Most importantly, she can see how she grew from relying on Keith for her happiness to becoming a self-sufficient, independent woman.

She soon settles into her new life. She loves taking care of the sweet and easy to please, baby. Sally is kind and generous and welcomes Kiki's presence in their home. Most evenings she comes with a menu where Kiki sits playing with the baby. 'What take-away would you like tonight? Chinese, Indian or McDonalds?'

One of her daily tasks is to open the door to receive the deliveries for the day. Parcels arrive from The Little White Company, Zara, Toys R Us, Sainsbury's and Tesco. Like clockwork, a box of fresh fruit and vegetables from Abel and Cole is delivered each Monday morning. Kiki puts the accompanying recipe in a binder file and puts the vegetables in the double door fridge-freezer.

Shelly, the lovely cleaner, arrives twice a week. She is the first cleaning lady Kiki has met in the UK. When she arrives in the morning, she is dressed neatly, smelling of perfume and wearing jewellery. Once she has greeted the over-excited dogs that lap up the treats and pet toys she brings, she changes into her work clothes. Even then she looks smart and elegant, her make-up and hair in place. It is obvious she loves being there as much as Kiki and Sally enjoy her company.

Minutes after Shelly's arrival, the dog walker rings the doorbell. More noise, more drama, more giggles and laughter. Finally, peace and quiet descend on the house; it is time to put the laundry into the washing machine and unpack the Tesco delivery.

Next to ring the doorbell is the dry-cleaner. He brings freshly laundered clothes on hangers and collects Donald's suits, shirts, and shorts that he has worn during the week to take to the shop.

The couple moved into the house a few months ago, but there are still boxes that need to be unpacked. In Kiki's room, there are boxes stored full of clothes, jewellery, books, and unused items. She goes through each box and asks the couple which items they want to keep. They find things they thought they had misplaced and to them it is like a discovery of long lost and newly found friends. Finally, she moves the remaining boxes against a wall and covers them with a black sheet: out of sight, out of mind....

Kiki notices a forlorn- looking suitcase in the dining room. They had left it there when they returned months ago from a holiday in Spain. It is full of clothes, shoes, perfume, jewellery, hats and handbags. It pleased Sally when Kiki offers to unpack it, but she is not interested in the contents; it belongs to the time when she was still pregnant. Kiki puts the contents away in Sally's dressing room.

It is a constant battle to get rid of the empty cardboard boxes used for packaging. It seems as if their bins always overflow; two weeks are just too long to wait for the garbage men to make their rounds. She looks up and down the street and notices the neighbours' small containers. A few bottles, neatly packed and folded cartons and paper are all kept in small boxes. Why is it that only *their* bins are so full? Foxes reach the black bags, rip them open, and strew litter, which must be picked up in the morning, all over the lawn.

After a few nights of gallantly doing night shifts with the baby, Sally throws in the towel: 'My friend's mom, Pat, volunteered to do a few "nights" for me. Her granddaughter is a few months older than Poppy and she has lots of experience with babies. I just can't do this anymore. The dogs wake me up in the night, Donald comes home in the early hours of the morning…. Oh my gosh, I am so exhausted.'

'Will Pat be sleeping with the baby in the lounge?' Kiki is a bit taken aback.

'Yes, she can sleep on the couch.'

It doesn't take long for Kiki and Pat to become friends. She hasn't had a female friend for a long time, and it is a welcome relief to speak to someone who also enjoys company. Soon, she looks forward to the nights when Pat arrives by taxi.

Sally really struggles to wake up during the night and soon Kiki becomes part of the night shift team. Pat does three shifts each week and Kiki sleeps with the baby in the lounge for two nights. Sally manages two nights every week. Somehow, the baby flourishes and it isn't difficult to wake her up twice during the night to feed her. Also, Kiki earns a few extra pounds since Sally's compensation for a night's sleep is generous.

The week before the family leaves for their holiday, parcels arrive with regularity at the front door. New suitcases, swimming costumes, kaftans, evening dresses, shoes, sunscreen, loads of baby milk and sachets of baby food are soon spread around the home.

'Why don't you rather take boxes of powdered milk? It will save a lot of space.' Kiki can still remember the days she went on holiday when her children were babies, and she wishes she could make a few suggestions. Wisely, she bites her lip and keeps quiet.

'Oh, we're allowed thirty-five kilograms of luggage on Virgin airways. Travelling business class has many advantages. It is much more convenient to take milk in sachets.'

When will the baby ever wear all these beautiful dresses and shoes? she wonders. Gucci shoes, out on display in Poppy's open wardrobe; Kiki has stopped converting the prices of these items into South African Rands, trying to put a value that she could understand on so many lovely things. She is as proud of Poppy's beautifully decorated nursery with the lovely clothes and toys, as if she were her own baby. It is hard to choose what to pack for the baby's first holiday abroad.

In the family's absence, she has time to paint, write, read, and watch TV. She sleeps badly; she is not accustomed to sharing her bed with three dogs lying sprawled at her feet. She goes out on day trips to London but must be back in time to feed them.

Harry, Sally's decorator friend comes to build a wooden deck at the back of the garden and when he has a break, they drink coffee and chat. By now she is also a confident bus commuter who holds a free bus pass. She enjoys the ride to the shopping mall in town where she goes for a haircut in a salon.

Then, one Sunday morning, she meets Carlos on a dating website. He is a nurse from Spain who works in Doha, Qatar. *That is so safe, I can talk to him,* she thinks and decides to build a friendship with him. He is too far away from her to influence her life, but she might mean something to him. Carlos is the divorced father of two young boys who live in Spain with their mother. Like Kiki, he is also a stranger living in a foreign country, thrown there by circumstances and bad luck.

On Monday when she opens her laptop, she notices he is waiting for her on the website. 'I've rushed home during my lunch break so that I can speak to you. I'm so happy that I've met you.' Against her better judgment, she starts to look forward to their conversations. She tells him she must get Indefinite Leave to Remain in the UK soon, or else she'll have to return to South Africa.

'I think that once you've all that in order, you must come to Qatar to visit me here,' he invites her. 'I may not go nowhere while I'm working here. My contract only allows me to leave the country to visit my sons for a few days at a time, but other than that, I must stay here.'

Oh, my word! I've just been invited to visit someone in an Arab country!

What are the chances that she'll do something like that? Only because she 'knows' Carlos, would she go there on her own. The whole idea is so outrageous, but still, it starts to play around in her head. Why doesn't she make this idea a goal, a plan of action? Nothing should prevent her except fear of the unknown or lack of confidence. Also, she would really like to meet this man, who has become such a good friend to her.

She asks the Google God information about Qatar. It tells her that she'll need a visa to visit, that she will have to stay in a hotel since it is against Qatari law to stay together as a man and a woman unless married. Really? They instructed hotels to obey these laws and there isn't any chance that Carlos may visit her in her hotel room in Doha.

Apparently only young unmarried couples may hold hands in public - even married couples must walk apart.

On her next visit to town, she enquires at a travel agency about plane tickets to Qatar. The potential she might return to the UK with a damaged heart or tearful eyes are huge, but how will she know if she doesn't take the risk? She also doesn't want to have a months-long internet relationship if there is no future in it; life is too short and complicated. Carlos is delighted with her progress, and they discuss possible dates that will suit them both.

She wants her stay in Doha to be short but powerful and exciting. If she takes the bank holiday in May with an extra day before and after the weekend, she will have five days' holiday, but will only be away for three days from work.

The wheels of bureaucracy turn slowly in Qatar and her visa might only arrive the day before her departure. Or might it not arrive in time at all? She is freakishly preoccupied and finds it hard to focus on her preparations. When the elusive document eventually arrives, Carlos says calmly: 'I told you that you'd get it in time.'

Finally, it is time for the taxi to arrive and to take her to Heathrow Airport. To her surprise Donald puts a generous bonus in her hand.

It is past midnight when the plane lands at Doha airport. It is an extremely hot night, and it takes forever for her suitcase to appear on the carousel. When she finally walks through the exit doors, she recognises Carlos immediately. He stares ahead of him, his eyes fixed on the revolving doors. When he notices her, his face changes from a look of worry to one of delight. She gets into his car and they talk and laugh, not knowing who is more excited; she or he.

Fortunately, it is late, and the chances of being detected by neighbours are slim. Still, she feels nervous and wonders what would happen to him if the police were to knock on the door of his apartment. He lives a simple life; there is little furniture and few utensils in the one-bedroom flat - only necessities. Like her, he can't carry too much stuff; he is a visitor in a strange country and will one day return to Spain.

In the morning, before he must go to work, he takes her to the hotel in Doha where she has booked her stay. Unfortunately, he has been informed that he must do an important exam while she is there, and he seems stressed about this unplanned event.

As they drive to the hotel, he tells her about the history of Qatar; the beautiful skyline of ultra-modern buildings and traditional souks is quite spectacular, and it is hard to believe it all came into existence after they found oil. She feels strange when Carlos leaves her in the foyer of the modern hotel to go to work, but she quickly pulls herself together. Carlos will fetch her later in the evening and then they will go out for a meal. Now it is time for sightseeing.

At the reception desk she asks for directions to the souk and though it is Friday afternoon all over the world, today is Saturday in Doha. The streets heave with men on their way to their evening prayers at the mosques. She is probably the only woman out in public. She feels as if she is carried on a wave of testosterone, but strangely, she is not scared. Carlos said that she will be safe as the moral laws in Qatar are extremely strict. 'An eye for an eye...'

The sun sets on the architecturally designed buildings, and she takes photos as she walks along. One lit up building that particularly interests her resembles a fairy-tale castle with turrets that twist about a hundred meters into the sky. She finds out that the building houses the Muslim Cultural Museum and visits it the next day. Walking here on her own empowers her, and she can't help but be proud of herself. She has not only afforded a plane ticket and payment for a hotel room, but she has proven that she has enough chutzpah to come here on her own.

When she returns to the hotel, she showers and changes. Soon Carlos will come and pick her up for dinner. He waits for her outside the hotel to avoid attracting attention and she goes outside to his car, where he awaits her.

They walk along the promenade, and it feels strange not to touch, to hold hands or walk too close to each other. It is a sultry evening, and they sit at a restaurant sipping non-alcoholic drinks as one can only buy wine at the European club or at certain hotels. The skyscrapers are beautifully decorated with neon lights and the boats ferrying people along the water are lit up with fairy lights. It is a romantic evening filled with sounds and smells that will be branded into her memory, but she feels strangely disconnected from Carlos.

'How come you think I am special, that I might be the one for you? What if you find that your true love, your special one, is still waiting for you?'

She is surprised at this question and does not know what to say. How should she answer this man with the dark, questioning eyes? She wracks her brain for something to say and finds, to her dismay, that for once, she is devoid of an answer. To protect herself from getting hurt or being disappointed at the outcome of her visit and meeting with Carlos, she cautions herself to just enjoy the experience, one day at a time: no expectations, no tears or sadness. And now, unexpectedly, she is confronted with a Pandora's Box filled with emotions and thoughts.

'And what if you are the one? How would we know we are not good for each other?' She is irritated with herself when her eyes fill with tears. She does not dare spoil this magical moment, but something tells her that it is already spoilt.

'We can enjoy this time together, my lovely Kiki, but only once we go our separate ways will we know if we are suited. Only when we are apart again, we will know if we miss each other.'

She did not expect this type of conversation so soon, and it surprises her that a man would speak like this. She is wary now, not knowing what to expect for the rest of her stay.

The next day she wakes up early and goes to the hotel's dining room for breakfast. After breakfast, she takes a taxi to take her to the Qatar museum. The beautiful building housing the museum is almost surrounded by water. She spends a delightful time there, getting lost in the peaceful, semi-dark building, wandering from display room to display room. Again, she pinches herself; she is brave and proud of her independence, doing this all on her own.

Later in the evening, Carlos picks her up at the hotel again and they then drive to the club for foreigners. Both must show their passports before they may enter the club. No locals allowed here!

'Have a look at the cocktail menu,' says Carlos and he shows her the selection of drinks available.

'Oh no, please!' She shudders at the thought of a mixed drink. 'Can I please have a glass of dry white wine?' They nurse their drinks for hours, talking, listening to the gentle slapping of the waves against the wall that separates the building from the ocean. The air smells salty and fresh.

They discuss their arrangements for the next evening. She will stay over at his apartment since she must be at the airport at half- past three the following morning. It involves her having to stay alone in his apartment-quietly, and all day long. Nobody must notice her presence. He will write his exam and since it is almost an hour's drive to the city, he can't drive back and forth to fetch her.

'Damn, this bloody exam my work has sprung on me! It's so important that I do well and to be honest with you, I find the English awfully hard. I hold a degree in nursing in Spain, but now it feels as if I know nothing! I am so sorry, Kiki. This is impacting on your visit, but there is nothing I can do about it. Are you sure you would not prefer to stay in the hotel tomorrow?'

'There is not much more that I want to see in the city. I spent hours in the souk, bought a few gifts, have been to the Islamic Cultural Centre where they tried to convert me to the Muslim faith…… I think I've seen and done enough. I would like to paint a picture of Doha for you while you are away at work. Remember, I promised you a painting, and I brought a canvas and my paints. That way the day will pass quickly. It is so hot outside and I need to rest before I return home on the long flight.'

Carlos appears stressed. He must drive to the city to write his exam, return to work until nine o'clock, have a meal, sleep a few hours, take Kiki to the airport, return to his apartment and later drive back to the city again. This was not how they had planned her brief stay and she wonders if this was maybe not the best time to have come. He makes her feel guilty but assures her he is fine and that it was better that she came now rather than

294

later. He will soon have to write another, even more important exam; there was no telling when the perfect time would have been.

She experiences a sense of dread when he leaves early in the morning. It is hot already. He locks her inside the apartment with strict instructions not to open the door to anyone and not to make any noise. She tries to sleep for another hour, but she feels restless and sad. She takes a shower and then sits on the cool cement floor while Skyping Lionel in South Africa. He is always there for her when she needs a friend to collect her tears in his caring hands.

'Can you remember what I told you? Just enjoy the experience...... You have now been to Qatar; you've had an interesting experience. This man is too far away for any future relationship. Just relax today, go home tomorrow and continue with your life in the UK.'

She packs her bags and makes sure that everything is ready for an early start the next morning. Later she cooks a meal and prepares a salad the way she saw Carlos does using lots of feta cheese, olive oil and tomatoes. When he eventually arrives home, he looks even more stressed.

'I bought you these perfumes today,' he says with his broad Spanish accent while taking three bottles of Qatari perfumes out of his bag. 'This one's for you and these two are for your bosses.'

She is very touched by this considerate gesture. They eat their simple meal of lamb chops and salad before they go to bed; the farewell already hanging suspended like a barbed wire between them - she, scared that she would not wake up in time; he, panicking that he won't be getting enough sleep to carry him through the next day's oral examination.

Neither of them can help the other on their lonely vigil and after a few hours of tossing and turning, her alarm goes off and she gets up to get ready for the journey to the airport. She wakes Carlos minutes before they must leave. Though it is still dark outside, they cautiously steal their way to the car, hoping that nobody detects them.

They chat amicably as they drive to the airport, reminiscing about the lovely time they have had, skirting away from any talk about the future. One last lingering look from Carlos and she disappears through the Departure door where her flight to Istanbul awaits her.

Chapter 19

UP IN THE AIR AGAIN

On the plane from Istanbul to Heathrow, Kiki becomes aware the woman sitting next to her is desperately trying to dry the tears streaming down her face. She doesn't want to embarrass her, but eventually she puts a tissue in her hand without saying a word. Kiki thinks, *my girl, I know how you feel. Get it out, let the tears wash you.* Is it just a woman thing? Is it so easy for a man to receive and then send you away; to continue with his life as if he doesn't need a special woman? She can't help but think that Carlos is keeping a secret – he is hiding something and certainly doesn't want to share it with her.

For all she knows the woman sitting next to her may just have lost parent. Perhaps she mourns the loss of a beloved pet, or she could just feel sad because she had to temporarily leave her lover? It doesn't matter what the cause of her sadness is, but somehow, by witnessing it, Kiki feel stronger. She cries inwardly, but there is no point in showing the world her tears. This time she brought the pain on herself.

She takes a taxi home from the station. She feels vulnerable and brittle sitting in the back seat of the car. Though she had a life changing experience, she knows the time ahead might be tough emotionally. It is with relief that she greets Sally, Poppy and the dogs before she goes to her room to change and unpack her case.

Her feeling of dread of abandonment is justified. She doesn't hear from Carlos for days after her return home. When he eventually sends her a Skype message, it is short and devoid of any emotion: 'I hope you arrived home safely.' How is it possible they were practically sowing words across the ocean and desert before she went to visit him, and now it has become impossible to meet on the internet at the same moment? How is it possible for magic to disappear so quickly?

After days of frustration and anxiety, she decides to do something almost unforgivable: she insults him as only a woman scorned can do. 'People laugh at me Carlos,' she tells him in a Skype message. They say: 'Are you stupid; did you not know what Mediterranean men are like? It is a well-known joke that waiters fall in love with tourists staying at their hotel, but once the next group of tourists arrive, they are ready for the next romance.'

That got his attention all right! After many tears, bitter words and then forgiveness on both sides, he tells her he is scared to fall in love, he doesn't believe in love, they might never see each other again. All is fine now, and they will always be in each other's heart, blah, blah, blah. She fees slightly better, but when Sally puts a book, called, 'The Magic', written by Rhonda Byrne, in her hand, with strict instructions to read it immediately, she obeys. She needs help.

After a few weeks, she tells Gordon, whom she met prior to her excursion to Qatar, she will meet him soon. He is over the moon. He has bought tickets for an outdoor concert at Leeds Castle in Kent where the Royal Philharmonic Orchestra and many other well- known artists will be playing.

Oh, what the heck, it is still a long time till July...... She needs to stay busy, redirect her mind elsewhere to help her to forget Carlos and Doha.

Gordon is very British – he is ex-army, drives a nice powerful car, lives on his own and is smitten with her. He has a part time job which keeps him busy during the week, leaving him enough time on weekends to ride on his bike and go for walks along the beach. He dresses well and has good manners. But he laughs at inappropriate times, and he is hard of hearing. Not one who normally takes an interest in star signs, it is Pat who points out like Keith, Gordon is probably a controlling, demanding Leo.

When Gordon invites her to visit him in Dover to go to the air show in Folkestone, she vehemently declines the offer. But Pat encourages her to go. 'You know Kiki, you should go and see where he lives. As a woman living the way you do, you are constantly at other people's mercy;

you never know what could happen to you and one can never have too many friends. What is the worst thing that could happen? Have a nice weekend and if it goes well, good. If you don't like it, what the heck, then you just continue with your life. He seems to really like you. I mean, look at all the cards that arrive at this house. There is one every bloody day! Look at these flowers he sent you today. My word, you should really count your blessings.'

Anything to get her mind off Carlos. She has always been totally honest with Gordon. But he is convinced that he can win her over - he just needs the opportunity to show her what he is like, he tells her. She needs to get out of the house every now and then and getting away for a day or two and seeing a town like Dover would be good for her mental health. Or what?

When Gordon sees her for the first time after six weeks, he is standing next to his car, overcome with emotion; clasping his hands: 'Oh, Kiki, you look so beautiful. My God, you are so gorgeous!' And there, in the street, he tries to hug and kiss her. She squirms and wriggles, trying to free herself from his eager hands. *Why,* she wonders, *oh, why did I ever listen to Pat's advice?*

'I have a few surprises for you my darling....' They are sitting on the couch in Gordon's lounge. He hands her a small parcel which she opens to find a pair of earrings wrapped in soft tissue paper. Next, he hands her a packet wrapped in brown paper. Inside is a packet of ginger biscuits. 'I read in the chapter you wrote; you love ginger biscuits.'

She must smile; she is taken aback that someone would take such an interest in her.

Before they leave the apartment to go to the air show, she has acquired a new pendant, a pair of matching earrings, a tennis bracelet, a packet of ginger biscuits, a pen engraved with her name and a silver card holder.

The day's prospects look good; they each take their camera and she, who has never taken a picture of an airplane in flight, is going to give it her best shot. Slightly intimidated by Gordon's long lens and impressive photographic gear, she turns her back on him to find the planes in flight, hoping she might catch just one single image. After walking on the Leigh, they enjoy a light lunch in a restaurant tucked away underneath the pavement. Close to the harbour they drink coffee at a café on the sidewalk. When they finally arrive at his apartment again, they compare their pictures of the planes they had taken that morning at the air show. She has done quite well. Gordon has no pictures on his camera. Something must have gone wrong……

In the evening they take a taxi to a restaurant in town and enjoy a lovely meal. They walk home through the night streets of Dover. She cannot resist the temptation to wonder if she could see herself living in this town. It is obvious that Gordon has visions of her by his side.

'I would love to go with you to South Africa when you visit again. We'll rent a car and then you could show me around your country. I looked on the internet and I'm bowled over by the beauty of South Africa. Wouldn't it be lovely if we could go together, my darling? Yes, I know you are worried about your Leave to Remain application, but once that is out of the way, then certainly you'd like to go for a visit? I'd love to meet your children.'

In her minds' eye, she pictures herself and Gordon arriving at the airport in Cape Town, and then driving in their rented car to her children's house. She can see them clearly sitting on their undercover patio, having a barbecue, their wine glasses filled to the brim, her grandchildren vying for her attention, the youngest sitting on her lap....

'No, Gordon, when I go to visit my children, I'd want to go on my own. I'm looking forward to seeing them so much. I'm very home sick and there is only one way I can be healed from that affliction. To be honest, I am not sure if I want to be with you at all. I am sorry to have to say this, but I think it is better that we discuss it now and you know how I feel about us.'

She sees the hurt in his eyes, and she hates herself for causing him pain. How could she be so mean? More importantly, how could she have been so silly to have come here? Yes, it is interesting, and perhaps only fair to have come to see where he lives, but there are just too many things that aren't gelling with her.

'Will you please still accompany me to the open-air concert in July? Please Kiki, I would really appreciate that.'

They are on their way home after a short visit via Canterbury. It is one of the places in the UK that she had really wanted to see, and she was not disappointed with the beautiful old town. But all the time she is weighing, measuring…. Could she see herself on the arm of this man who wants to display her as his trophy, who is making plans for their future because he honestly believes that she is in his?

Added to the other gifts lying in the boot of the car, is another bag with a beautiful skirt, a pair of khaki-coloured trousers and a cobalt blue cardigan which he chose and bought for her in a boutique in Canterbury.

'Please let me think about this. I'd love to go to the concert, but I need time to think about the relationship you want to have with me. I really appreciate everything you've done for me, but I'm not sure if this is what I want.'

The Satnav lady guides them through the traffic. Her voice is loud. Way too loud for her sensitive ears. But it still cannot mask Gordon's loud sobs. She cringes in the car seat and stares pointedly through the window at the green fields that pass by like fleeting pictures on a TV screen.

Poppy and the dogs are happy to see her again, and her bedroom is a safe retreat after the disastrous weekend. She plans to give all her attention to her Indefinite Leave to Remain application. She must present her application in Croydon on Thursday morning. Her stress levels are high, and she is grateful when Sally offers to take her to the Home Office.

Sally and Donald generously put four hundred pounds into her account towards her application. It makes a huge difference to her life. The money goes towards a 'same day' decision, which would take the burden off her shoulders by tomorrow evening. The alternative would be a postal application for which the results could take up to nine months. She would be without her passport during that period. If all goes well, she should be able to go home for a visit soon.

She sits on her bed while she once more goes through all her documents. Here is the page on the application form that Keith signed and here are his bank statements. Her eyes dart down the row of figures and she tries to read about her husband in these sums: what can she see that might interest her? He still enjoys the same lifestyle and has the same habits. She notices that he has paid for a few meals at restaurants. Interesting....... Plane tickets from Ireland to Heathrow.

'Oh, who cares what he does? She reads the instructions again. 'Please make sure that you have the right application form. They change from time to time.'

She printed this one in April and it is now July. What are the chances that they could have changed so soon? Thirty-five pages plus all the supporting documents.... She weighs the pages in her hands. This is her life on paper and compared to what she amounted to in her previous life, this is nothing. But it is a steppingstone to her future, and she reminds herself that should this application be unsuccessful, she has only a few months left to stay legally in the UK. In a way it would be a relief to hear she must go, but she knows on an intuitive level she is here to stay.

What would she do if she had to start again in South Africa? She has no idea, but similarly, she is beginning to wonder about her future in the UK. Her current position with Donald and Sally is precarious and won't last indefinitely; she can sense that.

You are too analytical! she reprimands herself. She should keep her head down and do her job; take one day at a time. Some days she wishes she were in love with Gordon. He is very persuasive and charming, and it would have been an easy way out of her situation to move in with him and live the rest of her days in Dover. The problem is that however hard she looks; she can't see an entrance to a tunnel that leads in that direction.

Chapter 20

LEAVE TO REMAIN

It is hard to believe the day finally arrived; she has prepared for this for such a long time. She booked (with difficulty) an appointment on the Home Office website to apply for Leave to Remain in the UK. Today is the day that she must throw her dice and watch where they fall.

She dresses with care and is pleased to notice that the woman staring back at her from the mirror looks elegant; not too smart but also not too casual. Though she fears the outcome of today's endeavour, she must appear confident and calm. There is not much more that she can do to prepare for potential questions about Keith's and her finances and their communal home in Wales-according to the address she is providing as proof.

Sally drops her off in front of the Home Office in Croydon. Kiki tells her not to worry, she will find her way home again. Having a Freedom Pass has given her confidence to travel on public transport. There are certain advantages being over the age of sixty when you live in the UK!

Luckily, she had taken a photo on her mobile of her appointment confirmation on the internet, because that is the first thing the man at the entrance to the offices requests to see. Then, after a security search like that at an airport, she may go to the third floor and announce herself at the reception desk.

'Where is your husband today? And where is his original passport?' Kiki is slightly taken aback at the enquiry from the Asian lady concerning the whereabouts of her husband, because on the application forms it states that she needs a full copy of Keith's passport - nowhere does it state that his physical presence was required.

Oh, darn, it does make sense - she should have thought of that. She looks around at the other people waiting in the queue behind her and can't see any other person standing alone other than individuals who look like solicitors representing clients. For the first time she wonders if she should have paid someone to assist her with her application, but it is too late now. She forces herself to stay calm.

'My husband is in Ireland today on business.'

'It states here that you are the spouse of a person present in the UK on the day of application for Indefinite Leave to remain. Your spouse must be in the UK today. I'll have to ask the manager what to do in your case since you are here now, and you have paid for your appointment.'

After about ten minutes - that felt more like two hours - she directs Kiki to the section where they process applicant information. Just before she might start feeling some relief, she hears the inevitable: 'Your forms are outdated. It changed in June. Here is the latest edition. Please complete this again and return to me once you are done.'

Kiki looks in dismay at the new application form the clerk hands her. It comprises of thirty-five pages. It took Kiki weeks of careful consideration to complete these forms and now she must redo it in the shortest possible time. She takes a deep breath and tries her best to focus on this task.

After they have captured her details into the system, the original papers of all the supporting documents are returned for her safe keeping. The copies and her application form are put into a file to be handed to a different department. They tell her to either wait in the cafeteria or go for a walk. It is bound to take two hours or more before she will be called again. Most of the people sitting in the waiting area of the cafeteria seem to be represented by solicitors. Is she missing something important? Two thousand pounds seems a lot of money if one can complete a form oneself and provide the required documentation. *Oh well, what must be must be.* She will just drink her coffee and wait till they call her number.

'Where is your husband today?' The same question. If she lies and says that he is in Wales and gets found out, she would be in trouble. Saying he is in Ireland is also not the correct answer, but she sticks to the truth.

'Please write his mobile number on this paper. Wait in the cafeteria again till you get a call from me.'

After an hour, her phone rings. 'What did you say again? Where is your husband today?'

Oh darn, why do I have to be tested like this? She thinks in despair.

'My husband is on business in Ireland today.' The truth and nothing but the truth will come out of her mouth. She has phoned Keith to alert him to the possibility of a call from the Home Office. Is doesn't seem as if anyone has contacted him yet.

After twenty minutes, they call her name on the intercom. 'Kiki Brown. Cubicle 5 please.'

'I am deeply sorry, but we can't deal with your application today. When you come again, bring your husband's original passport. Also, your husband must be in the UK on the day of your application. You don't have to make another appointment; you can come to the third floor and present yourself with his passport. Don't worry, everything will be alright.'

'Oh no! Do you realize I have been waiting for two years for this day!' she exclaims in dismay. She is on the verge of crying.

'I don't know why you waited so long, because you could've applied for this the day after you passed your Life in the UK test. You are here on a Settlement Visa and the rules are different for that category.'

Oh, my word! How come nobody ever told me this?'

Despite the disappointment, she is quite relieved. It seems there aren't any other problems regarding finances or the letters, and that is positive. She's convinced that Keith will help her with his passport. He will just have to come to the UK for a few days to visit his girlfriend in Wales. The other good news is that she doesn't have to make an appointment again; she may just arrive here. Good, now she can go home and gather her wits about her.

Standing on the sidewalk of a street in Croydon, so far from South Africa, so alone in the world on the day when she hadn't got Leave to Remain, nothing could have shocked her more than a pair of warm hands gently covering her eyes. Her mind is numb. Who could this be? Who would do this to her? She knows nobody in Croydon who would recognize her. She doesn't feel fear - on the contrary; she experiences a warm flow of love running through her veins.

Nothing could have shocked her more than to see Gordon, looking so confident and happy that he had surprised her like this. There, parked on the side of the road, is his car. She doesn't have to worry about how to find a bus to get home. If she wanted to, she wouldn't ever again have to worry how to get home.

While they drink coffee, she phones Keith. As she hoped, he offers to help her and undertakes to bring her his passport as soon as possible.

'Can we please go to the park now? I need to ask you something.' Gordon wears his black Stetson hat, looking handsome and appearing confident. The relief that the appointment is over, the optimism that she might after all be able to stay in the UK, that a man so keenly wants to be with her, that he drove all the way from Dover to Croydon to celebrate: is that the reason she said 'yes'?

'I brought you this to celebrate your Permanent Residency. Oh, well, you didn't get it today, but you soon will.'

They sit on a picnic blanket on the grass in beautiful Kelsey Park. She opens the packet Gordon offers her. Inside is a passport holder with a British flag and a wooden heart embellished with buttons. How thoughtful of him.

He talks about going to South Africa as soon as she is more settled and knows that she can stay in the UK. Where else would she like to go on holiday? Somewhere she has always dreamed of going. Oh, yes, if she wanted to, they could go on a riverboat cruise in Russia. He will get the brochure for that, but it will be after they've been to South Africa.

Once again, she experiences a feeling of dread.

Do I want this? How will it feel to depend on a man; to give up my freedom to someone that doesn't excite me physically – someone I will only go to because it will make my life easier, more comfortable, more secure?

She thinks these thoughts even before he presents her with a small box. Should she open it, accept it? He understands her better than she could imagine. Would she, should she, accept this beautiful, dainty, eternity ring? The diamonds glisten in the dappled sunlight, and she stares at it, feeling dazed.

She talks and can't stop herself. Kiki talks a lot. There are a few conditions, she tells him. Number one: he must wear a hearing aid. Number two: she will still work to earn her own money. Number three: she needs lots of space to do her 'own thing'.

When, oh when, will she come to Dover then, to live with him? He wants to know.

She thinks: *If you want me, take me NOW. Maybe today is the one and only day I might come to you.*

The ring fits her finger as if he knew her size. It is hard to take it off before she starts work the next day; it is so pretty. How come then, she doesn't want anybody to notice it? She should phone her children, tell them about this man who is interested in their mother. Surely, they will be happy too? Then again, this is not really an engagement – she is safe: she is still married to Keith.

She doesn't tell Sally about her 'engagement' either. She goes about her daily tasks as if nothing has changed. Except for the disappointment that her initial attempt for her application for Indefinite Leave to Remain had been only three quarters successful.

They joke when the post arrives, because inevitably every day there is a card addressed to her from Dover. When Shelly comes to clean the house on Monday, she requires an update on the 'gentleman' from Dover.

'He is so good to me Shelly. Why can't I get excited?'

'Oh Kiki! Any other woman would jump for joy. Think of it; you would have a house and no worries ever again. South Africa, you say? You mean he will take your there, and he wants to meet your children? I don't know, Kiki. If I were you, I would be really happy.'

'No Shelly, you have so much to be thankful for. When I watch couples go to the shops, I get jealous. You have someone who cares for you and your husband is always there for you.

She agrees to visit Gordon in Dover this weekend. He has had one of her paintings framed and wants to hang it on a wall with her assistance. She promised to help him rearrange his lounge. When he fetches her on Friday evening, he hands her the keys of his car.

'I've insured you as a driver of my car. I hope you don't mind but I saw your license peeking out of your bag the other day, and that's where I got your license number. I know you love driving, and I think it will give you confidence to drive to Dover today with me sitting next to you in the passenger seat. On Sunday afternoon, you can drive home by yourself. I won't need my car for the week.'

Her first impulse is to decline the offer, but she knows she must overcome her resistance and should take on the challenge. It's a powerful car and once on the highway, it's hard to keep to the speed limit. She's grateful, though, when they arrive safely at his apartment and Gordon takes the driver's seat to park his car with ease in his awkwardly positioned garage.

Years of practice of furnishing homes, occupying them and moving to different houses has developed her eye for detail. They move the lounge furniture to create a more pleasing ambience. Gordon is elated with the change and is now inspired to change his bedroom too. They go to town and on his suggestion make an appointment for an eye test for Kiki. 'You need a more flattering pair of glasses,' and she must admit that for once she agrees with Gordon.

Gordon insists she takes his car back to Penge. The following weekend, he and his daughter will drive there so that Kiki can meet her. They'll have lunch together and afterwards he'll return with his car. No protests convince Gordon that she doesn't want to drive back on her own, and that she doesn't like the idea that his car will be left unused on the street for a week.

Eventually, she feels proud of her accomplishment: she has driven on her own, albeit with the help of Mrs. Satnav, all the way from Dover to Penge. It seems as if she is regaining part of her old lifestyle. Someone is adding value to her life, but it is not she herself doing so, nor isn't it the value that she needs right now. The keys for the car lie on the bedside table for the week; she has no need to drive anywhere.

She can sense that change is lurking around the corner, but until the time is right, this is where she is supposed to be. She has a roof over her head and food on her plate and by some miracle her wages are still regularly paid into her bank account. The holiday the family has planned is still confirmed. They asked Kiki to look after the house and the dogs while they're away.

Life continues and twice a week Milton, the family's personal coach, comes to the house. After their workout, she helps Milton and Donald to make a delicious smoothie with green apples, beetroot, ginger, lemons, and crushed ice. It takes ages to clean the machine, and tidy the kitchen afterwards, but she enjoys being part of their efforts to enjoy a healthy lifestyle.

In the evening, a masseuse arrives with a portable tanning machine which she sets up in the lounge. The couple is eager to look tanned and healthy when they go on their holiday. Later, while Sally has her nails done, Donald gets a massage.

She has agreed to visit Gordon again this weekend. While she stands ironing in the kitchen, she ponders her reluctance to be with Gordon. Pat is here today, and she tries to explain to her why she feels so reluctant.

'If I don't feel better after this weekend, I'm going to call it off and discontinue the relationship, if one can call it one…. I'll give him one more chance. The only reason I really want to go is to have my eyes tested, but to be honest I could just as well do it here.'

The crease in Donald's shirt just won't go away and she frowns as she tries to press it out with the steam iron.

'Do you know what? I think nothing is going to be different this weekend. All it might do is make it harder for Gordon to accept it if I tell him I want to end the relationship. Why am I doing this? I should just call it off right now. Yes, I have decided. I will phone him tonight and break the news to him.'

'Oh Kiki! You're going to break the poor man's heart. I feel sorry for him! But if you aren't happy, follow your intuition and use your head. You know what Buddha said? The head comes first and then the heart……'

It is still not a simple task to tell Gordon about her decision.

'Are you still wearing the ring?' he asks her when he calls the next morning.

'No, I have taken it off and I will post it to you as soon as I can get to the post office.'

'Oh no Kiki! Please don't do that. Please wear it. I bought it for you, and I can't bear the thought that you aren't wearing it.'

How can she wear his ring? It will just give him hope and she dare not do that. She puts it back in its little box and keeps it in the drawer with her underwear.

Conflicting thoughts tumble through her head during the day. Though she feels sorry for Gordon, surges of optimism and lightness run through her body as she thinks thoughts about her freedom.

Eventually she agrees to meet him on Saturday morning at the coffee shop down the road. Sally and Pat leave her with strict instructions to contact them should she need help. Though they are in a public place, she feels most uncomfortable. He tries to hold her hand, he calls her 'my Darling', but all she wants to do is run away. *What about me? Does he not know how I feel or don't my feelings matter?*

She is convinced now that she should not date men much older than her. It is also patently clear to her she doesn't need anyone to 'save' her, and she wants to stay free until she meets that special person who she is convinced is waiting for her too.

'Stay away from men! Just leave them alone, they aren't worth it.' Sally and Pat try to convince her that all men are useless.

Again, once more, the day arrives that she must go to Croydon, to the Home Office. Though she is carrying Keith's passport in her bag and knows he is present today in the UK, she is still nervous.

What if? What if they won't allow me into the building because I did not make an appointment? What if they ask more questions about things, I just don't have the answers to?

Armed with a smile to hide her lack of confidence, she tells the official at the door why she needs permission to go to the third floor with her husbands' passport. After a short wait in the queue, she leaves Keith's passport at reception, declining their offer to have it returned by post the following day. She can just imagine how 'happy' Keith will be if she tells him, it will take a few days before his passport arrives in Wales.

She is waiting at the cafeteria again. It could take up to five hours before she will be called. After three hours of sitting restlessly, watching, writing two poems, chatting to a Pakistani solicitor who is waiting on behalf of his Australian businesswoman client for her outcome, texting Keith, Wayne, Sam, Pat, and Kit, she feels like quitting on the spot.

Maybe I should just return to South Africa. Yes, I will leave the first week of October. Why am I putting myself through all this? They can keep their permission. Do I really need it? How much longer do I need to sit here, feeling like a beggar? Surely, being married to a UK citizen should carry more weight than the applications of some of these people who are sitting here now?

Finally, after five hours of waiting she hears her name called on the intercom. Standing behind counter number four, an official wait for her. 'Mrs. Brown?'

'Yes....' She replies hesitantly, not knowing what to expect. He hands her Keith's passport, a bag with all the documents they required for her application, including her South African passport.

'Congratulations. You now have Permanent Residency. You'll receive your card within two days. Keep it with you when you travel overseas. It is proof that you may live in the UK without time restrictions.'

Oh, my word! I have it. Finally, I have it. I have Permanent Residency.

She has accomplished her first goal. Now it is only one more year before she may apply for citizenship and her British passport. To qualify, she and Keith will have to stay married or else she will have to either find another British husband or wait until she has lived in the UK for a total of five years.

Her legs feel wobbly as she walks to the bus station to find the bus to Penge. When she gets there, she goes to the post office to post Keith's passport to Wales. While standing in a queue for a further twenty minutes, she must resist the temptation to tell the man in front of her about her great achievement for today. He complains about the slowness of the service, and she stays neutral – this is her home now and she doesn't want to be critical. Whatever, she will find it hard to find fault with anything in the UK today, especially the triviality of the slow service in a post office.

She needs to celebrate. She needs a friend to say: 'Well done. Congratulations!' The one person who *would* have been over the moon doesn't even know that she has been to the Home Office today. Gordon doesn't need to know, but she does feel pity for him. Now that she has her passport back, there is nothing to keep her from visiting South Africa. As soon as she can, she will buy a plane ticket. On her return she will take a good look at her future. She views herself and her life in the UK differently now: she is someone who belongs, who has the right to live on this side of the wall.

After so many months of worrying and planning, it feels strange not having to think about achieving Permanent Residency anymore. She texts Keith to thank him for flying from Ireland (albeit to visit his girlfriend) but still; he trusted her with his passport, and she is profoundly grateful for his assistance. He gave her the only thing he had to offer, and all she is asking him now, is that they stay married for a while longer.

She opens a bottle of red wine that she had kept for the occasion. She cannot expect anyone to understand how she feels tonight. Only she knows what it took out of her and what it means to her. *Cheers! Well done, Kiki, congratulations.*

Chapter 21

MAGIC AND MAGICIANS

The first letters she writes to him are polite and studious and not very spontaneous. She finds his openness attractive and when he confesses to her that he sometimes drinks too much beer and wine, she is surprised. Red lights, like large helium filled balloons, wave in her face. Like debris on a wave pushed there by the tide, she relentlessly moves closer to her next significant encounter.

Mike attracts her attention on the website because he is an artist, an enigma, and an author who has published a few books. He also presents danger, and she knows that she must be careful. Her instincts warn her to stay away, but at the same time it is as if this is predestined, something she has no control over.

When his son was still a young boy, he was an involved father, but now his son is a young man and has flown the nest. Mike feels that the time is ripe to start a new relationship. According to Mike, his mother is psychic, and he inherited the ability to 'see' things from her. That will then explain his interest in magic and the occult. Previously these were taboo topics for her, but now she wants to learn as much as possible about everything - even dark forbidden topics.

There is no rush for either of them to meet and for weeks they send each other the occasional letter, pictures of their art and different interesting topics. She is interested in his acoustic paintings, a form of art using melted, coloured bees' wax to create intricate images. To Kiki, the most impressive fact about him is his knowledge and experience of self-publishing. In fact, he has published four books and says he is prepared to help and guide Kiki, who wants to publish a book of her own poetry.

In a sense she doesn't expect to meet him physically; she is cautious about this mysterious man. But one Saturday evening he surprises her with a phone call. They chat for a long time and eventually they agree to meet in London the following day, Saturday.

'I'll be waiting for you under the clock at Waterloo Station at noon.'

By now she is quite adept at travelling by train from Penge Station to Victoria Station. Today the tube stops at Westminster because of work being done on the tracks. She must ask a stranger for directions to get to Waterloo Station from there.

'Just walk across the bridge. Waterloo is on the other side.'

To her surprise the beautiful building of Westminster is situated just outside the station. *Oh, my word! There is Big*

Ben, and the bridge is no other than the one that crosses the Thames. Thousands of tourists mill around, and she knows that she is here today because she is an adventurer, someone who wants to experience life. *How privileged am I!*

Mike is shy; he holds a book in his hand like a weapon; ready to protect himself from enemies lurking behind rubble. He is dressed in black and when she looks at his longish straight hair, it is as if she recognizes him from another lifetime. He reminds her of the man in a picture she painted almost a year ago. It is of a man with a cat sitting on his shoulder. Mike looks like that man.

The day is pure magic, and they discuss many different topics. Mike chose a Mexican restaurant on the banks of the Thames where they eat a meal and drink beer and wine. Their hands touch ever so lightly and before long they sit close to each other, wrapped in a cloud of togetherness. Their fingers enjoy the luxury of the silkiness of each other's skins.

Too soon it is time to go home again. They stand at the railings of the river Thames before they say their final good-bye. She shares with him a spiritual experience she had many years ago. In his dark eyes, through layers of curtains, she can see that he knows what she is talking about. His face changes in front of her eyes and he looks completely different from the shy man she spent all afternoon with. He looks at her intently. She is not sure if she knows how to interpret what's happening between them. The sun, sinking in the west, sprays light beams across the Thames changing everything it touches into gold.

'My god!' He exclaims. 'Look at you! You transformed in front of my eyes! You look as if you are seventeen years old!'

'And so do you!' she says in amazement.

Later, when she sits on the slow train from Victoria Station to Penge, she realizes that she still has his book in her bag. It is her token, a promise of future contact with him. As she walks home from the bus stop, she experiences an overwhelming feeling of sadness wrapping her as if in a cloak. Their souls touched for a moment and now she feels as if she has lost something precious.

When they chat on the phone again, he seems distant. 'I am in crab mode. I need time to digest what's happening between us. Please visit me at my apartment this weekend. I want to show you my books and art.'

He shares a birthday with Nelson Mandela, the South African President who spent many years in prison after being convicted for acts of terrorism. Mike is a typical Cancerian. She will soon learn that though he always returns from his hiding place, it is hard to know for how long she, a Pisces, must swim on her own, until he is ready.

On Saturday morning she feeds the dogs and then leaves by train to meet Mike in Walthamstow. The visit can only be for a few hours before she must return home to feed the dogs once more. Mike has an early morning shift at his work in London and will wait for her at the station after work.

When she steps off the escalator at Walthamstow station, he stands at the bottom waiting for her, holding his book in his hand. They board the number forty-eight bus and sit quietly next to each other. He is shy again, as if they've never met before or held hands. He points out his apartment as they drive past it. They are on their way to the canal where he wants to show her the narrowboats. When they get off the bus, he takes her hand to hold in his. She doesn't dare look into his dark brown eyes, afraid that she might scare him off, like a bird caught unawares by a pouncing cat. He can hardly contain his excitement. He wants to show her everything. Music, art, books, more books, more music. She listens to his favourite band, the Fall. He tells her about the Poison Girls, a rock group he admired in his youth, when he wrote about music and published and sold punk rock magazines.

He cooks a delicious vegetarian meal for them and forbids her to clean up afterwards. He shows her how he makes an acoustic painting and encourages her to experiment. Though she finds it interesting, she realizes the art form isn't for her – she prefers to draw and paint a picture.

She is in awe of this man who has no appreciation for convention and lives a plain and simple life, interspersed with art and writing. Before they leave the apartment to go to the bus stop, he takes her in his arms and holds her tightly against his lean body. He looks intently into her eyes. 'I am here for you Kiki. Don't ask too many questions. Just enjoy our friendship, one day at a time. I am your Magician, and you are my High Priestess,' he says.

He accompanies her on the forty- eight bus to Walthamstow tube station. 'See, there is the Dragon, the pub where we'll meet on Friday evening when you come for the weekend. It will be more convenient to meet there than at the station.'

In her bag she carries one of the books that he wrote and published. She starts to read it on the train, and though it is interesting, she finds it hard to concentrate; her mind is still digesting the richness of the few mystical hours they shared today.

Back at home she downloads the pictures that she took of the narrowboats and the selfies of Mike and herself. She can't help to wonder if these pictures are the beginning of a happy relationship or if it will only be a reminder of a fleetingly sweet moment in her life. Does it really matter? It appears to her as if she thrives on pain; her deepest memories last longer and hold more value than the easy, glib ones.

She sends him a piece that she has written about her experiences. He returns it with written comments: 'I get so angry with Keith when I read how he has treated you. I could happily give him a kick up his ass.' And then later: 'It makes me jealous to read this. I know this is your past and I shouldn't allow it to affect me, but still, it isn't easy……'

Despite his late-night calls, the tears and confirmation that he misses her, she feels that it is time to visit her family in South Africa. She hasn't seen them for nearly eighteen months and though there is no doubt in her mind that she will return to the UK, this is something she must do. Once she has returned to the UK, her life can continue and, hopefully, Mike will be part of it. Maybe then she will be able to move on and find a 'proper job.'

Though she is concerned that her job won't last much longer than just another few months, she's convinced that she's doing the right thing when she takes the bus to Bromley to visit a travel agent. They look at possible dates for flights to Cape Town via Istanbul from Gatwick airport. She selects a flight and return date and buys a ticket. Sally and Donald are still away on leave, and she sends a text with the news that she has planned to go away for three weeks the following month.

Her children will sort out suitable dates between them; they are all excited at the prospect of her visit. Though Mike isn't happy, he tries hard to release her: 'Damn you! How can you leave now? We've just met! Three weeks is too long!'

'It will pass quickly, you'll see. I'll phone you almost every day and we can speak on Facebook and email each other. Once I'm back, we can take it from there and this separation will just be part of our relationship.'

There is still one more weekend before she must leave. He invites her to visit him at his apartment.

'What are you going to wear? He asks her.

'I don't know. I have not decided yet. Probably black....'

'Yes, I want to see you in black - wear everything in black.'

He has made a disc with pictures of her paintings accompanied by music. 'Show your son this; let them see what you've done. I'm also making a compilation of music for your daughter and copies of my art that I'll post to her address. Keep your eye on the post. I'll send you many cards.'

They spend the weekend in his cave, reading, talking, listening to music, and making love. He shows her a draft of the book he is writing, a suspense novel set in America. She reads the chapters out loud while he is busy cooking a vegan meal in the tiny kitchen. Being together like this is so idyllic and she fears that it will be over too soon.

'Listening to my story being read out loud by you is so self-indulgent,' he says, while she traces the outline of the ankh tattoo on his shoulder with her finger.

She arranges for a taxi to take her to the station in Croydon. From there she takes a train to Gatwick Airport. She is so much more confident when she does her transit at Dubai Airport than she was the previous time and, fortunately, the stay over time is only three hours. Soon she is on the flight to South Africa and her mind is free to roam amongst the clouds until, half dazed after a sleepless night, the plane touches down at Cape Town airport.

She is delighted to see her grandson who looks at her shyly through his long lashes.

'What would you like to eat tonight?' Her son-in-law offers her a choice of lamb chops or snoek. He realizes that she would've missed both these favourite meals while living in the UK. When they arrive at their home and she greets the rest of the family, it feels as if she has never been away. Except for the centimetres each grandchild has grown and a few changes to the décor of the house, everything is still the same as it was before she left.

The following afternoon her eldest daughter and her husband come to collect her to take her to their farm for a visit. That evening, while sitting on her bed in their guest room, her second daughter phones her. It is wonderful to be able to chat with her, knowing she is not too far away. Though they laugh and giggle she realizes that, although she misses them all while she is in the UK, they are all busy, doing their own thing. Perhaps she is here more for herself than for them. She needs to experience their daily rhythms and everyday existence, put it into her heart and then, replenished, move on again.

Once she has seen the new baby, she feels satisfied: mission accomplished.

Her son is on holiday in Croatia and once he returns towards the end of her visit, she will stay with him and his family for a few nights in Muizenberg before she returns to the UK.

Soon she drives the grandchildren to school and sporting activities. It makes her wonder how her daughters manage every day. It must be awfully hard to juggle their careers between being dutiful wives and mothers of growing children.

When she notices the winter sales in the shops, she goes on a spending spree. The polka dot suitcase is much emptier now since all the baby clothes Sally sent for the new-born have been handed over, and she has room for a few winter bargains.

Her youngest's life is also terribly busy. Having a full-time job and looking after two young children is not an easy task. If only she could have been here to help them all.

One evening after work they go to Franschhoek to visit her mother's grave. Her youngest brother accompanies them. Finally, she puts flowers on the hard soil where her mother lies buried next to her father's grave. Being of French Huguenot descent, it is apt that they are buried here. The valley was previously called Elephants Corner, when elephant herds would come down from the mountains to calve there in summer. But when the Huguenots came here with their Bibles, vines wrapped in cloths and extensive knowledge of wine farming, the name changed to 'French Corner.'

It is windy and cold tonight - as it usually is in spring in this beautiful town. Dark clouds rush down the mountain towards the valley as if they're on the rampage, needing to attack all and sundry. She takes her time to say the 'goodbye' that she couldn't achieve last year in October when her mother had died.

Since the children are safe at home in the care of their nanny, they can enjoy a meal in one of the town's many trendy restaurants. The pleasure of speaking Afrikaans and being in the company of family is almost too much for her to bear.

The following day, she receives an email from Sally. They have experienced some bad luck, and though she will give her an excellent reference, and will do her best to assist her to find another position, they can't keep her on as their au pair any longer.

Oh my, what bad timing! It was so expensive to take this holiday, for which she waited so long, and now this has to happen! When she tells Mike the news, he sees it as a bad sign and tells her in his typical 'Mike style' what he thinks about the situation.

'My dear Mari Celeste, as your Sorcerer, I have a message for you that I want you to take seriously. The fact that you have now lost your job while you are in South Africa is a bad omen. Why don't you stay with your family in South Africa? What do you want to do here in this God-forsaken wet island in any case? Looking on Google maps, seeing what a beautiful place Cape Town is with 'Coffee' Table Mountain, I think you'd be crazy to come back here. This is surely a sign that you shouldn't return. I'll visit you there one day......'

'I hear what you say, but I'm not inclined to want to stay, Mike. If I had really wanted to, nothing would've prevented me. But right now, I feel I have a task to finish, and whatever it is, I want to be there to complete it. Don't be concerned about me, I'll soon find another job.'

'Whatever your decision, know that should anything go wrong, you are welcome to stay with me until something comes up. I could never let you be destitute.'

'Don't be concerned Mike. I've always found work when I've needed it and you'll see, it won't be necessary to help me. I do appreciate your gesture but trust me, I know I'll be fine.'

Whether he is convinced or not is not her concern. All she knows is that she could never disturb the crab in his cave; it would freak him out completely! Once again, this struggle is hers, only she can figure out her next steps.

So, the next day she opens the Au-pair website once more and unhides her profile: 'I am 64 years old with 25 years' experience as an estate agent. I hold a degree in Psychology and worked as an au pair in various places in the UK the last two years. I am the grandmother you have been looking for to care for your children.'

The website has been kind to her more than once before and lo and behold, Jack, a single father, is looking for a driver to take Danny, his six-year-old son, to school and back. He would also like his new au pair to do the shopping, laundry, cooking, and general housekeeping. Kiki tells him that she'll get in touch with him as soon as she is back in the UK.

Though it all seems positive, she has an uneasy feeling about her future. The sensation of dread regarding Mike is also getting more intense each day.

Soon she'll see her son and she start to focus on their imminent meeting. When they finally collect her on Saturday it feels as if they had seen each other only a few weeks ago. *If ever I were to live in South Africa again, I wouldn't mind living on this side of the mountain, underneath the shadow of Table Mountain.* It is a very cosmopolitan area, and the rough sea touches the hem of the mountainous terrain which makes the scenery completely breath-taking.

For the duration of the flight back from Cape Town, first to Dubai, and from there to Heathrow airport, she is annoyed that she chose a window seat. The irritating thing is that she must ask the Japanese student and the British lady, returning from Australia, to leave their seats when she needs to use the toilet. But then, as the plane descends above London on its way to Heathrow, the clouds open briefly and there, like a spotlight shining on sparkling diamonds, lie London Bridge, Big Ben, the Wheel and the Thames, all greeting her with smiling faces. This was the reason, then, why she had to sit here: so that she could see these sights and burn them into her memory forever.

'Here we are Mike: me and my polka dot suitcase. We have made it through the tunnel.' She is standing on the plane, texting him as they wait to disembark. She is in a rush, counting the days before she can see him again. How nice it would have been if she could have gone directly to Walthamstow! Technically she doesn't have a job anymore and though she will have to work for her lodging, she doesn't expect to be paid. Hopefully, she and Jack can sort out her new position soon so that she can stop worrying.

She walks with trepidation to the front door of the house that has been her home for the past eight months. Though she has a key to the front door in her bag, she doesn't feel at ease to let herself in. She rings the doorbell and Pat's daughter comes to open the door.

'Oh, look! It is Kiki!' The dogs are happy to see her. The baby's smile is hesitant and guarded. She reminds herself that three weeks was quite a long time to have been away for a child of her young age.

Pat is visiting Sally and though they enquire about her visit, she senses a slight tension between them and her. She tries hard not to show her discomfort, commenting on the couch that has been moved to the open plan kitchen area, and the baby's new play pen that covers half the floor space of the room.

She carries her luggage upstairs to her room and then brings down the gifts she has brought from South Africa. The next day she tackles the laundry and ironing and does the tasks just as if she were still going to be paid. It is hard, though, to unpack and settle in, when she knows that she must leave soon again. Initially she doesn't tell them that she might have found another job, hoping against all hope that they might have a change of heart and invite her to stay on.

As the weekend draws closer, she starts to feel paranoid and stressed about seeing Mike again. She finds it hard to focus on her 'work' and wishes precious time away. She only relaxes once she sees him standing at the bar counter in the Dragon where he is buying drinks.

Mike likes the African burial mask and the Mandela fridge magnet she brought him. He is also delighted to see her again. His usual initial shyness wears off quickly and he sits close to her while they ride together on the bus to his apartment. They spend the rest of the weekend inside.

Early on Saturday morning he leaves her still sleeping to go to work for a few hours. When she wakes up, she washes the dishes and sweeps the dust off the bathroom floor. It had bothered her since the first time she came to his apartment. Though attracted to his bohemian lifestyle, she is essentially a homemaker and to her, dirt is something that needs to be erased.

'So, what have you been up to while I was away?' He looks suspiciously in the direction of the kitchen and notices that the dishes are washed and left to dry on the side of the basin.

'Mm, I have to earn my stay…. I swept the bathroom floor too,' she admits hesitantly; afraid that he might think that she was in any way disapproving or critical.

'Why did you have to do that Mari Celeste? Don't you know that dirt is just part of life? Why would you waste your time cleaning when you know it will just return? Leave the dirt!'

Unsure of what to say or how to react, she smiles and shrugs her shoulders - she is at a loss for words.

'I'm a cleaner you know! This is what I do for a living. I take care of children and I clean and tidy homes.' She walks into his outstretched arms, and he holds her close, but she suspects that she has broken an unspoken rule.

'Jack will fetch me on the fifteenth. I have too much stuff to carry on a train. I think he is so relieved to finally find someone who will help him, that he will do anything to get me there in one piece. So, we have one more weekend before I leave. How on earth shall we manage to see each other once I live in the country?'

'Don't worry Mari Celeste, I'll visit you wherever you are. We might even find a nice place en-route where we can stay together for a weekend. I'll find you; you'll see.'

Before she leaves him, he hands her three discs of music that he compiled plus six laminated caustic art pictures that he copied. He walks with her to the bus stop where they hug and kiss each other as the bus pulls up. As the bus drives past his front door, he already stands in front of it. He waves at her, but she doesn't wave back as she knows he can't see her where she is sitting.

This isn't a good time for me, she thinks. She feels terrible. Not only is she sad to have to leave Sally and Poppy next week, but she feels anxious about her new position. The prospect of moving to a new family is always scary: she never knows what awaits her.

But the biggest concern for her is the intensity with which she misses Mike. It is an unease, one that she suspects he might also suffer from. They are both terrified of being hurt and though they're attracted to each other, neither one of them welcomes or enjoys this feeling.

On Tuesday evening she receives an e- mail from him: 'I am in crab mode, but you can phone me if you want to.'

Her mouth is dry, and her heart feels heavy. Having to stay here with the family this weekend will be difficult when she had pinned all her hopes on a visit to Mike's cave. She depends on his hospitality. After all, he had offered to let her stay with him until she found a new position. Now that she doesn't need that anymore, surely it won't be a problem if she stays for just a weekend. The phone call doesn't go well. He asks her when she wants to come, Friday or Saturday? She says that he should tell her when he wants her to come.

'My son wants to visit me this weekend. I'm also missing my friend Ricky; I haven't seen him for a while,' he tells her.

'Mike, tell me on Thursday when you want me to come. Decide when you want to spend time with your son; I don't mind that you must work on Saturday; I just want to see you before I leave. But, if you feel that I'm crowding you, I'll understand.'

She decides not to contact him again and waits for him to phone her. It's not easy to stay calm and she practices her breathing. She keeps looking at her phone in case he leaves her a text or WhatsApp message. She only opens her emails the next morning after a restless night.

'I know this is probably going to mess with your head, but I've decided to terminate our relationship. I'm not ready for this; I've been on my own for too long. I would still love to see your book come to fruition, so please send me your poems to read. I hope we can still stay friends.'

Kiki goes into complete denial. Feeling trapped, she realizes that she had to get out of the house. Clay, her South African friend from Nottingham, has invited her many times to visit him and his family and she has always made excuses. This is then the ideal opportunity to visit. After the weekend it will be three days before Jack will arrive to fetch her. She will start to pack on Monday.

On Friday afternoon, instead of taking the tube from Victoria Station to Walthamstow, she goes to St Pancras International and takes the West Midlands train to Nottingham. 'No tears, no tears, no tears,' says the speeding train. She buries her nose in Anais Nin's book, Delta of Venus, which she had borrowed from Mike.

Clay is the perfect host and spoils her by showing her around and taking her out for meals. They drive around in the Nottingham region, and he tells her about the Industrial Revolution which began in England in 1760. They eat lunch in an ancient pub, Ye Olde Trip to Jerusalem. It is built into stone caves, filled with memorabilia to match the historical building and resident ghosts. Too soon, he must take her to the station again and she travels back to London.

Tired and desperately hurting for and missing Mike, she retraces her steps back to Victoria Station, looking longingly back at the blue Victoria line leading towards Walthamstow. *I should have been returning from there tonight.*

As Kiki boards the bus to return home from the station, she puts her Freedom Pass in her purse. It's probably the last time in a long while that she will make use of public transport. There are still so many places she wants to see and visit in London. Maybe later, maybe one day she will return.

Chapter 22

THE LIE OF HOPE

Kiki put everything she owns in the hallway. She takes a picture of her belongings with her mobile phone and sends a WhatsApp message to her daughter: 'Here are all my possessions, ready for my new home.'

The polka dot suitcase that is always at the centre of her moves shows signs of abuse – who knows where else it will travel to before it finally breaks. She doesn't know why she feels embarrassed about the amount of stuff she owns. Very few women could fit all their worldly possessions into the boot of a car. Hopefully, Jack drives a big car with a huge boot.

Her old room looks bare and empty without her paintings and bits and pieces. Just to make sure she hasn't forgotten anything; she goes upstairs one final time. During her eight- month stay in this room, she cried many tears. She also often smiled and praised herself when things went better than expected. From this room, she undertook two long distance trips: one to Qatar in May and one more recently when she visited her family in South Africa. Obtaining her Permanent Residency was probably the biggest achievement managed from this room. She also made new friends and left a few old ones behind, those who did not fit into the place where she found herself at this stage of her life's adventure.

Today she has to say goodbye to her little girl - dear Poppy, whom she met when she was still a seven-week-old floppy and uncommunicative baby. She is such a little star and Kiki would have loved to have seen how she grows and develops.

Sally joins Kiki to wait for Jack's arrival. When they hear a car drive past the house, they look out of the window to see if it might be him. The dogs have been put into their cages in anticipation of his arrival. Finally, Kiki receives a text to tell her he has arrived.

After a last hug, she returns Poppy to her mother's arms and put her keys into her outstretched hand. This is it then – time to step off the cliff....

Though she had hoped that by now her life would be different and she would have her own place to live in and a different type of job, she still has many things to be grateful for.

This moment of leaving a familiar place to step over a cliff to reach the next, the unfamiliar, must be the most daunting time for a new au pair. It makes it easier if she closes the door behind her, cuts the ties and stops comparing the old with the new. What is in the past is in the past. She is blessed to have wonderful memories of living with this young family.

She is lucky that each time that she has moved, her situation has improved. Her workload becomes more manageable – thank heavens for that, since she is getting older and finds she doesn't enjoy doing repetitive tasks. Despite the sense of dread at the thought of what might wait for her behind the locked door of the new house, she hopes she will be happy there and that life will at least treat her with respect. She is much stronger emotionally than the day when she left Wales nearly two years ago and she is incredibly grateful for that alone.

She marvels at the way Jack drives through London without consulting the Satnav or a map. He seems to know every street on their way! When they cross the Thames over London Bridge, she is once again completely enthralled.

They arrive at her new home. There is a room waiting for her; a family waits for her to serve them. There will be daily school trips, food shopping to do, laundry, ironing and companionship for a boy who reaches out to her for her attention. Long days stretch into evenings while they wait in front of the fire for Jack to arrive home from work. She attends parent's evenings and gives feedback late at night when he arrives home.

While an exhausted Jack sleeps in over weekends, Kiki stays at home to keep the boy company. Often, while the boy is at school, she escapes the house and goes on trips to the Chiltern Hills. Kiki tells herself that she's doing all right, she's fine. She writes poems; she paints and works hard to forget that Mike ever entered her thoughts and life. One morning she takes his books, his paintings and gifts, tears everything into the smallest pieces possible and dumps the lot into the rubbish bin. There, finally he is gone, there is nothing physical left to remind her of him. That night rats choose to go running in the ceiling just meters above her bed, keeping her awake long after her usual sleeping time.

Her major goal - to get her British Passport - is only three years away. One day she will get divorced from Keith and surely many opportunities still await her.

During the seven months she stays in the basement room without a door, she saves a few pounds. She can take long walks, listen to kites call their mates, but she must wonder where she is emotionally positioned in all of this. It's a long, hard winter and each day her toes are clad in thermal socks. Waiting, always waiting for Spring, which seems to take forever to arrive.

The mysterious world of a website for lonely souls holds its own mysteries; an ebb and flow of life, hiding risks of either mental anguish or moments of joy. Like the kites calling above the trees, she calls for a mate, a life partner. And, one day, she meets him.

'Hi. I realized I missed you,' his message reads on the dating website. They met for the first time a few months ago, but then he disappeared again.

'Hi. It's nice to see you here again. Why did you leave after we got on so well?' she asks him. She's intrigued. When they first 'met' virtually in June, they were very attracted to each other. Though she felt safe with the distance between them, she enjoyed his intense, direct conversations. Although he said he would come to meet her in London one day, she knew the chances of this happening were very slim. After all, Scotland is not just down the road. And then, one day, he disappeared from the website and blocked her on his Facebook Page. For days she pondered this and eventually conceded he must have a reason and there was nothing she could do other than accept and respect it.

'I was developing feelings for you, and I wasn't ready for it.'

'Are you ready now?'

'Yes, and I'd like to get to know you better.'

It doesn't take long before they close their profiles on the website. Sean phones her every evening and they stay in contact during the day via texts and WhatsApp.

'Next year I'll fetch you and then we'll be together forever.' Her ears strain to hear these words and her heart races when she hears how he pronounces her name.

'I have a big family and we're awfully close. You'll become part of my family and they'll accept and love you.'

Finally, she has something to look forward to. Someone is prepared to share his life with her and wants her to be part of his family. Sean's phone calls become her lifesaver during her dark moments. She doesn't want a long-term relationship without meeting the object of her desires and she suggests that they meet in Scotland after Christmas. She needs a break, but she also needs to push her boundaries to see if there might be a hole in the wall.

Keith texts her from Spain. He moved there to start his new job as an estate agent. He wishes her a happy Christmas, but she banishes thoughts of him. Whatever. He ignored her request to let her have the car that was bought with their joint money and is now (she imagines) standing unused in Wales. Recently, she and Jack jointly completed a practical course on positive attitudes. As one of the tasks she had to perform, focusing on positivity in their relationship, she had to write Keith a letter. She remembered many happy moments in their marriage, and she thanked him for those good times. Though a hard thing to do, it made her feel good and then, thinking nothing of it, she sent him a copy. To her surprise, he replied to her letter the same day. 'Thank you very much for this. I'll always keep the letter.'

In a few hours, she will be flying high in the open sky as far North in the United Kingdom as one can go. Perhaps the Scottish Highlands will invigorate her and give her a new perspective on her life. Also, she will finally meet Sean in person! Their plan is to spend the next five days together and they are both beyond excited.

Once she hears the engine of an approaching car snaking closer on the snowed-under road leading to Jack's home, the first layer of worry abruptly drops off her shoulders. With relief, she slips into the heated front seat of the Mercedes. The other layers - to be stripped off her like the peels of an onion - will be to board the plane, find the taxi at the airport in Scotland and finally meet Sean in person. Then, and only then, will she be able to relax.

Lately she has noticed that she is less fearful of being on her own in this country. Living here now is somehow different; the mystery and attraction of England have become slightly tarnished. Its petticoats are a bit tacky, as if protruding from beneath the hem of a dress. It took her a while to realise, but the people who live here are just ordinary people, the same as anywhere else in the world. It is not the magical place that she was so overawed about when she first came here.

'Madam! Unzip your laptop bag and place your handbag inside with your laptop.'

It is hard to believe that EasyJet is serious about their 'one bag only' rule. Really? Is this the solution? While clutching her laptop bag against her chest with her handbag sticking out, she feels thoroughly unglamorous while boarding the plane. Now she carries one bag only and she isn't breaking any airline rules.

Oh, what a glorious feeling it is to fly high above the UK! Beneath us I can see rows and rows of homes where people are sleeping right now, dreaming about what to do with the leftover turkey from yesterdays' Christmas lunch.

As if on cue the carpet of clouds opens above Scotland. The plane glides over mile upon mile of white, snow covered mountains. Her eyes fill with tears. *This is so beautiful. I didn't expect to see this spectacle at all.*

There is still an hour to think about her expectations of meeting Sean. Her tummy takes a tumble. Once again, she reads the text he sent her early this morning: 'My darling, I'll wait for you outside the Wetherspoon's in Hope Street. I'm so nervous, but I know we'll get on fine. I can't wait to see you for the first time.'

Jack was concerned about her and for her safety. 'Don't worry Jack. I'll be fine. It's only for five days and whatever happens, I'll stay in the hotel where I'll rest and relax. However, I think I know this man by now and honestly, I've never met someone who has been there for me every step of the way as much as he's been. He ticks all my boxes and I just know we're meant for each other.'

The weirdos and unsuitable men she's met or spoken to on the internet deserve a whole chapter in a book, but they have made her realize that Sean is genuine and sincere.

Trying to ignore the sceptical look on Jack's face, she looked down at her hands. Why do they look so old and the skin so dry? She should take better care of herself. This is her life, her path to travel and only she can walk it.

Still, as the plane glides above the snow-covered mountains, she can't help but wonder if her impressions of Sean are going to match the person she is shortly going to meet.

Almost too soon, the town becomes visible from her window and the plane lands at the small airport. The taxi driver has transported too many passengers from the airport to the town in his lifetime and he isn't interested in her small talk. Instead, she marvels at the snow-covered trees and plants along the way.

'I'm waiting for you, my darling. I'm outside already. Oh, my word! I'm so excited....'

She knows this man; it is as if they've known each other for a long time. They greet like old friends and the taxi driver, putting her case down on the sidewalk, would never have guessed that this was the first time they had set eyes on each other.

Sean takes her case and pulls it into his regular watering hole. 'This is where I usually sit with my friends.' He points to a table where a group of men huddle over their beers. However, he steers her case to the furthest side of the room, and they take place at a table, sitting opposite each other. It is the first time they can take a proper look at each other. Their eyes meet and they glimpse simultaneously at each other. He looks slightly different from the pictures she has seen on Face Book. He is shorter than she is, has a short ginger beard and little hair on top of his scalp that look a bit straggly around his ears. Wouldn't he have had time to trim it, or doesn't it bother him? She banishes these observations to the back of her mind and says while she looks into his light blue eyes: 'We'll be okay.'

'We'll be okay,' he agrees. He leans across the table and gently kisses her on her lips. 'What would you like to drink?' His soft and gentle voice makes her want to drink fountains of dry white wine. She is so relaxed now; she could sit here with him for the rest of her life. Right now, she feels proud of their achievement, of doing this thing. Proud of her journey here to the other side of the UK, and filled with anticipation for him, Sean, joining her here.

'My son lives with me in my apartment and since he sleeps on the couch, the place isn't tidy.' That makes sense, but she wishes she could see where and how he lives.......

They finish their meal and walk across the bridge towards the other side of the river to the hotel where she has reserved a room. It isn't far to walk and as they go along; he points out places of interest to Kiki.

'This is Ranger's, the pub where we'll come later tonight to listen to Scottish music. There is the castle and over there is the pedestrian bridge that bounces when many people cross it at the same time.' He greets familiar faces; people he says he knows from previously working with them.

Who would have thought that Scotland would be so Scottish? There are many tourist shops specialising in selling tartans, scarves, souvenirs, shortbread, Celtic jewellery, postcards of the castle and memorabilia of Loch Ness. If she were to ever live in Scotland, she would probably wear tartan skirts and scarves!

Sean takes her to visit Leakey's, the famous bookshop. It is in the beautiful building that was built in 1793 as a Gaelic church. Now, thousands of second-hand books are displayed on shelves placed against the walls of the building, almost touching the high ceilings.

In the evening Kiki and Sean stand side by side at a bar listening to traditional Scottish music played by a bagpipe band. The bar is packed with interesting punters, locals and tourists.

Sean has arranged an excursion to visit Loch Ness on Sunday afternoon. They join a group of tourists on a bus, which travels to the river where they board a boat. Though it's bitterly cold, they witness a gorgeous sunset through the glass windows of the boat. She pinches herself! Here is she, Kiki, in Scotland, sitting close to Sean on a boat sailing on Loch Ness while she takes photos of Urquhart castle. It is freezing cold as they walk around the castle area. Afterwards, they visit the curio shop where they view a movie about the castle's history. As the movie ends, curtains open to reveal the lit-up castle, etched against the night sky. The sight leaves her and Sean speechless - what an unexpected gift of beauty!

The fact that her maternal great grandmother was of Scottish descent connects her to this country and she is eager to learn more about her ancestors.

On Monday morning Sean must go to work and Kiki wanders around the shops on her own. When he arrives back at the hotel after work, they are delighted to be united again.

'I love you darling, and I want to see you again once you have returned to England.'

She gets tearful at the thought of leaving him behind in Scotland. Sean surprises her and shows her his newly bought train ticket to her place of residence and work. 'Look what I got today! I'm coming to visit you for your birthday in February.' It's still a while, but at least they have something to look forward to.

Too soon her five days in Scotland are over, and she must return home. When Sean greets her in the morning on his way to work, he places around her neck the silver Celtic cross that he always wears on a chain around his own neck.

'Keep this with you until we meet again, darling.' This is the type of thing *she* would normally do, and it touches her deeply that a man would want to link himself to her in this poignant manner.

It takes one and a half hours to fly to London, but her mind travels far and wide during this short time. How different her life has become since that day in January 2012 when Keith and she were pushed into a corner and forced to look at different options for their survival. She doesn't have the inclination to think how things could have worked out differently if they had made other decisions – she is just glad they didn't take options one or three – that she didn't have to live in the Transkei as a hermit or have to walk into the cold ocean to end her uncompleted life!

She has come a long way since then. Never in her wildest dreams could she have imagined that Keith would leave her, and she would have to take care of herself in a strange country. It took a while to reach closure, but she now realizes that he had other intentions and did her a great favour in the long run. What would she have done then if she had realized then that this, the fourth, undiscussed option would become her reality? Would it have been easier or wiser if she had stayed in South Africa on her own? Would she have come to the UK had she known how hard it would be to find a position as an estate agent there? *Would she, Kiki Brown, have become an au pair? What an unlikely idea!*

And yes, though it took a lot of pain and time, she has changed so much. She is much stronger and more independent now. At least she can take care of herself - albeit not perfectly; but she is learning about her capabilities and how to deal with unique challenges.

Perhaps she really needed to come to 'soft' soil and pour herself into it. Who will ever know how much she really meant to others? She is appreciated and valued where she lives and works now.

Though she is often asked why she doesn't return home to live with her children, her reply to that question is always straight and to the point. *While I am strong and capable of making a life for myself in the UK, I want to experience life here and see as much as possible of the country. Soon, my goal will be realized when I can apply for British citizenship.*

Since she has met Sean, she has given up her internet friendships. It was time to let go of that addiction. The lessons she needed to learn about dating and relationships have been learnt. Some of the friends she has made are amazing and she can only thank the Universe for putting her in touch with them. Many make her smile, some make her cry, and some are simply ridiculous.

Finally, though, she has met someone special who says he wants her to be waiting for him when he returns home from work. 'You can paint and write, and I just want you to be happy. You will never have to look after someone else's baby or live with other people in a spare room in their house where you always feel like a guest. I need you in my life and we're going to have so much fun……'

It is obvious to her she'll soon move to Scotland.

'Can I be your Wednesday man for one more time? If you're free on Wednesday, I want to take you out for lunch.'

She has a few hours free on Wednesday. It would be so nice to see Kit again. It's quite strange, but she doesn't feel guilty that Sean is in the dark about her arrangement.

She is starting a new chapter in her life – she is done with living with other people in their homes. Finally, she will live in a place with someone who wants to have her there to share everything with him.

'Stay in touch with your friends,' a little voice in her head tells her. 'You never know when you might need them.......'

Chapter 23

DISILLUSION

Kiki is surprised to see how strained Sean appears. He is waiting for her at the airport arrivals hall. She forgot they were both the same height, but now her boots make her appear slightly taller than him. He has taken a day off from work to fetch her.

She gets another surprise: the feeling of elation she expected, after an absence of ten weeks, isn't there. When they met up in February in London, they agreed that the next time they would see each other, it would be 'next time... forever.' Now, finally, after packing her cases, posting her boxes to his apartment, stressing about the travel arrangements, and craving a change in her circumstances, she has finally arrived in Scotland to start a new life with Sean as her partner.

As they walk towards the bus terminus, she fights the impulse to hail a taxi. After all, she had a tough time getting here, and she is in a hurry to get to her new home. But now, being with Sean means she must accept that they will make use of public transport wherever they go. Though they never really discussed finances in finer detail, she must assume that taking a bus to work every day defines their mode of future transport. Soon, she should have a job and then they can buy a car. She will have to be the driver since Sean doesn't hold a driver's licence.

Sean decides that they should first go to Wetherspoons for a drink. Today the ambience appears to be unfriendly and dismal, which doesn't lift Kiki's spirits. She wonders if she might persuade Sean to occasionally visit a different pub or restaurant. She realizes that food and drinks are cheaper here, but sometimes one should celebrate in style and in an unfamiliar environment.

Eventually they're ready to go 'home.' An Arctic wind rushes down the street from the direction of the snow-covered mountains. It teases her hair and blows a strand into her mouth. Kiki huddles deeper into her thick coat. 'If this is spring, I wonder what summer will be like?'

'Summer?' Sean laughs. 'My darling, you'll soon notice that summer is a season that comes and goes without being noticed. Come, follow me, this is where we go in.'

Her heart, already heavy after noticing the dismal street where the only decorations are blue and green garbage bins, the cold wind, a future without summer and the reality of Sean and her pulling her two cases towards her future home, takes a further battering when she notices that the concrete floor leading towards a blue door at the end of the corridor is bare and unpainted.

Sean unlocks his front door, and they step inside the small reception hall. She looks around with anticipation, but only the kitchen is visible. There are three doors, each one shut. Kiki finds the smell of stale cigarette smoke overpowering and she suppresses a sneeze. Sean opens the bedroom door and puts her cases down inside the small room. He closes the door again and opens the lounge door to reveal a small two-seater couch covered with a throw, a round glass- top table with three chairs, a display cabinet, a bookshelf, and a small television set.

'I cleared a wardrobe out for you and bought a couple of clothes hangers. Now, darling, you have your very own space where you can do your own thing. This is the sofa where I sat every night watching TV, waiting for you to arrive. From now on, we'll sit here together.'

His words sound hollow as if they're tumbling through a tunnel - like leaves blown there by a malevolent wind. Sure, she'll have her own wardrobe, but the room is so small that she struggles to open the door and not scrape it against the bed. She unpacks her suitcases. *What is stored in the boxes on top of the wardrobes?* The wallpaper, partially stripped off the wall facing the bed, makes Kiki wonder what inspired it. Why would anybody tear wallpaper off a wall and then leave the project incomplete?

When Sean goes to work the following day, she begins her investigation. There is hardly any food in the fridge and the coffee container is almost empty. *What will we eat for dinner tonight?* Something is amiss and she must search for clues. *A shortage of funds? A lack of money? Or maybe he is just clueless.*

After all, they come from different backgrounds and cultures. Does he need her to direct and guide him? No, that is not what she thinks and nor how she sees her future. She remembers their conversation about the prospect of maybe living in South Africa one day…… 'Life is awfully expensive there. We'll need lots of money to survive. I don't know about you, but I don't have enough savings, yet to be able to afford it,' she told him.

'I have some savings and my pension will be paid out shortly. First come here, my darling, and then we'll discuss our future. Once you're here, I'll pay for a subscription at the gymnasium for you.'

She is convinced there is an explanation for the lack of food and material possessions. But she needs to eat properly. Maybe he is waiting for his next pay- check at the end of the month. She hopes he isn't under the impression that she is wealthy. But why didn't he tell her what the lie of the land was?

On Saturday morning, they go to the shop to buy milk and coffee. She needs a few personal things and so her spending starts. From the moment her bank balance dwindles, she realizes she must find a job as soon as possible.

Kiki puts her details on a website for childcare. There are a few positions to consider as a babysitter and she completes the required forms online. Within days she takes a bus to meet a single mother for her first interview.

They drive in her car to the boy's nursery school. Naomi shows Kiki where to get on and off bus number sixty-eight. It sounds daunting, having to collect the boy from his nursery school and taking him back to his home, but her employer offers to pay her seven pounds per hour and beggars can't be choosers. She'll have to pretend she is stronger than she really is. At least there is the prospect of a few pounds to be earned while she searches for a proper job.

She wakes up in the morning to stare at the torn wallpaper. She thinks of the dismal street where she now lives and feels thoroughly depressed. Sean has taken ten days' leave to show her around the town and be able to spend time with her. It is impossible to suppress her tears. Sean comes to sit next to her on the side of the bed.

'What's the matter, darling? Why are you crying? You should be happy that we're together now. I know this is a big change for you, but please, try not to cry.'

'When I look at the torn wallpaper, it makes me depressed. I worry about money. What is your position, Sean? You told me that I could relax and won't have to work initially, but now it seems as if you can't afford to have me here. The little money I have saved isn't enough for us both and really, that wasn't my idea when I came here.'

'Don't worry darling. We'll be fine.' She is baffled that she struggles to blend the image of the person she met online with the actual person who sits here next to her. It's difficult to imagine that she planned to spend the rest of her life with him. The situation seems like a biscuit with a cream filling that bulges between the two sides but refuses to make one whole biscuit.

But she can't help but worry. She is concerned about his lack of openness with her. This isn't what she pictured nor what she dreamed of. She's shocked to find her heart has grown cold so easily. What happened to the love she felt over a long distance for this man who supported her so wonderfully? Is she shallow, so materialistic? What happened to the woman who thought she would live in a cave with the right person if she loved him?

Sean has a work interview scheduled for a more senior position. His friends and work colleagues tell him he is the best candidate for the job. On the morning of the interview, he dresses with care; she bought him a new shirt and tie as a token of her support. She senses his anxiety. He really wants this opportunity, and her heart goes out to him. A few days later he arrives home with a serious expression on his face. His hopes are dashed. Somebody else has been appointed and he must continue to work for the same salary doing the same monotonous job.

She spends her days searching for jobs in both the newspaper and on the internet. Maybe she should make one more attempt to find a position as an estate agent? Perhaps they are not as ageist in Scotland as they appear to be in England. She applies for three different positions and promptly gets invited to an interview. The franchise also operates in South Africa, and she understands their modus operandi. Sean walks with her to their office and on the way there, they go to the local NHS surgery. The receptionist is obese and has masses of facial hair. Kiki must provide proof of address to be registered as a patient. She changed her address at the bank a few days ago but will have to wait for a letter to arrive in the post. She feels reluctant to register at this surgery. Perhaps she should wait awhile; she has enough medication to last her for a few weeks.

The owner of the property company explains that she must put down one thousand two hundred pounds deposit to join them as an agent. That is not all – they also expect a monthly desk fee of one hundred and fifty pounds. Obviously, she will also need to buy a car.

'Would you like any referee's contact details or see my property related certificates?' She is surprised at the woman's eagerness to employ her. Is she only interested in her one thousand two hundred pounds?

'No, I'm happy with what I've seen. There is a training course in fourteen days in the city. If you want to join the company, you could do the training then.' Kiki isn't convinced at all that this is the position for her. She'll have to keep searching....

Sean shows her where Iceland, Poundstretcher, Poundland and all the 'cheaper' shops are located. Defiantly, when she must buy food, she goes to Marks and

Spencer's and shows him how, for a few pennies more, they can make a fresh, quality meal. She feels like a spoilt brat. *How hard will it be to adapt to a life of skimping, of getting by... of not having.* She has already given up so much; how much more will she have to forfeit? What will she receive in exchange for it? Love? Is this it? She resists the 'poor' mentality and struggles to come to terms with this strange twist her life has taken.

Eventually, after many sleepless nights, she relents and admits defeat. When her daughters phone her on South African Mother's Day, she cries pitifully and is pleased Sean doesn't understand Afrikaans: 'I've made a huge mistake. It's not at all what I expected it to be. I'm furious with myself.' There, she has made an admission to the world and to herself.

She asks their opinion: should she invest to improve the material lack of comfort – should she buy rugs, paint the walls, do things to make the flat look and feel cosier?

'No Mum. If he isn't bothered, leave it as it is.' She already bought towels, a throw, two gold rimmed wine glasses, porridge bowls, olive oil and other bits and pieces.

Even though she is preparing herself mentally, she is in no rush to leave. Something is bound to happen. She might find a good job as an estate agent; she might even adapt to her new life in Scotland and get used to the man who was so different from the one she had got to know on the internet. Perhaps the sides of the biscuit will move and shape themselves into a third person. Maybe she will get used to the cold, drab life she is enduring now. She must be patient and not rush into something she might later regret. As things are now, she doesn't have many options. She has nowhere to run to, nowhere to go to when she leaves here.

She sleeps badly. The noise in her head and the fluttering of her heart take a long time to subside when she wakes up in the middle of the night, damp with perspiration despite the freezing cold room. Seagulls trample with their webbed claws on the roof in the middle of the night. *What are they doing here so far from the sea?* She wonders. But it is not far from the sea. The ocean is just a block away from their apartment. It isn't the type of sea she is familiar with though.

Through the paper-thin walls she can hear the angry voices of the arguing neighbours. She listens to the front door opening with a thud and then the sound of boots treading down the cement floor in the corridor. She cries and crawls closer to Sean, who wraps his arms around her.

During the day, Sean communicates with her by sending her texts from his place of work. He finds it easier to send a message rather than to talk in person. He appears baffled at the way their relationship has changed. She doesn't know how to comfort him or how to calm his fears because she also doesn't have any answers. Her replies to him are stilted and feel unnatural.

When she goes to collect the boy at the crèche for the first time, she worries about the outcome. She takes a bus at the town centre and rides to the outskirts of town. It's hard to know exactly where to get off the bus but the friendly bus driver points towards the crèche and she walks in that direction. When the boy recognises her, his lovely smile disappears from his face, and he promptly cries. Kiki tries to stay calm as they walk towards the bus stop. With no idea when the next bus will arrive, she tries to calm him. Even the 'Frozen'-themed lollipop she had bought for him doesn't appease him. Finally, the bus arrives, and they take their seats in the front seat. Still, he cries. She worries about the commuters' thoughts: 'Who is this woman? Who is this crying child? Where is she taking him?'

Her heart beats faster as they approach the terminus where they must disembark. From there, they still have to walk about half a mile to his home. *Please, let me get the code right at the entrance to the apartments. How will he react when we get home*? Luckily, he is so tired that he soon falls asleep on the bedding lying on the floor next to his mother's bed. She waits in the lounge until finally his mother arrives home at nine fifteen. The next bus to the city only arrives at ten o'clock and to stay warm, she paces up and down in the bus shelter until it eventually arrives. Sean waits for her at the corner closest to the apartment and when they get home, she is ready for a good crying session. She wonders why she is so depleted: is it because she is tired, relieved to be home safely or just angry that she must put herself through all of this?

Within a few days she must do it all over again. One night she volunteers to sleep in the spacious guest room while Naomi is at work. In the morning, she reverses the routine and takes the boy to the nursery. It pleases her when it goes well and within days Naomi puts her wages into her bank account.

One day an advertisement on Gumtree for a live-in Nanny position in Elgin, a town in the Highlands, catches her attention. Though she needs a regular income, she still doesn't really want to be away too far from 'home.' It is easy, though, to press the buttons on her laptop and she puts in an application for the job.

'If I get this position, I could stay there during the week and come to see you during weekends.' She broaches the topic gently but is surprised at how well Sean takes the news. Ironically, she is looking for the type of job that she hoped she would never have to do again.

Kiki is pleasantly surprised when the advertising agency contacts her. 'Unfortunately, that position has been filled by the clients themselves, but we have a wonderful position in Aberdeen that I think would suit you perfectly. The family has two girls who need to be driven to school every day. It is a mansion with ten bedrooms, but you will stay in a separate cottage. There is a car available for you to use on your free days. Please send me copies of your passport, Residency Permit, and referees. I'll arrange for a Skype interview between you and my client.'

The Skype interview goes extremely well, and after the hour of conversation, she's convinced that she'll soon move to Aberdeen. She asks The Google God how she can get there, and he shows her the way. Sean says that he'll come to visit her there when she can't make the journey home to visit him. She stares at him with her blue eyes and decides not to reply. Would she want him to visit her? She isn't convinced.

Despite it being hard, she now must wait for the client's husband to conduct a Skype interview with her. The agent said she would contact Kiki's referees. At last, she can feel optimistic again. She and Sean feel happy and relaxed. Soon, very soon she will feel valued and appreciated again, while earning an income. To make a good impression for the interview, she has an awfully expensive haircut in the city. Unfortunately, John can't make it to the interview, and she has to face the possibility that this position is not to be hers.

The week passes without contact from the agent. Kiki phones her and it surprised her to hear she has had problems getting hold of her referees. Kiki gets in touch with them, warning them of a potential call from an agency in Scotland. After two days, the agent phones Kiki to tell her she has spoken to her referees, and she would contact Kiki soon. There is another family in Perthshire who is also looking for a nanny and should this position not work out, she will put Kiki in touch with them. Kiki does some research and wonders whether the place where this family lives in the country might be too isolated. Maybe this isn't quite the right place for her after all.

She waits and waits. She and Sean check her phone regularly to make sure it is connected. Nothing happens. The weeks pass and she looks at Nanny jobs in London. If Scotland is not opening for her and she keeps on resisting to open to Scotland, she'll have to move on. The sun has started to shine in England; it is nearly summer there. Should she go home? Where is home now?

At this stage she wants to shout and kick. How is it possible that the agency is so slack? How is it possible to be so callous about someone else's life and future? What would it take to make a call or send an e-mail even if the message is 'thank you but no thank you?' She can remember the days when she closed 'deals' to put buyers and sellers together to conclude a sale. This is not much different and as a businesswoman she is appalled at the poor service she is experiencing.

Being on her own during the day, she has ample time to think about her situation. Some days she must go to the shops to buy food. She rushes home quickly because it is wet and cold outside; her main concern is reading her e-mails. Naomi asks her to baby- sit for her in the second half of the month, but it feels like an awfully long time to wait for an opportunity to earn. In the meantime, she spends too much money. It is hard to admit, but she is concerned she might get used to this type of life. She realizes it will eventually get to her like some form of painless cancer gnawing away, until one day, it will spurt its venom at her with full force. How long should she wait before she throws in the towel? How long before she has passed the point of no return?

A few more weeks pass, and she is more convinced than ever she won't stay in Scotland. The longer she stays here with Sean, the harder it's going to be for them both when she eventually leaves. Naomi sends her a link to apply for an admin job at her workplace, but she doesn't tell her she hasn't any intention of staying in Scotland.

Feeling desperate and remembering the little warning voice from months ago, she contacts her old friends. She sends a WhatsApp to Ernest, her South African friend who has lived in the UK for many years. She explains that she made a huge mistake and now wants to return to England. The pull of 'love' is not enough for living life in a particular way. Or is the real reason that she can't pull this off that she is too damaged and maybe too scared to commit? Why does she run away when things close in on her? Is she knowingly damaging herself? If she runs now, where will she run to?

'You are welcome to stay with me for however long you need to. Here you'll be able to rest. You can go for walks on the beach, sit in the sun and relax, cry, or do whatever you need to do to get well again. Stop being so hard on yourself. We all make mistakes from time to time and sometimes it isn't actually a mistake, but a learning curve. You tried something – it didn't work out the way you anticipated and now it is time to move on again.'

'Thank you, Ernest. If I don't get this position at Aberdeen, I'll definitely consider your offer. I should hear from the agent this week. She has contacted all my referees and I expect a work offer soon. But let's see what happens. Thank you. You've given me hope.'

Not used to such unbelievably bad service, Kiki keeps hoping that the agent will want to redeem herself. But after five days, she still hears nothing from her. She tells Sean that she is considering going to Colchester to stay with Ernest. She isn't sure if she notices a tear glimmer in his eyes – one that says: 'thank the Lord, this is not working for me either' or is it saying: 'oh Lord, she is going to leave me here by myself. It's all over. Where did it go wrong? What can I do to keep her here?'

Ben Nevis is the tallest mountain in the United Kingdom. On Saturday morning, they take a bus to visit Fort William. On the drive there, she admires the miles of green and water masses, typical of Scotland. She reminisces about her role as a tourist, a wanderer, a gypsy. From their window seat at Wetherspoons in Fort William, they watch tired mountaineers dressed in hiking gear, purposefully walking to their hotels or restaurants, gloating with accomplishment; 'I've climbed the highest mountain in the UK today!'

They both realize that this is probably their last excursion together. They try their best to pretend that they're happy. Before they return home on the bus, they buy marmalade, shortbread and postcards of a thistle and a steer at a gift shop.

Kiki realises that her time in Scotland is over. It has been profound and dramatic. Six weeks felt like six months. She arrived here with great hopes and a heart filled with love. She'll leave with shattered dreams and icy feet. Her boxes are packed and Sean volunteers to post them to her as soon as she sends him a delivery address. This time she'll travel by bus to England and hopefully she'll be able to marvel at the beautiful Scottish countryside. Ernest offers her a haven with no strings attached. Once settled there, she'll have time to gather herself and plan her next move.

Hopefully, God will guide and direct her. He knows by now what she needs to survive as a single woman: a job, a place to stay where she'll be provided with her basic needs and, if she's lucky, a gentle sprinkling of happiness too. Somewhere, she'll find a hole in the wall and once again she'll attempt to reach the other side.

HEADING SOUTH

Heading south again. But how far south this time? Would Colchester be a destination or a via point on this part of her journey?

Kiki stares over the changing countryside from her window seat on the bus; countryside changing just as her life keeps changing. She craves the comfort of being settled, of not having to search for cracks of light through holes in walls, of not having to creep through holes and sometimes being made to retrace her steps. Of not having to pass through endless tunnels.

Her search is ongoing, but what is the prize at the end of the quest? Is it companionship? Love? Is it self-respect, independence, self-assurance, pride in herself? Or is it just the joy of living a life of fulfilment, surrounded by family and friends, being a member of a greater circle?

She drifts off to sleep, rocked to the lullaby thrum of wheels on the tarmac.

They enter a tunnel, she's sure of it. It's long, cold, dark and silent, the carapace of the bus protecting her from the whoosh of passing traffic.

The tunnel is endless in her dream-like state, but suddenly a pulse of light disturbs her slumber, and she opens her eyes to see fleeting scenes of the English countryside, peppered here and there with ice and sprinkles of snow. And here and there a patch of blue in the cloud-decked sky. And suddenly a ray of light from the sun – a cold shard of light, but one that gives her hope for the coming seasons and days.

Is the tunnel of her own making, a figment of her imagination? Must she continue looking for cracks in the wall, holes in the structure, endless tunnels?

It's time for metamorphosis. It's time to find and capture the light at the end of the tunnel.

AKNOWLEDGEMENTS

Many thanks to my children, their spouses and my grandchildren who believe in me and encourage me to experience life to the fullest. You have been my inspiration to publish this story. Some stories need to be told and this is one of them.

I am grateful for all the many friends I have made during my interesting life experiences. Your loving kindness, your care and interest, means the world to me.

Thank you, Janey for helping me shape the ideas and words, making this adventure readable.

Printed in Great Britain
by Amazon

69676508R00220